I0670922

Aftershock

Blood Never Lies

an *Eye of the Storm* companion novel

written by Dianna Hardy

Aftershock
Blood Never Lies

Copyright © 2018, Dianna Hardy
The moral right of the author has been asserted.

Published by Satin Smoke Press, October, 2018
First Edition | ISBN 978-0957540484
This print version updated August, 2023

Written in British English.

All rights reserved.

In this work of fiction, the characters, places and events are either the product of the author's imagination, or they are used entirely fictitiously. Any resemblance to actual events or locales or persons, living or dead, is entirely coincidental.

No part of this book may be reproduced by any means or in any form whatsoever without written permission from the author, except for brief quotations embodied in literary articles or reviews.

This book is set in 11 pt Cormorant Garamond Medium by the Cormorant Project Authors, licensed under the SIL Open Font License, Version 1.1.

A CIP catalogue record for this book is available from the British Library.

Satin Smoke Press
(an imprint of Bitten Fruit Books)
South Hampshire, UK

www.satinsmoke.com

A Brief Recap

Dear Readers,

This section acts as a brief recap for those who have read the *Eye of the Storm* series, and serves as a background to the characters of Pete and 'Claire' for those who have not. While you do not have to read *Eye of the Storm* to enjoy this book, it is highly recommended that you do to gain full understanding of everything the characters have been through to get to this point. If you do wish to read it, do not read the section below beforehand, but come back to this book after you've read the series. If you do NOT wish to read it, the below should help you with *Aftershock*.

The following contains huge spoilers for the *Eye of the Storm* series...

Pete is a werewolf, and an older one at the age of fifty-three (though, being a werewolf, he looks much younger as they can live up to around three hundred years when mated). He's had, for many years, a reputation for being reclusive, which also includes darker elements of his personality, leading to rumours of 'what he likes to do to women'. Things that involve whips and blades. None of this is helped by the physical deformity he carries: burns which scar half his face and throat.

Claire was previously known as Beth (or Bethany). She's a human who was best friends (since childhood) with Sarah who unexpectedly passed away at the end of *Reign Of The Wolf* after a fatal car accident. Devastated by her death, Beth vowed to protect Sarah's newborn baby (born on her deathbed), Jasmine.

Beth has always had a crush on Pete, ever since she first laid eyes on him, despite his burns; perhaps even because of them since she's never liked lies and pretence in her men – or cowardice. The burns are 'honest' as far as she's concerned; something he can't hide. Being a huge dog lover (and animal lover in general), she immediately connected with his wolf and saw beneath the rumours and his silence, finally learning how he acquired his deformity: escaping (and killing) his mentally ill and violent mate who burnt him during one of her frenzies one full moon.

Always cautious around Beth, Pete began to let his guard down after she was attacked by a rogue wolf near his cottage one night. Suffering from grave internal injuries, he shared his blood with her under Dr Hendrickson's advice, leading to her full (human) recovery and drawing them yet closer.

The end of *Eye of the Storm* saw them rushing to the hospital having heard of Sarah's car accident. Unfortunately, Sarah was already brain-dead at this point. The doctors scrambled to save her baby, which they did, but knowing the baby – a girl – had grown at an unnatural rate over the last twenty-four hours, and knowing the supernatural nature of her conception (her father was a *Trident), they stole her from the ward and disappeared, with a new identity for Bethany Michaels: now known as Claire Appleby.

Below, I have recounted the last scene in which we see Beth and Pete, escaping with baby †Jasmine in *Eye of the Storm*. It leads straight into the Prologue of *Aftershock*, which begins two years after that fateful night.

Enjoy!

Dianna
March, 2018

*Tridents were horrendous beasts, genetically engineered with the help of magic, by Dr Evan Trident, over two hundred and fifty years ago. They were monstrous versions of the werewolf, driven by base animal needs and not much else. They craved violence and were steered by lust. All Tridents were finally exterminated two and a half years ago from the point this book begins (the prologue).

†What readers know that the characters don't: Jasmine's father was Amil. He was a Trident, which all the characters know. But what only the readers know is that Amil was actually a God called Himet, and Sarah (Jasmine's mother) was a Goddess called Yemet. 'Amil' and 'Sarah' were the physical incarnations that forced them apart and ensured they forgot their true heritage, for they were forbidden from being together. Their true identities were remembered by them both on Sarah's death, and what Sarah recounts from her past tells the reader that Jasmine was actually physically conceived by her human husband, Taylor, and that the 'seed' of her conception was frozen in time by the Egyptian Gods, Anubis and Sekhmet, in a bid to buy time for Sarah (Yemet) to once again reconnect with Amil (Himet). This reconnection would (so they hoped) break the curse keeping them apart. When they did reconnect (and shared their love physically), their joining rekindled the 'seed' within Sarah, and the baby began once more to grow. Thus, baby Jasmine is a biological product of Sarah and Taylor, but was sparked into creation by the souls of Himet and Yemet, as well as the magic of Anubis and Sekhmet.

~*~

Rain battered the roof of her car.

Where the *hell* had this storm come from? Beth couldn't

see a damned thing for the downpour. She strained to find Pete in the distance, but steam and water clouded her window pane.

Cursing, she rolled her window down, grimacing as she got splashed by the unforgiving rain.

She looked at her watch. Five minutes to ten.

She started the engine, keeping her lights off for now. "Come on, Pete."

Thunder cracked so loud, it startled her. This wasn't going to help the bloody traffic.

She heard a muffled bark.

Springing into action, she leaned over and opened the back door, pushing it wide. Nothing happened for a moment, but then a blurry mass leapt into the car, carrying...

Bloody hell, he'd done it! He had the baby!

He barked again. Beth knew exactly what that meant: *Go.*

She took the handbrake off, dropped the gear into first, and did her best to not spin the wheels as she accelerated.

Pete shifted in the back seat, then reached for the door and shut it.

Beth found her seatbelt and pulled it across her. "Is she okay? Are you okay?"

"Wet, but fine. We need to get the hell out of here."

She risked a look over her shoulder. She caught sight of the little girl still swaddled in the blanket. "She's not crying," she said, not sure if she should be worried about that.

Pete let out a low laugh. "Little tyke slept through everything."

"In this weather?" Lightning streaked across the sky; she knew another roll of thunder would follow.

"She seems quite at home with it."

"Are we being followed?"

"No. I don't think so. No one saw me take her, but I had

to leave the window broken behind me. It won't be long before they find that, and once they see she's gone, they'll pull the CCTV straight away. Let's just get as far away as we can. Take the back roads and country lanes."

"In *this*?" She stared at the downpour.

"No bugger will be on them."

"I hope the lanes don't get flooded."

His hand, wet and gritty from the ground, squeezed her left shoulder. "We'll make it, Beth. We're gonna make it."

She swallowed a lump as tears fell.

They were. They *were* going to make it.

"I've left clothes for you on the parcel shelf."

"I see them. Do you know the way to the garage in Weybridge?"

"Yes." She'd memorised it – her phone and its SatNav might be the first thing the police checked, so she'd switched it off and taken the battery out. She knew the plan. She'd exchange her car there, then she'd become 'Claire' – goodbye Beth.

Eyes stinging, she squeezed his hand back, then brought her focus back to the road. Turning right on to another residential street, she caught sight of the hospital in her rear-view mirror, fading into the distance.

The baby gurgled, and then sighed.

Her broken heart filled with something she couldn't quite describe. It was bittersweet; devastating, yet hopeful.

She checked her mirror again. The hospital slipped from view.

Goodbye, Sarah.

Aftershock

Prologue

Dragonfly... She giggled as she chased the glimmering flash of blue and green as it buzzed ahead of her.

Mummy had said these colourful flying things were called dragonflies, and Jasmine loved them! She'd almost managed to catch one once in her small, two-year-old hands, and it hadn't stopped buzzing, vibrating against her skin, making her giggle more than she ever had. But her hands had been too small, and it had broken free before she'd been able to form a cage around it. Not that it mattered, because she didn't want to catch them to keep them or hurt them – she loved seeing them fly free. She only thought if she caught one, maybe it could be her friend; maybe it would love her like a pet cat or dog. She didn't have any friends.

The dragonfly darted into the woods ahead of her. She stopped, frowning. Mummy had told her not to go in by herself. She looked back. She could see the house from here. She could also see the frames of Daddy and his friend Aiden. It was Aiden's house they stayed in. Mummy said Jasmine had been born here. She'd told her that more than once. She'd also told her that if anyone asked her, that's what she should tell them – that she hadn't been born in a hospital like most babies were, but here in Aiden's home.

Daddy was a wolf. That was something that was a secret. She was allowed to say that she'd been born in Aiden's house, but she was not allowed to ever tell anyone that Daddy was a wolf because most people were not wolves and would not understand. She didn't know why they wouldn't understand since many of Mummy and Daddy's friends had pet dogs, and being a wolf wasn't really any different to having a dog. But Jasmine knew the secret was important, and she didn't mind looking after the secret because Mummy had explained that it kept them safe, like washing hands before eating, or cleaning a wound. The secret was just another part of the day to remember.

The frown still on her face, she turned back to the woods, narrowing her eyes to try and pierce the darkness between the trees. That's where the dragonfly had gone. Is that where all dragonflies lived? Could there be many in there?

She hesitated.

She wasn't supposed to go in there, but she'd also heard Aiden say before to her Daddy that the woods were not big - *"only a small clump of trees, really"*. As long as she could still see the house, she would know her way back. All she'd have to do was go towards the house and try not to fall over.

There was that familiar buzzing again. She smiled as another dragonfly sped past her shoulder, making her squeal in delight. It captured her mind and all thoughts dashed out of her head as she dashed after the magical-looking creature, towards the trees. She wanted to move faster. She didn't want to lose it this time. She kept her eyes on its darting body and translucent wings with one single thought: *go where it goes.*

There was a really strong gust of wind. That's what it felt like. So strong, she couldn't keep her eyes open, so she squeezed them shut and tucked her chin in, letting out a small muffled sound that could have been a scream when the gale picked her up and carried her through the air.

Was that what had happened? It must have been because when the gale dropped her and she finally opened her eyes as she landed on her bottom – her nappy taking the brunt of her stumble – she was no longer where she had been.

Her eyes filled with tears and her bottom lip trembled. She could feel herself wanting to cry even though it had been a little bit fun ... but she *was* a little bit scared.

Lip still trembling, she turned around and saw the trees now behind her, not in front of her. In front of her, there was a clearing of grass which eventually dropped away, although she couldn't see into what.

Little gasps turned into attempts to stop wailing, which was the sound her tears always wanted to make.

Buzzzzzzzz. Buzzzzzzzz.

Her eyes widened, and a small smile threatened to break through the tears. It held back the wails at any rate. Her dragonflies were back, and there was more than one. Maybe this *was* where they lived.

They soared upwards and circled above her head in unison – so pretty.

And then, she saw it. *It.*

She didn't have a name for 'it', but she shivered in excitement – or was it apprehension? Whatever it was, she'd seen 'it' before. Her toddler mind tried to conjure up the word for it, or at the very least the memory of where she'd seen one before, but it felt like so long ago. Yes, it must have been a very, very long time ago, even before she'd been one year old; maybe even before she'd been a baby in her mummy's tummy. It circled above her in the same way the dragonflies did, but much, much further away. And it was big. Huge. She knew it was, although she couldn't remember how she knew. She also knew it could see her as clearly as she could see it.

A rustle of leaves and foliage behind her made her turn. Her daddy sprinted out of the woods as a wolf, heading straight towards her. She could sense his worry. She was very used to Daddy's wolf.

He changed into her daddy as a man and sat back on his bottom, letting out a sigh of relief. "She's here!" he called out. "I've got her!"

Still looking at her daddy, she reached up to the sky and pointed.

"Jasmine, sweetheart … you know you mustn't run off like that, and never into the woods where Mummy won't be able to see you."

She was sorry, but she had something important to say – more important than sorry. She creased her eyebrows in concentration trying to remember the word she needed to explain, but she couldn't, although it was on the tip of her tongue. It made her feel angry and powerless. Her chin wobbled with her frustration, but she kept pointing up. "Big bird," she said, though she knew that wasn't right. "Big bird, Daddy. Big bird." And she was crying now because she had no other words to match the grand vision in her mind of the magnificent creature gliding between towers of sand against a regal orange sun.

She looked up past her pointing finger. It was gone.

The wails came now because her tears always made that happen anyway. When her mummy ran out of the woods, looking at her like she was very scared, the wails got bigger.

"It's all right, pipsqueak." Daddy picked her up into his large arms and cradled her against his chest. He placed a kiss on her head. She loved him so much.

"Oh, thank god," she heard her mummy say.

Daddy stood up, taking her with him, and she felt very safe in his arms. He was strong. "I never lost track of her scent,

Claire."

"How did she get all the way over here?"

"Kids. Always faster than you think." He let out a small chuckle. "Be thankful she can't shift – she'd move ten times faster."

Mummy's face still looked all stiff.

She probably shouldn't tell them about the gust of wind picking her up and speeding her through the trees. She thought it might make Mummy even more scared.

Before she knew it, she was in Mummy's arms, her familiar smell comforting her as much as her daddy's arms had. Daddy was still there though, right next to her. He dropped a kiss on Mummy's head now. Daddy looked after them all.

"Let's get inside," he said. "I'll make warm cups of tea and some dinner, what do you reckon?"

"Sorry, Mummy," she whispered into her neck.

She felt Mummy relax. Her muscles went a bit softer. Another kiss on her head, this time from Mummy. "It's okay, honey. Just don't do it again, all right? It's important you can always see me or Daddy while you're playing."

She nodded against her chest, and was happy to be carried all the way back to the house.

She yawned.

Mummy rocked her a bit as they walked, and she yawned again.

When her tears had dried, it was a small smile that took over her face instead, as she thought of blue and green shimmering wings dancing above her head.

Her eyes closed.

Other wings filled her mind. The one that belonged to the big bird that was not a bird at all. Giant wings – so giant that when they flapped, the wind they made could lift you right off the ground. Wings that were warm to touch – hot, even. Dry and hot like the sand of those towers against the sun.

If she were to sit in the middle of those wings, on the big bird's back, she wouldn't feel the wind they made, but the wind of the whole world as it sped past her while they both soared as one.

As one.

Chapter One

"Claire," she said, raking her fingers through her shoulder-length, dark blonde hair, to pull out the last knots of the day. "Claire."

It was a ritual of sorts. Every evening before bed, she repeated the name as she stared at herself in the mirror. Perhaps one day, the name would fit. Perhaps one day, she'd wake up and simply *be* Claire without thinking; without feeling the burden of everything that had been lost.

"Claire."

They'd agreed that, to be on the safe side – so they could get used to the change without any errors, for errors could cost them their lives – she would be Claire all the time, even in the privacy of their own room; even against each other's skin as they made love. A necessary sacrifice – they had a little one to think about – but it felt like plaster ripped from a wound every time her lover uttered a name that wasn't hers. It wasn't the name itself per se; it was the lack of time afforded her to lament the tragedy of that night two years ago. Denying Beth – who she had been – meant denying Sarah in some ways; denying her death, and everything she'd stood for in the nearly thirty years she'd known her.

Beth had died, too. In an instant.

And 'Claire' had muscled in with her no-nonsense atti-tude, vowing to save the unsavable and put everything right. Claire had been needed, but not wanted.

Yet, Claire was now Jasmine's mother. Jasmine needed Claire. Sarah was just a whisper in history, and Beth could not chase a whisper.

"Claire."

In the mirror, a dark shape emerged from the bathroom which adjoined the bedroom. Pete met her eyes in the reflec-tion of the glass. Tall, muscular and lean, he wore his history – or part of it – on his skin for the world to look upon and guess at: burnt flesh that scarred the left side of his face from this throat to his scalp.

Her own burns remained hidden, as did her scarred heart.

In nothing but boxer shorts, and black hair framing his face and spattering his chest, Pete looked daunting and enti-cing all at the same time. More than that though, he held her gaze with a silent compassion and steady love. The kind of love one had to earn for he didn't give it freely. This very private male had opened himself to her in beautiful surrender, al-though he laughingly joked every now and then that he'd had no choice – she'd bulldozed her way into his life, his heart, his soul.

"What are you doing?" he asked, his voice gruff – a legacy of the burns around his throat, and another reason strangers regarded this imposing man with wariness. But he already knew the answer to his question – she'd been repeating this mantra every night for over two years.

His arms found their way around her waist as he sidled up behind her.

She sighed. No one had ever held her with such surety.

She'd spent her life too tall, too independent, too honest, too brash, too full-on for most men. Maybe she *had* bulldozed into his life – she probably bulldozed into everyone's life – it's just that her intensity had finally met its match in this ... werewolf. She inwardly smiled. It *had* to be the werewolf with the flame-licked face – no human male could take the force of her nature, and it was a nature she'd battled with, but ultimately, refused to dull.

"Reminding myself who I am." She couldn't hide the sadness that tinged her words, and it annoyed her. She needed to be stronger than this, but this afternoon had shaken her – she thought they'd lost Jasmine, and with that realisation, the walls she'd placed around the last two years had come crashing down. She'd been unable to fully restore them.

One of his hands replaced hers, running his fingers through her hair; then he pulled her strands to one side and kissed her neck, his teeth nibbling the delicate skin around her vein.

Another sigh slipped from her mouth.

He trailed his tongue down her neck and along her shoulder, every motion with care as if he was savouring every centimetre. "I know who you are. Your scent hasn't changed. The way you taste hasn't changed."

"When we couldn't find her, for a split second, fear was all I knew and I imagined her dead. In that moment, I wasn't Claire anymore, but I wasn't Beth either. I don't know who I am without her."

"We'll never be without her." His fingers stroked her navel; travelled lower past the waistband of her sleep shorts; dipped beneath the cotton of her underwear until her sigh became a gasp. She took in his movements in the mirror, her vision glazing as heat rose. God, she needed this. She needed his complete understanding of what drove her in life; an understanding she saw in his eyes daily.

His tone darkened, meeting the depths his fingers explored. "I'll remind you who you are."

A moan escaped her as she rocked her hips against his hand. "Does our predicament ever bother you?"

"What predicament?" he muttered, his lips back on her neck.

"That I'll be doubled over with age before you've sprouted another grey hair?"

"Hush. That's decades in the future." He sank his fingers fully into her, taking her gasp a little higher. "I'd much rather live in the now."

Hell, the 'now' sounded good. And felt good. She couldn't complain about the now when he so fully encompassed it.

He eased his fingers out of her, turning her around, pressing her back against the vanity table as he tugged down his boxers. His gaze smouldered; pierced her every damn time he looked at her.

"The door," she whispered.

"Closed. She's not strong enough to pull the handle down yet."

And Jasmine was asleep. If she woke, she'd cry for them before she got out of her cot bed.

"I want to be inside you," he growled softly. It was a demand. It was urgent. And she felt it, too, in that moment – *his* fear at Jasmine's near loss, though he'd kept it hidden from sight; had focused on keeping them all calm.

Her need for him tripled, as did her heat, the ravaging liquid fire for this male reminding her she'd never felt this way for any other before him.

His mouth captured hers, tongue seeking entrance, and she happily opened for him, groaning at the feel of him sliding her underwear down her backside.

He pressed against the back of her, guiding her into position. She fell seated on the table, her legs rising up to hug his waist; pull him in; her need for him as great as his was for her. "Inside me," she whispered.

He complied, hungrily.

She moaned long and low as she felt him enter her in sure, swift strokes until he was fully inside her, his hips against hers, completing her, completing him, and erasing all fears that hovered in the recesses of the last two and a half years. There was just *them*, and fire… "Pete," she stuttered, hoarsely. "More."

Embedded deeply, he thrust, redefining completion altogether. "Fuck … I love you."

"I love you, too. Say my name."

He knew what she meant. Sadness shone for a moment in his gaze, but then he smiled a wisp of a smile and thrust again. "I love you, Bethany."

Hell, yes.

A wayward tear she hadn't known was there slipped from the corner of her eye. She grasped his shoulder with one hand, his hair with the other.

His pace increased, his movements exacting, intimate, loving… He brought his forehead against hers, pupils wide, that telltale glowing golden ring around his irises exciting her and calling to some wildness inside her only he could access.

Her gaze dropped to his mouth. She knew his fangs would grow next. The thought of their emergence sent a wave of euphoria tumbling through her, threatening to take her to the crest of her bliss far too soon.

"Mummy?"

SHIT.

They both froze, not daring to move an inch.

Pete shook himself out of the shock of their interruption first, and grabbed the cushion from the low vanity chair, smacking it against their hips. Their nudity might now be hidden from the toddler in the corner of the room – not that Jasmine was looking; she was too busy sleepily rubbing the slumber out of her eyes – but god damn it, her lover was still hard inside her. Denied orgasms were the worst.

"Jasmine, honey ... er..." She couldn't form words.

"Mummy and I ... we're ... just having a small cuddle before bed. Are you all right? Did you have a bad dream?"

She needed Pete out of her.

He met her eyes, disappointment evident, but also a hint of amusement. He pressed the cushion tighter against them.

"Can I have a cuddle, too, Mummy?"

"Wait, wait," Claire snapped. "Um ... stay there. Sweetie, the best thing is to go back to your room and as soon as you get back into bed, count to ten. You can count to ten, can't you?"

Jasmine nodded.

"Good. I'll be there to give you a cuddle as soon as you reach number ten."

She frowned, her dark brown eyes looking even more mysterious than they usually did in the low light. But to Claire's relief, Jasmine didn't argue. "Okay." She turned, stumbled a little, then waddled away from them.

Claire sighed, but then Jasmine stopped in her tracks. "Door, Mummy."

"I'll get it," Pete mumbled, finally pulling out of her with a pursing of his lips at the sensation of withdrawal, cushion firmly in Jasmine's line of sight despite the fact she was turned towards the door.

Claire crossed her legs, still on the desk, and stretched her vest down over her hips so it wasn't obvious her shorts and underwear were strewn on the floor.

Pete moved the cushion to his front and held it fast against his crotch as he made his way to the door and reached for the handle.

Jasmine rubbed her eyes again and yawned, not taking in anything out of the ordinary.

Pete opened the door, and Jasmine toddled out, making her way to her own room.

Claire went cold as a realisation took root.

From the other room, she heard Jasmine begin to count.

Pete turned back to her, shoulders sagging as he let out an abated breath at their successful escape, then looked concerned when he took in her bewildered countenance.

The dread in her grew, and she saw the moment Pete caught on. His eyes widened as he tried to piece together what exactly had happened.

There must be an obvious explanation, but she was drawing a blank. They hadn't heard the door open; they'd heard nothing at all, and Pete had werewolf hearing.

Jasmine couldn't open doors yet.

The door had been closed.

"Ten, Mummy! Ten!"

Her eyes met Pete's. He shook his head because he had no answer.

She asked the question anyway. "How the hell did she get into our room?"

Peanut butter and jam on toast: the most scrumptious breakfast ever according to Jasmine.

It wasn't only on her toast though – it was on her fingers and hands, her chin and the tip of her nose, a little on her cheeks, and Claire thought she spied a bit clinging to the strands of her dark hair.

She smiled to herself and took another sip of her coffee, entranced by the carefree way kids took to the world. She only hoped it would last, knowing full well it never did.

"Jasmine, sweetie, would you like more juice?"

The girl looked at her half-full beaker and shook her head. "No, thank you, Mummy." A large corner of her toast went into her mouth.

'Making love' hadn't been quite the heated affair after Jasmine had been tucked back into bed last night. Instead, Pete and herself had discussed the practicalities of the next few years. After the chaos of Jasmine's birth, they had made their way here – Aiden being an old and trusted friend of Pete's who fully knew of his animal nature – and laid low for nearly five months. When word had finally reached them that the Surrey pack had survived the attack on Lawrence's land – and more than that, that Lawrence and Lydia were getting married, publicly and lavishly – they'd used that distraction as their chance to uproot. With all of theatrical high society's focus on the wedding, they'd packed bags, headed for the coast and followed it all the way to Wales, then Scotland and back. As a family, they had trekked across the United Kingdom for the past twenty-four months, staying here and there for weeks or months at a time. Camp sites were the preference, but even open fields – ideally near a stream – and their tent, did the job. Money was made doing odd jobs on farms and in cafés. Pete had the strength and stamina to keep farm owners more than grateful, and Claire didn't mind the labour – it reminded her of the days backpacking around the world in her youth, some of which she'd also done with Sarah.

They'd returned, here, to Aiden's B&B four weeks ago to recoup and plan the next few years. Despite the safety and relative anonymity to living off-grid (or mostly off-grid), they both knew they couldn't continue to do this. Jasmine was growing – she'd be three in a few months – and they needed to find somewhere to settle; she needed to go to school, make friends... The thought of it all sent a river of panic coursing through Claire, but it simply wasn't fair to keep Jasmine from stability if stability was possible. With so much time having passed, and riding on the rumour that Lydia had given birth herself – that everything seemed to have settled, and be thriving, for everyone – Pete had contacted Bill and Marco in California.

California – that's where they were headed.

Between the deserts surrounding Las Vegas and the national forests leading up to Oregon, Bill and Marco had found land to build a home, with plans to open a wolf sanctuary to help preserve the species once they were able to cut through all the red tape and acquire the right licences. A sanctuary for *real* wolves, not werewolves – although any werewolf in that area would certainly gain some security from the project by default.

And that was where they came in: Jasmine needed security, and Bill and Marco could offer it; both Pete and herself could work the land, keep tidy the log cabins for hire, and help with the project. Pete assured her they'd be welcomed with open arms. It was a new pack – a new life.

She didn't doubt they'd be welcomed, but the thought of structure and routine, and fully using her new identity as Claire Appleby after having lived so freely and anonymously for so long, made her anxious.

"Penny for them?" Aiden's voice pulled her out of her thoughts.

She looked up at the man who'd just walked into the breakfast room and smiled. At fifty-two years old, his hair still retained most of its blond, even if his face held the weathered lines of the outdoors. His handsomeness was only accentuated by those creases, but it brought home to Claire that Pete's age was nearer Aiden's fifty-two than Claire's thirty-one, even if Pete didn't look it owing to the longevity of his werewolf gene.

"I'm just trying to get my head around the trip to America. I never thought I'd be living out there, especially not in recent years with all the earthquakes being reported."

"Oh, don't do what everyone else is doing and make mountains out of molehills. You know how it is: the news says this, rumours say that; things go viral and grow way out of proportion. But when you actually go and experience it, it's nothing like how it's reported to be."

"I know you're right. I've travelled enough – even went through the Middle East over a decade ago. The people were some of the friendliest I'd met; I know the press has a habit of colouring things their own way." Though the earthquakes...

With everything going on, she hadn't been keeping abreast with it all, but about five years ago there'd been a spate of earthquakes around the globe, even in countries that didn't usually suffer from earthquakes. She remembered feeling one or two right here, in Great Britain. They'd died down since, but environmental and political groups had both jumped on the bandwagon – hell, even religious groups had – and 'the quakes' were still talked about. California was one of those areas talked about the most. Five years back, they had suffered one of the worst tremors with many casualties. Still, Bill and Marco had said the tremors were few and far between now, and so small they were barely noticeable to humans – animals could feel them, werewolves could feel them, but Jasmine should be fine and no further damage to buildings or the land had been caused since that one big one.

"I do have a friend in the States who says it's safe over there – Holly. And she's ... well, she's up to speed on everything, including everything that happened with us at Lawrence's place. She knows as much as you do about the way of things."

Holly was a university friend of both hers and Sarah's. The news of Sarah's death had hit her hard. Although she'd been in Britain and with them when they'd met Pete and discovered werewolves existed, Holly's contact with them had gradually faded over the past two years, Sarah's passing too great a wound to rekindle their history without pain. While she didn't think Holly would turn her away, she wasn't altogether sure how their moving to America would be received. Holly and herself had a habit of winding each other up.

"That's good. You won't be starting from nothing. Is she in California, too?"

"New York, mostly, but I believe she has quite a few friends in Los Angeles, so I don't think it would be too difficult for us to catch up. We've, erm, always had a bit of a tumultuous friendship, though," she laughed. "We *are* friends, but we can rile each other up if we're not careful."

Her smile faded a fraction as she thought of how Sarah had always been their mediator. Good-natured, sensible Sarah.

Fuck. It still hurt too much.

"Nothing wrong with those friendships. Sometimes we need people to fire us up and get us motivated, even if it's by aggravation. Takes all sorts to make the world go 'round."

"Indeed it does."

"I popped in to see if Jasmine wanted to feed the geese with me." He affectionately ruffled her hair. Having seen her as a newborn, and knowing the hardships they'd all been through, he'd grown quite a soft spot for her. "What do you think, pipsqueak?"

"Geese!" exclaimed Jasmine as the last of her toast went into her mouth.

Aiden laughed. "I'll take that as a yes, then."

"After I clean you up," said Claire.

Jasmine nodded and slid from her chair to present her goo-covered face as Claire reached for the wipes.

Aiden pulled Jasmine's chair out for himself and placed his large frame on it. "Have you got your flights booked yet?"

"I think Pete's sorting it out now with Marco on the phone."

"Isn't it the middle of the night over there?"

Claire smirked and threw him a look.

He caught onto it straight away. "Of course – the full moon is tonight."

No wolf slept easy on the full moon, even if the effects of the orb were not as powerful as they used to be before the annihilation of The Trident. Whatever had gone down at Lawrence's mansion the night Jasmine was born, through the tumult, wolves had earned themselves the invaluable reward of peace. The Trident that hunted them were gone, and so were the debilitating mating pains – *any* pain – that had biologically ruled over wolves every month. The females of the species were no longer beholden to a life of agony and death without their mates; Pete had also heard that mating itself was now a choice. Sure, scent still dictated who was best for whom – their animal nature still very much dominant – but without the pains, mating itself could be something nurtured over time and at a wolf's own pace. It was a gift never afforded any wolf before.

"Mummy, are we going on a plane?" Jasmine asked as Claire ran the wet wipe over both her hands.

"We are, yes."

"To live in Meric?"

"America. Yes." She pulled out another wipe for her face.

"Fly like birds?"

"We'll be going higher than the birds, sweetie."

She frowned, then smiled. "Fly like *big* bird."

Claire laughed. "There's no bird bigger than a plane."

"Big, *big* bird."

"Come on, squirt," said Aiden, getting up. "The geese are hungry."

"Thanks, Aiden. We'll see you for dinner?"

He nodded. "I'll be back late afternoon." Divorced, with no children of his own, Aiden ran the B&B and small farm on his own with a handful of part-time staff. Although he hadn't said outright, she got the impression he'd enjoyed their company the past few weeks and would be missing them when they left.

"Thank you for everything you've done for us over the years."

"Ach," he shrugged away her gratitude. "Save your goodbyes 'til it's time for goodbye." He winked at her as he ushered Jasmine out. "It's one of many favours I owe Pete, but favours aside, he's a good friend, and so are you now. You'd both do the same for me."

Claire smiled and nodded, then waved her daughter out, not that Jasmine was paying attention as she held both arms out either side and pretended to fly out of the room to a mantra of "big bird, big bird". So immersed was she, she collided into Pete's legs as he opened the back door from outside.

"Whoa, steady. You being a rocket?"

"Big bird," she corrected.

Pete grinned. "A little too big for the house, I think."

She ignored him and 'flew' out the open door.

Aiden chuckled. "She'll be giving the geese some lessons in a minute. I'll see you at dinner."

"See you then," Pete nodded. His eyes met hers as Aiden followed Jasmine out of the house.

Pete shut the door behind them, then made his way to where she was seated and bent down for a kiss.

Claire melted into it. "Good morning, gorgeous. How are the cows?"

He sat down in front of her on the chair Aiden had vacated. "Milked, and sprightly this morning. Reckon they had a better night than we did."

She laughed, pushed herself out of her seat and straddled him on his own. "We've probably got about half an hour if you want a quickie?"

"A quickie?" His eyes gleamed with amusement. "As appealing as that sounds – and believe me, it does – I'm waiting for Marco to call me back with confirmation of the flight. He can book it cheaper his end." His lips met hers in another, much needed kiss.

She moaned softly into it.

"So, as much as I'd love to thrust us both into a mind-numbing orgasm" —he let out a groan, his words clearly eating him up— "yet another interruption's going to ruin me for the rest for the week."

She smiled into his mouth. "The rest of the *week*?" she teased. "My..." She ground herself down on him, able to feel him already straining behind the denim of his jeans. Hell, this male consumed her, and she was bloody glad for it.

He exhaled, and nipped her bottom lip. "Wench. That's just mean."

"Now, now..." She delighted in the sounds that escaped him as she worked her lips down the side of his face and throat. "Would a mean person" —she slid off his thighs and crouched in front of him— "do this?" She popped the button of his jeans, caught his eye, and slid his zipper down.

Gold flashed heatedly around the rim of his irises, sending a bolt of pleasure through her; his breath hitched. "What are you doing, woman?"

She was having trouble with her voice, her need for him mounting faster than she could think. "We can't have you ruined for a whole week." On her knees, she glanced at his bulging crotch and licked her lips, which told him *exactly* what she was about to do.

She heard him curse – a wanton whisper – then he ran a hand through her hair, love and lust ablaze in his eyes.

His phone rang.

She bit her lip, hiding a smile; also hiding the disappointment that raced through her. She'd never get enough of him – never.

Pete's next curse was less wanton, and less of a whisper. He leaned forward and yanked the device from his back pocket. "It's Marco."

"That *was* quick."

He mumbled something unintelligible, and she rose up and planted a kiss on his lips. "I'm going for a shower."

His head snapped up as he searched her out with a torn gaze. "You're killing me here," he said.

She laughed. "No – not for *that*. I'm saving that for you. I'm going to head into town with Jasmine; I want to freshen up first."

"Hey, hey, hey..." He grabbed her by the belt loop of her trousers. "You'd *better* save that for me."

She hid her grin at the territorial show of dominance, because it was clear he was only half-joking. The other half of his tone held a definite warning, and she loved him for it.

"You'd better make it worth saving, mister." She winked, turned, and walked away, smiling at his growl which swiftly turned to a vocal greeting when he finally answered the phone.

Her smile faded a fraction when she spied Jasmine from the hallway window halfway up the stairs. They never had got to the bottom of how she'd entered their bedroom last night.

Pete had concluded he couldn't have shut the door properly, and that it must have swung closed behind her after she'd walked in. They were old, oak doors, almost as old as the house itself – they *did* swing on their hinges, and they slipped on their catch sometimes.

While it was unusual for Pete's wolf hearing not to pick up on the noise of the door opening and closing, they *had* been rather lost in each other at the time...

Pulling herself away from the sight of Jasmine happily throwing grains for the geese, she carried on up the stairs. That had to be it. What other explanation could there be?

Chapter Two

"Relax – we made it through," whispered Pete to her left as she carried Jasmine down the long metal walkway leading to the aeroplane. His large, warm hand, low on her back, offered her some comfort.

But she was still tense. Going through passport control had had her holding her breath so tight she thought she'd pass out. Any suspicion of her fake identity would mean so much worse than jail: it would mean having Jasmine taken from her. And Pete, of course. That would end her.

They'd been ushered through with no problems, though, and she knew she needed to try and relax for Jasmine's sake. The poor girl had only just started to realise that moving to America meant she wouldn't be seeing Aiden again – at least, not for a long time – and she'd been in tears over that fact for the last ten minutes. The two of them had had a wonderful connection. It had brought the point home to Claire that they were doing the right thing – she was getting too old to move around every few weeks; Jasmine instinctively wanted to plant roots and build bridges. It was time to settle.

"Honey…" She kissed her on the side of her head as she spoke softly in her ear. "We'll see Aiden again, I promise – just not for a while. Be brave. We're going on a new adventure –

there'll be so many new friends to make. It's going to be fine."

The girl gurgled against her shoulder, still hiding her face. Claire was glad she'd packed another top in her hand luggage, 'cause toddler snot was a force unto itself.

"Look," said Claire, aiming for a new angle. "We can see the plane!"

After another sniffle, Jasmine tentatively looked up towards the floor-to-ceiling window Claire was pointing at, curiosity getting the better of her. She clutched her favourite soft toy – Marlo, the lion – in her hand. Claire had won him for her at a funfair a few months ago. That had been a good day out.

"It's big, isn't it?"

She nodded, her eyes widening a little as she blinked the last of her tears out.

"It's going to fly with us inside it. Have you ever seen anything that big that can fly?"

She sniffed again. "Big bird," she whispered.

"Well, it must have been a *very* big bird," replied Claire, humouring her.

Jasmine nodded, then rested her head back on her shoulder.

"Want me to take her for a bit?" asked Pete.

Claire shook her head. "It's okay. We'll be in our seats soon."

"We will." He clenched his jaw. He didn't like flying at all, and she suspected no wolf took to it that easily. They were born for running, not soaring through the air.

He glanced at her. The look in his eye said, *I'll be glad when my feet are back on the ground.* He'd never let Jasmine see his anxiety, though.

Riding on the rush of love she suddenly felt for him, she shifted Jasmine onto her other shoulder and right arm, then took his hand in her left one. "I love you."

The tension in his shoulders eased a little, and he smiled back at her with thanks. "I love you, too."

He ignored the way the flight attendant by the aeroplane's door stared at his face before glancing away.

Claire squeezed his hand, and caressed his thumb with her own. "Relax," she whispered. "We'll make it through."

It was a blessing that Jasmine had fallen asleep within half an hour of take-off, because Pete had very nearly broken the armrests by clenching them so hard. He'd gone silent as he'd battled with the pressure build-up in his ears and head, his body rigid, his eyes closed, and Claire wished she could have been more attentive towards him, but she'd had a bouncing two-year-old to deal with. Having done a hundred and eighty since the plane left the ground, she'd had to stop Jasmine from head-butting the cabin window in her excitement to look out.

Claire reached over now from her window seat, across Jasmine's sleeping form taking up the middle seat, and placed her hand on Pete's thigh.

He turned his head towards her and opened one eye.

She smiled. "The worst of it's over – we're in the sky."

"Just tell me when we land."

"Really?" She raised an eyebrow. "You're going to sit there like stone for eleven hours?"

His gaze was pleading.

She patted his thigh, then blew him a kiss.

Finally, he forced his right hand off the armrest and reached for her cheek.

She shifted her head until his palm rested against the back of her neck, and sighed at the feel of him. "Do you want to swap seats? I know you're scared, but seeing how beautiful it all is from this height might help."

"Are you fucking kidding me?"

She grinned. "Consider it a 'facing your fear' exercise."

"I can face it from here, thanks."

"Fair enough. At least Jasmine's settled down. I thought I was going to have to put a leash on her."

They both looked at her in the seat between them. She hugged Marlo to her chest which rose and fell peacefully.

Pete caught Claire's eye. "Any chance she'll stay like that for the rest of the flight?"

"About as much chance as you taking the window seat."

"Bugger."

"Indeed. Did Marco ever get back to you about our Visas?"

"They're still being processed, but since he's hiring us directly, he doesn't foresee too much of a problem with us being accepted for them. It's a case of being patient with bureaucracy. If it's not sorted within three months, we might have to fly home and start the whole process again, but he thinks he can pull a string or two to speed everything up. He's not worried. He also mentioned he knew a woman – can't remember her name now – Cathy, or Katie, or... Anyway, she works at the local nursery school. She said they weren't full this year; they have room for Jasmine if we wanted her to start there straight away."

Jesus...

She couldn't stop the tears that rose to her eyes, even though she tried to blink them away.

"Hey ... are you okay? That's good news, isn't it?"

"It is ... god, it really is, it's just ... we're doing it. I can't believe we're really doing it, you know?"

He nodded and smiled. His hand slid down to her shoulder. "I know. We kind of got used to it, didn't we? The traveller's life; moving from one place to another... This is going to take a bit of getting use to in some ways."

"It sounds so stupid, but it sort of feels like ... growing up, or something." They both laughed. "But also ... becoming trapped. And I know that's the fear part – that's the illusion, right? I just really hope that never happens."

"It's in your nature, Claire."

"What do you mean?"

"I mean you're adventurous and free-spirited by nature, always looking for the next challenge to conquer, and you get restless if there isn't one."

Her eyes widened as she took in his words. "I don't think I—"

"It's not a bad thing. It's just who you are, and I love you for it. I admire it no end. As much as I love the outdoors, I do need my territory – more than you. I need a home to guard and nurture, to see bloom... My point is, it's natural you feel this way. I won't ever entrap you, I swear it. One of the reasons I chose this place with Bill and Marco was *because* of the potential challenges for you. We'll be living among nature – in the reserves – and much of it's wild and has never been managed. I figured it would be the best way for you to feel at home within our home, if that makes sense."

Her mind was blank. She was stunned, to be honest. "You ... thought about all that? You thought about..." She couldn't quite form the words for his impeccable consideration and care of her. He'd placed her first. Jasmine, too – that went without saying – but he'd placed *her* first; had read her like a book and made sure the next chapter would do her justice. "Peter..." 'I love you' wasn't enough.

She shook her head, but he smiled, reading the gratitude in her eyes correctly. "Nothing makes me happier than seeing you happy. I haven't forgotten how much you've lost."

The stupid tears were free-flowing now. "I don't know what I would have done without you." She placed her hand on his, still resting on her shoulder. "I gained so much more than I lost. I know I get sad over Sarah still, but you and Jasmine are the world to me, and I wouldn't change that for anything. I hope you know I really mean that."

"Course I do."

She bent down to kiss the top of his hand, then froze.

Fear was something she'd never truly known until she'd become a mother to Jasmine, and right now, it was all she could see and feel. "Peter ... oh god."

He jerked forward the same time she did, his face mirroring the fear she felt.

How it was even possible, she didn't know, and now wasn't the time for her mind to try and piece together the impossible. Ignoring the seatbelt sign, still lit up, she undid hers in a frantic hurry. Pete followed suit.

"Pete ... where..."

"Jasmine?" he called out, already striding up the aisle as Claire scrambled to get out of her seat. "Jasmine!" She kicked something soft with her foot. Looking down, she saw Marlo poking out from under the seat, dropped.

Dumbstruck, she looked back at where their daughter had been sleeping between them, her seatbelt still fastened; the girl in it, gone.

There was no reasonable way to explain why or how Jasmine had gotten out of her seat, so Claire found herself in front of two of the air hostesses, trying not to scream and rave – that would help no one – as she explained her daughter had slipped away while they'd been napping: she must have gone exploring.

Yet a quick search up both the aisles proved futile.

Almost ten minutes later, and Jasmine was nowhere to be found. None of the other passengers had seen her toddling around. Claire was about to lose her mind.

Pete had wandered up the other end of the aeroplane with an air steward to confer with the pilot.

"She's done this before, though never in an unfamiliar place. She's very good at sneaking off; I don't even know how she slipped under the seatbelt – she must have then crawled under our legs. She's *got* to be somewhere here, this is an enclosed space." She was rambling, but it was necessary for the sake of her sanity.

"We'll find her." The air hostess handed her a plastic cup of water. According to the badge on her striped blouse, her name was also Claire. It made her feel claustrophobic. *That's not my name! That's not my name! It's* her *name – not mine!* "Here ... try to be calm. Your daughter's probably having a giggle in some nook or cranny thinking this is the best game of hide and seek ever." Real Claire's voice was way steadier than her own. And how many nooks and crannies were there on an aeroplane?

A fourth air hostess was speaking to each row of passengers as she made her way up the plane with a huge smile on her face, calming them all down and asking if they'd seen a child hunkering under their seats.

The *ping* that came before an announcement sounded. The voice over the speaker was the most terrifying thing she'd ever heard. "Claire Appleby to cockpit station, please."

The other Claire smiled – as if her daughter might not be hurt; as if everything was all right. "I'll take you there. The station's down this end."

She followed the hostess down the aisle, then saw Pete standing at the far end beside a curtain which she assumed covered the door to the cockpit. He waved at her. His smile held relief; on seeing it, she finally let out a breath. *Please be good news.*

After a brief word with the air steward, he made his way towards her. "It's all right," he said as he approached.

"Pete?"

"She's asleep."

"Asleep?"

"Come and see."

He took her hand, and she followed him to where he'd been standing previously, and let out a little gasp at the sight of their daughter curled up on the floor to the left of the aisle beside the drinks trolley, just in front of the curtain. Tears surfaced. "Oh, thank god."

But how on earth was she asleep? It looked as if she hadn't woken up at all, which clearly she must have to have gotten here.

"Thank you so much," she directed at the staff. The air steward nodded, and the 'Claire' hostess smiled as she looked on Jasmine's sleeping form.

"Bless her, she must be exhausted. I suspect she wanted to see the pilot. I've been doing this job for eight years – it's not the first time we've had to steer an excited child away from the cockpit."

She didn't think Jasmine even knew what a cockpit was. But she just nodded her thanks. "I'll wake her up and take her back to her seat. I'm so sorry to have caused so much trouble."

"Don't worry, it happens. We've got a short form for you to fill out, though, if that's okay – just detailing what happened for our records. There's no rush, though – we've got eleven hours," she added by way of a joke. "Get yourselves settled first."

"Of course. Thank you again."

They courteously moved back to give Claire and Pete

some room.

"Jasmine, honey..." Claire knelt down by her side and ran a hand through her hair and across her forehead, instinctively feeling for anything untoward like bruises or a fever. She seemed fine, though, and her breathing was steady, as if she'd been sleeping for a while. She shook her gently. "Jasmine."

She turned where she lay, eyes still closed, murmuring in her sleep. She had no idea of the havoc she'd created.

With a sigh, Claire leaned in and scooped her up into her arms.

Her eyelids fluttered open, though she didn't look as though she wanted to keep them open. "Mummy?" she mumbled.

"It's okay. I'm taking you back to your seat. Why did you leave your seat, Jasmine?"

She rubbed her right eye with a small fist, looking confused. "Mummy..." she repeated.

With child in arms, she followed Pete back to their seats, trying not to meet the eyes of all the other passengers. Relief was fast giving way to acute embarrassment. She'd stumbled into parenthood, and it never felt more obvious than during moments like these. While some of the gazes falling on her were sympathetic and understanding, many held judgement: *What kind of parent loses their child on an aeroplane?*

Her cheeks burned.

Pete went ahead of her to undo Jasmine's seatbelt.

Claire placed her back in her seat with no protest from Jasmine, thankfully. "Sweetie, look..."

She blinked as she looked down at Claire re-fastening her seatbelt. "You have to stay in your seat with the belt done up until we say it's okay to undo it, all right? Please don't wander off again."

Pete handed Marlo to Jasmine who took her lion from

him.

Claire found herself frowning as she pulled the belt tight. *How in the world did she manage to slip out of it?* She couldn't figure it out.

Jasmine looked towards the window. "Are we there yet?"

"No, honey. It's only been an hour – there's a long way to go. We'll be able to take the belt off again soon, and then you can sit on my lap and look out the window again, okay?"

She nodded, sleepiness still colouring every inch of her face.

Pete sat himself down in his aisle seat. At least the whole debacle had been a distraction from his anxiety of flying.

"Jasmine?"

Her daughter looked up at her, her gaze starting to become more aware as sleep was chased away.

"Do you remember why you left your seat and went for a walk?"

She didn't reply straight away, but stared at her with those large, dark brown eyes, a shade darker than Sarah's had been, but looking so much like hers in shape and intensity. When she did reply, Claire couldn't explain the small shiver that ran up her spine.

"No, Mummy ... no walk."

Chapter Three

Two and a half years on...

If heaven could be found on the earth, it would be here among the national parks and forests that made up the east stretch along California, right up into Oregon. Lakes, pines and firs, snow-capped peaks to the north, and desert rocks and dunes to the south towards Nevada, made up only a small portion of the largely untamed land that any wolf would be proud to call home. And the September sunshine made everything look stunning.

Days ago, a handful of gray wolves had roamed silently in and out of where Pete, Bill and Marco currently trotted. Unless there were trackers on the wolves, they were hard to spot if you were human, but as werewolves, they could track them by scent. Marco had told Pete that their population had tripled over the past half-decade in the rugged wildness of the foothills between the Plumas and Lassen national forests. Human tallies did not hold this information; it belonged to the confidential records Bill and Marco had begun when they'd first arrived. And *they* could identify each wolf from their personal aroma – no man-made device needed. There was no marker more accurate.

A small pack of werewolves led by an Alpha called Tristan – *the* Grand Alpha between here and Chicago, Illinois – had long kept their home in the woods surrounding Portland in Oregon. They oversaw the growth and migrations of their animal cousins down to Sacramento and into Idaho, but such a large area to cover was taking its toll, and the states further out remained devoid of any werewolf packs, so near to extinction they'd all been.

Bill and Marco had met with Tristan when first seeking residency in America. They had fully filled him in with the happenings in Europe and the new Gunvald reign. Bill and Marco were subsequently welcomed as overseers in the State of California, and having steadily established their new roles over the past five years in both the werewolf and human worlds, Bill and Marco had received their official "pack" status just a year ago: they *were* the California pack now. They had a duty to expand their pack number over the next few years, and any werewolf seeking entry into California were expected to report their whereabouts and intentions to them.

In these early days, Pete, Claire and Jasmine had been included as part of their new pack, officially increasing their numbers, despite Claire and Jasmine's human status. The destruction of the old werewolf rules after the death of all the Trident had given birth to a much freer way of living among and managing packs. In the unlikely event Claire happened to become pregnant with Pete's child, there was a minimal chance the child *may* inherit the wolf gene. No matter how small the probability of it all, in these post-near extinction times, it was an important enough reason to absorb them into pack society.

He and Claire had been endlessly grateful, and Jasmine had taken in her new home with that curious delight exclusive to children. They had all settled in more easily than they could have hoped for, and those roots they needed to make for Jasmine's sake were already furrowing deep. Claire had driven into town half an hour ago to pick Jasmine up from school.

Marco shifted into his human body a few yards ahead of them; Bill followed suit. Pete relished the form of his wolf and everything it offered for another few seconds before giving in to the twist of muscles and crunch of bones as they realigned.

On two legs, and not much else, he strode up the bank of long grass towards his two companions, both of whom held similar gaits and dark brown hair and eyes. Marco, though, was of Italian descent; Bill had been born and bred in London to an Irish father and a Scottish mother, his dark hair and paler, almost marble-like skin – not too dissimilar from Pete's own – inherited from his Celtic lineage.

"I can't smell any of the gray wolves today," said Pete as he came to stand by them.

Bill shook his head. "Neither can I. I think they've moved on, and not a moment too soon."

Hunters had been rumoured to be trespassing over the next few days. Bears, foxes, deer, and wolves were all prime targets until they could catch the bastards out and ensure their arrest. That meant calling in law enforcement since Bill and Marco didn't have any authority to make arrests.

Other than the initial needed work Visas five years ago, they had had no issues securing employment with the U.S. Forestry Service. Marco's Forestry degree, Bill's Masters in Environmental Sciences, and a glowing reference covering years of employment and experience with the Gunvald Estate in Britain, had landed them both with full time work which they had chosen to take on seasonally so they could spend the rest of their time setting up their wolf conservation project which was just starting to become recognised. They also relished the extra time with each other as a couple – something they could now, in werewolf society, express freely. Last month, they had publicly announced their engagement.

"Do you often get hunters trying to sneak in?" asked Pete.

"Poaching happens, though not too much around here, and Tristan has a tight rein on that kind of thing up north. Not sure on the source of the information – we got an anonymous tip-off – but we'll need to be vigilant over the next week. While they might be after the gray wolves, there are still so few of them here, they tend not to bother – the poachers are usually caught before they manage to catch the wolves – but they could be after the black bears. And the Bighorn Sheep are further south near the desert – they're poached for their antlers. There's still a chance the rumour's just a rumour, and nothing will come of it."

"Any reason the source would lie?"

"None I can think of. Even kids pulling pranks don't bother rangers with that kind of thing – nothing in it for them." He headed for the clothes they'd stashed between a cluster of rocks.

The ground rumbled.

All three of them stopped, instinctively looking for their centre of gravity for balance even though it wasn't needed for such a small tremor. It was a strange thing to feel a quake as an animal – like you were part of the earth itself, not separated from the movement.

"Not even a two on the Richter scale," said Marco. "We and the wildlife are the only ones feeling this. Humans can't."

"Could this be why the wolves ran?"

"Doubt it. You've felt them – they happen every day and have done since the Great Quakes started nine years ago. All the animals are used to it now. They feel more like micro after-shocks to me – and ongoing."

Pete nodded, noting how the ground settled quickly

enough under his feet. No rock or stone had been shaken; no leaf had been left shivering.

Bill grabbed his T-shirt and shoved it on. "We've been out here for hours; let's head back. We can always scout at night if we're still worried."

This was true. Being werewolves had so many advantages, the ability to track in the dark being one of them.

Two minutes later saw them fully clothed and heading back towards their Range Rover. "How has Jasmine settled in to her new school?" asked Marco. She'd just started kindergarten, having turned five three days ago. Thankfully, she didn't seem to be struggling despite the fact she was one of the youngest in her class. She took it in her stride.

"Very well. She's made a couple of new friends – a girl and a boy, both in her class. I think the change has been good for her – she can retreat into herself if not pushed a little. But she seems to be integrating well with the other kids."

"Good to hear. And Claire?"

Pete sighed, but smiled. "Claire and 'integrating' ... she's never found it so easy blending in to the background."

"Who says she needs to blend?"

Pete laughed. "Look at my face, Marco. I can tell you that standing out makes it *harder* to make friends and be accepted, no matter how much we think society's moved forward. Wariness of anything different is a natural defence mechanism, though. I don't begrudge anyone for it. And Claire's used to it – she's always been gregarious and outspoken. I worry she dampens it all for Jasmine's sake."

"Surely Jasmine wouldn't care."

"Course not, but all those new friends we want her to make? Their parents might."

Bill stared at him through his sunglasses as they all got in the car, one eyebrow raised in amusement. "Is this before they find out you're a werewolf, or after?"

Pete grinned and shrugged. "We have no plans to tell anyone."

Marco clapped him on the shoulder from the seat behind him as Bill fired up the engine. "Doesn't matter – they still know *something's* off about you, even if they can't put their finger on it. Obviously, they won't think 'werewolf'. In your case, they'll think it's to do with your scars because that's what's visible. In our case, they put it down to the relationship we have. The judgement's there no matter what excuse they make for it. But there are good people, Pete – ones who don't have judgement of that ilk in their nature. They'll just accept you for you off the bat, and even if they're few and far between, they're worth holding out for. Take it from us: it's better to have no friends, than many friends who can't accept you for who you are. Remind Claire of that if she's struggling."

"She knows, but I'll remind her – thanks. It's just that Jasmine comes first, you know?"

"And she will for the rest of your lives. But what are you teaching her if you hide the things that make you *you*?"

"Do you prance around telling everyone you're wolves?"

Marco laughed heartily behind him. It was Bill who answered. "No. But we do now prance around not hiding we're gay."

Pete chuckled at that.

"There'll be a time we can prance around as werewolves, too. Just probably not for a very long time. But we'll get there. Not by hiding though – not completely, anyway."

"Yeah. I get it."

They fell into a comfortable silence on the drive home. He knew that the reason Bill and Marco had chosen this route – nature, the land, the wildlife, and the wolves – was so they could more *publicly* be who they were: werewolves. No, of course they didn't 'announce' it. But they could *live* it as members of the human world with the jobs they had without anyone raising too many questions. It was for this very reason he felt Jasmine would find the right home here.

He suspected she'd feel 'different' as soon as she started to make friends and have that point of comparison, and she *was* becoming aware of her 'differences'. The hard part for them was that they didn't fully know *how* she was different. Anatomically and physiologically, she was human. But they all knew that was only a half-truth, and there was no point kidding themselves otherwise – soon, they wouldn't be able to kid themselves at all – and as he'd predicted, she was beginning to show signs of ... not being entirely comfortable in her skin. What that would mean in months and years to come was anyone's guess, but here, amid the sanctuary of Bill and Marco's home, they could explore Jasmine's needs unfettered. That was a gift.

Twenty minutes later saw them pulling into the long drive that led to the house. Claire's car was already parked at the top, and his heart leapt at the thought of seeing both her and Jasmine – his two girls. That never got old.

The porch door swung open and Jasmine sped out of it, clutching something in her hand, clearly having heard the car rolling up the drive. "Daddy!"

He took in Jasmine's huge smile; her bouncing hair as she ran, accentuating her excitement at his arrival. That was love, that was. Pure, unadulterated love, and god help him, five years ago, he never thought he'd have this. He thought his past had ruined him for everyone. He was one lucky bastard.

Bill brought the car to a stop, and Pete opened his door.

"Daddy! I drew a picture in quiet time and Mrs Myers loved it so much I got to show the whole class!"

"Wow!"

"Do you want to see?"

"Most definitely." He caught her as she leapt into his arms, not giving him any time to get out of his seat.

"Look!" She held out the slightly scrunched up piece of paper.

He took it from her and smoothed it. A drawing of two people – stick figures with huge heads and saucers for eyes – stared back at him. He pointed at the tall one with browny-blonde hair. "Is this Mummy?"

"Yep."

"And..." He moved his finger to the shorter one with dark hair. "This is you, right?"

She beamed her smile. "Yes!" Her joy uncontainable, she rammed her own finger at the other figure on the paper. This one had four stick legs and a snout. It was big and she'd drawn lots of lines for fur. There was a heart above it. "And this is you!" Then she lowered her voice, though it still vibrated with excitement. "Don't worry, I didn't say you were a wolf. I said it was a big, friendly dog I love that lives with us." And even though she was brimming over with happiness, her eyes widened a little in concern as she searched his face to make sure she hadn't done anything wrong.

Fuck. His heart cracked. He brought her in for a hug and a kiss to her head.

He spied Claire in the doorway. She gave him a small wave, then turned and headed inside.

"I love it," he told Jasmine. "It's an amazing picture. Can we put it up on the fridge?"

Her smile regained its wattage. She nodded with pride.

Pete caught Bill's eye as he carried her out of the car with him, his friend's look a knowing one.

Like any child, Jasmine wanted to share the things she loved; the things that mattered most to her. To hide who they were was to deny her that chance and it left him hollow. He didn't want her to learn not all the world was so loving.

They'd made the right choice moving here. They'd take it slow – baby steps. They didn't have to hide everything here. They could teach her in stages. And maybe Bill was right: one day, some day, maybe none of them would have to hide who they were at all.

"How's Mummy?"

"She's good. Daddy, can Diego and Molly come round to play?"

"Are they your two best friends in class?"

"Mmm-hmm," she nodded, tracing the wolf she'd drawn with her finger as he carried her up the steps to the house.

"Course they can. I'll speak to Mummy and see if we can sort something out with their parents."

She placed her arms around his neck in a hug. "Thank you, Daddy."

"Is your room tidy for dinner?"

She looked at him, sheepishly. They always tidied it before dinner – saved a huge amount of hassle just before bed.

"Why don't you spend ten minutes putting some toys away while I say hello to Mummy."

"Okay."

He placed her down. "Shall I take the picture for the fridge?"

She handed it to him with a smile, then skipped off up the stairs to her room.

Pete found Claire in the living room, going through a box on the coffee table. "Hey, you."

"Hey," she greeted, turning her head up for a kiss, which he gladly gave. Her blue eyes were lit with her familiar inner-strength; her cheeks rosy from the fresh mountain air. Jesus, he could look at her all day. "Did you find the wolves?"

"Nope. We think they've left for a new habitat for the moment."

"Because something scared them off, or a natural progression?"

"Hard to say, to be honest, but we'll keep an eye out over the next week or so. How was your day?" He sat next to her on the sofa.

"Not bad. I took a couple of new bookings for two of the cabins and brought all the paperwork up to date. Current guests are leaving tomorrow, so I'll have to leave Jasmine with you after picking her up to sort that out."

"No problem. What are you doing?" He nodded at the box she had her hands in.

"Trying to find some photos Holly wants." She sighed. This weekend, Holly was flying in for a visit for the first time since they'd moved here. Claire was sure she'd been putting it off on purpose over the past two and a half years, and finally ran out of excuses. "Photos of Sarah. I don't know though – in the move, they all got a bit scattered, and I think some of the ones she's asking for might be at my mum's back home." She caught herself and glanced at him apologetically. "I mean, in England."

He threw her a half-smile. "Come on, you know I get it. It's only been two and a half years – can't expect it to feel like home straight away. It takes time."

She put down the two photos she was holding and sidled up next to him on the sofa. "You feel at home, though – I know you do."

He looked at her. He wondered if his features took on the warmth his chest did at her nearness. "I feel at home because you're here."

She stared at him a bit, then smiled, softly, her cheeks going a bit redder.

"It's true. England, here, Canada, China, the bloody North Pole – wherever we end up, it would only be home with you."

That soft smile of hers grew. She rested her chin on his shoulder. "What did I do to deserve you?"

"Came at me like the fireball you are, obliterating my fear of the damned element." Inside, he cringed. Shit. That sounded like fucking bad poetry, but it had just come out of his mouth 'cause he meant it.

She didn't seem to mind though. With another sigh – this one content – she leaned forward and kissed the side of his face, right on that old burn, as if her brand of fire could heal the trail of rage the old one had left behind. Maybe it could, but somewhere within, he couldn't stop the way he shrivelled up a little. How could she be proud to be seen with him when she tried so hard to fit in? He'd never fit in – couldn't even pretend. The difference was right there all the time.

She swore she'd never be 'less' of herself. They'd both changed, though. Their independence, self-centredness, pride, all came second to Jasmine's needs now; to their love for her. Was there a way being less of yourself could mean being more for your child? He wasn't sure.

"Don't change, Claire. Promise me. Be that fireball."

She raised her head, stared at him, then lowered her eyes, her smile fading. "But I have changed," she whispered. "Claire is Jasmine's mum."

"No – Claire's just a name; a label. Beth was the one who blazed her way to that hospital to save her best friend; Beth's the one who blazed away from it with her best friend's baby. *That's* her mum, no matter which name she wears. But if the name bothers you so..." Was he really going to say this? To hell with it – yes, he was. "Marry me."

Her eyes widened in shock. Her cheeks went even redder.

"What?"

"Marry me. I've loved you since the moment you traipsed into my life talking my hind legs off with your nonsense, I love you more than ever now, and I'll love you 'til the end of both our lives. I love you as Beth, as Claire; I'll love you if you're Gertrude."

A laugh broke through her shock.

"I love you if you're a best friend, a mother, or a lover. So have my name instead of the one forced upon you. *Choose* my name. Forget Claire Appleby; be Claire Cryer and have it mean something."

He'd rendered her speechless – not a mean feat. Hopefully her dumbstruck state was due to his bad poetry, and not the fact he had no ring, or even a fucking plan, 'cause he'd taken a leaf out of her book and just sprinted head first into what he wanted: her, and her happy, forever.

Her grin suddenly split her face into the same thousand watts Jasmine had offered him earlier. "Yes."

Shit. His heart hammered against his ribs; he couldn't hold back his own grin. "Yes?"

"Yes!" She got up and straddled his lap. "I never thought I'd marry anyone, but you're not anyone." She took his face in both her hands. "You're my wolf." She kissed him, her kiss affirming her 'yes' and everything they'd been through to get to this point.

"Guys, please…" Bill threw his keys on the table, his teasing voice pulling them apart. "Get a room. One's being freed up tomorrow."

Marco's huge grin told him they'd caught the last of their conversation. "Copycats."

"Couldn't let you have all the glory."

"Congratulations!"

He took Marco's outstretched hand while Bill kissed

Claire on the cheek, the joyful laughter lifting the mood of the last few hours. "Double wedding?" Bill asked her.

"Maybe ... I'm going to need a few days to think." She glowed. She looked the happiest he'd seen her in a while.

Pete swore he was fucking blushing. Ha – the burn scars were good for something: hiding the fucking sap in him. "Any decent ring shops around here?"

"I don't need a ring," Claire said, overwhelm tingeing her tone.

"I'm getting you a ring."

It was Bill's turn to shake his hand. "One hour's drive into Redding – quite a few there to choose from."

"What do you say, Claire, shall we have a look at the weekend?"

"And take Holly with us? She'll insist on going. No way – she'll end up choosing the ring. Let's go next week after she's left."

Small feet sounded as they bounded down the wooden stairs. "Daddy, I've tidied my room."

"Come here, pumpkin. Mummy and Daddy have some news."

Jasmine approached them, looking curiously at everyone's smiling faces. He could stare at Claire's all day. He hadn't seen that smile on her since they'd first met.

Claire motioned for her to get on her lap, which she did. "Sweetie ... Mummy and Daddy are getting married."

It took a moment for the words to sink in, and then her dark brown eyes got big and round. "Oh ... oh!" She clapped her hands in excitement. "Will you look like a princess?"

Claire froze for a moment. Tears sprang to her eyes, her demeanour easing.

Pete's worry piqued, but then her smile was back and she

tenderly stroked Jasmine's cheek as she blinked the tears away. "Or perhaps a ghost, but I'll give princess my best shot."

Chapter Four

"Y ou're happy?" asked Holly as they both leaned back, half-sitting on a rock that overlooked the most magnificent view across fir trees. A lake peeked out from between the foliage.

"Yeah, I am. I mean ... as much as I can be. I miss her. Sometimes I wonder if it was all a dream, and I'll wake up tomorrow."

"You mean a nightmare."

Claire said nothing, not rising to Holly's blunt pessimism. She didn't want her happiness over her engagement to fade. Two days in Holly's presence and her visit was already starting to take its toll, but Claire battled her annoyance out of respect for Sarah above anything else.

Out of the three of them, Holly had taken the news of the existence of werewolves the least well, preferring to push the whole ordeal to the back of her mind, despite the sheer impossibility of that. Sarah's death had hit her as hard as anyone else, and although Holly hadn't said anything, Claire suspected she blamed the werewolves – at least in part. Never mind that it was Tridents who had hunted her, not wolves, and never mind that her death itself had seemed to be the result of a very bad car accident rather than anything supernatural. Admittedly, the arrival of Jasmine as well as the events of that night put the 'bad car accident' theory to the test. But no one had found any answers as to why Sarah died, so 'bad car accident' it was.

"Jasmine keeps us occupied. And she's a real delight."

"Oh, she is, isn't she? And, my god, Beth, she looks *so* much like her."

"Claire. You'd best stick to the right name."

Holly rolled her eyes, and brushed a strand of her dark brown hair off her chin. "Because we're surrounded by people who'll whisk your kid away and slap you in jail in case you're *that* Beth that no one even knows about?"

"Come on, Holly, I mean it. Not even Jasmine knows, and if *she* starts going around calling me Beth, we have a problem."

"What problem? It was five years ago, and *no one* is looking for that baby taken from the hospital."

Claire winced.

"The people who might still be looking saw a huge dog run off with her. *That's* what they're looking for."

"My car was there. It was even reported afterwards, I think."

"How many Beth's are there in the world?"

"Fitting my exact description, and from England? Hmmm..."

"All right, all right ... *Claire*."

Jesus, Holly was difficult.

"I'll call you whatever you like, but I can't get used to it."

"I'm not used to it either, but it is what it is. So..." She desperately wanted to change the subject. "How are things with you and Tim?"

Holly shrugged. "Yuuuugh ... you know."

"I do?"

"It's fine, I guess, just ... it's weird to know this huge

secret about the world and be with someone who doesn't."

"You mean the existence of werewolves?"

"Oh, so it's okay to talk about werewolves, but not call you Beth?"

She shot her a look.

"Fine. Yes – werewolves. It feels like half a relationship – I can't talk to him about one of the most significant discoveries ever. But it's going to be like that with anyone I'm with from now on, so I just have to suck it up and accept the fact I'll never be in an equal relationship again. You're lucky being with Pete – you can talk about it all."

"There must be hundreds of other things to talk about."

"Yeah, there are, but..." Holly looked over at her, then looked away; started fiddling with her rucksack for something. "It gets lonely. And I can't go back to *not* knowing. I'm not like everyone else anymore. I feel weird and awkward, and ... oh, my god! I'm *you*." She pulled out her water bottle.

"Nice."

Holly grinned at her from behind her huge sunglasses. "I'm teasing."

Half-teasing. She ignored her. Holly had always been the one who cared most about fitting in and being liked, and it pressed Claire's button that she, herself, had swayed the same way in recent months.

"Are you ever going to tell Jasmine you're not her parents?"

"Holly!"

"I'm curious."

"What would I tell her instead? Your father's an evil monster who lied to and slept with your mother, then ran off and left her pregnant? Then later, she was in a horrific car crash and died?"

"Well, maybe not *now*. But when she's older?"

"What purpose would it serve? Pete's been more of a father to her than most fathers are to their daughters."

"I can see that, but the truth has a nasty way of coming out, don't you think? I'd want to know if it was me."

"But to what end? It's not like she can seek her parents out, they're both gone."

"So tell her you adopted her because both her parents died – she was still wanted and loved. Why would that ruin her?"

"I guess it might not, but—"

"It just means she's prepared when the truth *does* come out in a way you can't control. And it will – it always does. Besides, while her dark hair and eyes *could* pass for Pete's, her skin tone's a bit darker than either of yours and she looks not even a little bit like you. You don't think she'll notice when she's older? She will. And she'll wonder; she might even ask about it. And when you show her pictures of your parents and their parents, she'll notice she looks nothing like them either. Though she *might* notice that she's the spitting image of Sarah since she's in almost every photo you guys ever took together."

"So, I won't show her any photos," she snapped.

"None? That'll make her even more curious – she'll look for the photos herself."

Claire sighed, though it came out more of a hiss. "Holly, we'll cross that bridge when we come to it, okay? She's too young now." And she hoped she'd put enough finality into that last sentence so Holly would shut up about something that was none of her business. But she'd always been like that, hadn't she? The delightful personality trait was more pronounced without Sarah here to diffuse the tension.

Holly took a swig of water, and they both fell into a heavy silence, making a pretence of admiring the view, and Claire wondered if Holly was also feeling the frustration of their friendship dynamic without Sarah here. This was the first time they'd met since Sarah's death. In fact, it had always been quite rare for them to meet up without Sarah at all – she'd been their glue – and it wasn't half noticeable.

Footsteps and voices sounding behind them had Claire standing and turning, perhaps feeling a bit more wary than was necessary. Pete came out here much more than she did, and she didn't know the routes as well as he, but it surprised her, somewhat, to find it occupied by others this Monday morning. Casual hikers and boondockers weren't that common here. Most campers registered their stay with the Forest Service, and Bill and Marco had access to that register. No one was due to be in this area today. Pete's warning about poachers replayed in her mind.

Two men kitted out for hiking came into view along the trail from its bend. They stopped talking when they saw them, but waved with a smile and headed their way.

"Maybe they're lost," said Holly.

Maybe they're hungry, thought Claire, as images of Tridents in beast form sprang to mind. Fuck. She gave her head a small shake to get rid of the unwelcome visual. All the Trident were dead. All sources pretty much guaranteed that to be the case.

"Hi," the slightly shorter of the two called out. "Is this the trail that leads up to East Quincy?"

"Yeah," replied Claire. "Follow it north – might take you most of the day, though."

"No, that's cool. That was the plan: take in the wild country and get fit," he laughed.

"What's up in East Quincy?"

"We're just passing through. Actually heading up to the golf course north of Lake Almanor. Do you know it?"

"I've not been there."

"Aah, well, there's this reunion happening there in a couple of days – we're meeting some friends. They're going to drive us back down to Sacramento the day after the party."

"Sounds nice."

"Right." The two guys now stood in front of them, the taller one relieving himself of his backpack. "Should be good. We haven't seen them for over ten years. You're not American, right?"

"No. I'm from England."

"What brings you all the way out here?"

Friendly. He's just being friendly. "We have friends here, too, and the change of pace and lifestyle was exactly what we were looking for."

"Our friends work here as foresters," shot out Holly.

Claire's back went up. She threw her a look. Talk about giving information away.

"Awesome. Guess you know who to call if you ever encounter trouble."

She wasn't sure if there was an undertone of ... something ... in his sentence, or if she was being paranoid.

"Well, we'd best get going, right, Steve?"

His friend nodded. "Two more hours, then stop for lunch?"

"Sounds good."

"Good luck, guys. Have a great party."

"We will. It was good to meet you." They continued on up the trail, and then the shorter guy – not Steve – stopped suddenly, turned and headed back.

Claire wished she felt as carefree about this kind of shit as she had years back. *It's just chatting, they're just being friendly, strangers are not a threat, the chance of them being a danger is minimal ...* but no matter how many times she repeated the script, it didn't undo the past five years; it didn't undo the existence of a paranormal world she was now a part of – a world where you could be found if there were those who wanted to find you, if not through normal means, then by supernatural means.

"You know," he started, "it occurred to me to ask ... is there a direct number for your friends? I mean, we have a general number to call if we come across anything we can't handle – overprotective mama bears and the like – but—"

"The general number really is the best number. You'll get through to someone straight away."

He eyed her with interest, and now she was starting to think she had reason to feel uneasy after all.

"Good to know. Thanks. And if I happen to bump into some British foresters, I'll know they're your friends."

The unease she felt grew, and she couldn't shake the feeling there was some kind of veiled warning there. Her mind scrambled for the right thing to say until they were all distracted by another figure emerging from the wooded area to her right, off the beaten track.

Also male, and appearing to be of Native American descent, this new stranger held his hand up in greeting when he spied them. He made his way to the group.

"Ma'am," said Steve from behind his friend, tilting his hat to her in 'goodbye'. "Thank you kindly for your help. Come on, Liall."

The shorter man tore his eyes from the stranger, something that looked an awful lot like hatred shining through them, nodded once, then turned and left with Steve.

"Wow," whispered Holly. "What was *that* about?"

Claire finally snapped. "What the hell did you tell them about Bill and Marco for?"

"What? I didn't! I never named them; I said you had friends who worked here. I figured if there was any ill intent on their part, that might put them off doing anything bad."

"You gave way too much detail."

"Are you kidding me? When did you get so paranoid?"

"The moment they referred to our friends as British. We never told them that."

"So they assumed. Is it such a crazy leap to take after telling them you're from England? And *you're* the one that told them that, not me."

"How could I have said anything else? My accent gave me away, there was no point lying. But *you* didn't have to say we had friends who worked here. If they're poachers unsure of who to look out for, you gave them a huge helping hand."

"Two bears take food from one another," the man said, just metres from where they stood.

Claire and Holly both shut up and turned to greet him. He seemed to be in his late-thirties; his hair, long and black, was braided in two places. He wore jeans and a T-shirt, the belt around his waist holding a leather pouch. Two silver chains adorned his wrist.

"Hello," said Claire. "I'm sorry, we're just—"

"Hungry?"

After a moment, Claire laughed, an unusual sheepishness – not one of her regular traits – colouring the laugh. What must others think of Holly and herself together? Lord, even Pete had a habit of walking out of the room after five minutes.

"Hi." Holly held out her hand. "I'm Holly."

He took it with a warm smile. "I'm Elkoyti. Everyone calls me Elky."

"And I'm Claire."

He took her hand next. "Come now, you say your name with hesitation."

A bit bewildered, she pulled her hand back. "I do?"

"Names have meaning; we wear them like skin."

"What does yours mean?" asked Holly.

"I'm afraid the meaning is rather gruesome, but like all things, it has two sides to it."

They waited for him to expand on that. He didn't, but changed the subject. "I have family in Gregstown; I stay with them sometimes. I do prefer to camp out here under the stars, though."

"Isn't Gregstown the ranchería?" A ranchería was a native village or settlement if she understood the term correctly.

"That's right. I'm a descendant of the Maipeke people from this area."

"I think Marco might have mentioned the Maipeke when we first moved here, but only in passing. I think he was taking us through Indian Falls at the time."

"It's beautiful country around here." He smiled again. It reached his dark eyes. This man pretty much exuded nothing but warmth and ease. "I think I know of you, Claire. I've seen your husband – tall, dark hair, scarred face – and I've seen your daughter, too."

"He's..." She hesitated, unsure how much to reveal to this stranger, but he all at once seemed less of a stranger than the other two. "He's my fiancé. We've just gotten engaged."

"Congratulations."

"Thank you."

Holly stared daggers at her. She knew exactly why; she could read her internal dialogue. *Oh, NOW it's okay to go giving away secrets?*

"Did you know the two men I saw you speaking to?"

"No. They were asking for directions. I..." She hesitated again, then carried on. "I didn't feel too comfortable around them, but can't put my finger on why. I did hear about potential poachers in the area, though."

"Hmmm," he nodded. "They might be poachers; they

might not. Perhaps the better question is what would they be poaching?"

"I heard bears are the favourite in this region."

"Yes. And new creatures unseen."

Holly tried to surreptitiously nudge Claire with her shoulder. She'd have a fucking embolism in a minute.

"Holly!" she snapped.

Holly rolled her eyes, but quit the nudging.

She got it – this was mysterious and weird. It still felt better than their conversation with the other two. "What do you mean 'unseen'?"

"Exactly that." He placed his hands in his pockets and rolled back a bit on his heels, contemplating both of them. "There's a hotel along that trail through the woods – less than half an hour's walk. They serve unrivalled coffee. Fancy joining me?"

She could tell Holly didn't. Perhaps it was the bitch in her, but that made her mind up for her. "Sure. I've got a couple of hours before I need to go. I might grab lunch, too, if they're serving food?"

"Yep. They do a mighty fine rice and nachos dish."

"Sounds perfect." She picked up her rucksack, only to have Holly tug hard on her arm.

"I'm sorry … Elky," smiled Holly. "Can you give us half a minute?"

"Sure." His look told Claire he knew the score. "I'll wait for you at the top of the trail."

When he was far enough away to be out of immediate earshot, Holly placed herself in front of her. "What. The. Fuck."

"Is that a question?"

"You don't *know* him. You went all scared rabbit on those other two, but he's safe?"

"Seems safe to me. Look, I'll phone Pete now and let him know where we're going and with whom."

"And he's going to be okay with that?"

"He's not the boss of me. Bill and Marco have probably heard of this guy, especially since he knew of them and Pete. My gut says we can trust him. Besides, didn't you get the feeling he had things to tell us?"

"About poachers?"

"About 'creatures unseen'. Maybe it's important."

"Christ, Claire. We're going to walk through the woods with a stranger because your gut says it's okay?"

"Look." She held her phone up, the ringing through the earpiece clear to hear. "I'm phoning Pete right now."

Holly went to protest, but she cut her off when the phone went to voicemail. She left Pete a message, then hung up and pocketed the device. "Let's do this." She strode towards the trail where Elkoyti waited.

Holly hurried behind her, tutting furiously. "Because the *last* time we followed a guy through the woods ended so well?"

It had ended with pain, death, and destruction, but also... "It ended up giving me a family I cherish."

Chapter Five

The shrill sound of the recess bell pulled on Jasmine's ears – or that's what it felt like anyway: noise could be so loud it pinched and stretched your ears out. She wondered if that was how Daddy's ears felt when he was a wolf. She knew dogs had super-good hearing.

She'd asked him once if she would be a wolf, too, when she grew up, and he'd said she wouldn't, just like Mummy wouldn't. That made her feel a little sad.

Jasmine did her best clearing up the pots of paint she'd been using, so she could get outside as quickly as possible.

"What have you painted for us today, Jasmine?" asked Mrs Myers.

"It's still wet," she answered, knowing that wasn't the question she'd been asked, but it was the most important answer, because Mrs Myers could answer the other question herself: she could look at the painting and see what it was.

And that's exactly what she did while Jasmine wondered if she could get away with *not* washing the splatters of orange paint off her hands – it would take too much time, and playing outside never lasted long enough.

"Wow, I love the sun you've painted, and this is a really huge bird!"

"It's a dragon," she corrected. She used to call them big birds herself, but she remembered now what they were really called.

"That's even more amazing. You have a great imagination."

She smiled, then concentrated on drying the paint on her hands with a paper towel.

"Don't forget to wash your hands, Jasmine."

Oh. She let a frown replace her smile, but did as she was told and headed for the sink at the back of the room, trying not to bump into the other kids who were rushing to get outside.

"What made you decide to paint a dragon?"

"I'm going to ride a dragon one day."

She couldn't see Mrs Myers' face from where she stood with her hands under the tap, but she could hear the amusement in her voice. It was the same way all adults talked when they thought she was joking. She wasn't joking though. "You're going to *ride* one?"

"Yes."

"Well, aren't you going to need to catch it first?"

"No."

"Then how are you going to ride it?"

"It will land in front of me, kneel down, then I'll climb up and sit on it."

"But you might fall off," she said with a laugh.

"I won't. I'll hold on, and he won't let me fall off."

"So, your dragon's a 'he', not a 'she'?"

Jasmine nodded, but didn't reply out loud. She was starting to feel uncomfortable, like she was giving away too many secrets about the dragon, or something. "I've washed my hands now, Mrs Myers. May I go out and play?"

"Of course. I'm going to write your name on the painting

and put it on the rack to dry, okay?"

She nodded again. "Okay." Then before her teacher could ask more questions, Jasmine walked as fast as she could out of the classroom.

She felt better once she stepped out of the building and could see the sky above her. She quickly scanned the expanse of blue, but wasn't expecting to see what she wanted to see. She'd come to learn that dragons were a bit like werewolves: people thought they were make-believe. That meant she'd have to keep it a secret the way she kept her daddy's secret. That was okay – she was starting to get used to the fact grown-ups didn't see the world the same way she did. Even some children didn't see the world the way she did. She thought that might mean *she* had some kind of super power, too. She wasn't a wolf, but maybe she was a dragon? Though, she didn't *feel* like a dragon... But Daddy had told her that girl werewolves didn't change into werewolves until they were teenagers, so perhaps it would be the same with her – maybe she would change into whatever she was when she was older.

"Jasmine!" Her best friend, Diego, called her over to where he and Molly stood. It looked like they were playing hopscotch, and because that was one of her favourite games, and Diego made everything fun, she smiled and ran over to join them.

~*~

Bloody hell, these actually *were* the best nachos she'd ever tasted.

Claire was starving, and it only now occurred to her that she hadn't had much of a dinner last night.

Holly was picking at her salad, sitting in her chair, stiff as a board, while Elkoyti relayed stories about his Native

American heritage, and his own journey growing up in Los Angeles, only in early adulthood to be told about his people. It was fascinating. Claire could listen to him all day, the warmth he emanated, as strong as any sun. It radiated with honesty, and maybe that was why she'd taken to him so. She couldn't sense a deceitful bone in his body.

Holly maintained her wariness.

"With hindsight, I was grateful," he said, his voice, though deep, carrying a lightness that came from an acceptance of life's challenges. "My natural interests lay in history and culture, so I studied both, and also religion, at university. Once I learnt about my true heritage, I had a fountain of knowledge to dip into, and it's quite something to learn about your own ancestry without any personal judgements to colour it, which I think is what my adoptive parents always intended. My biological grandparents remember, as children, the still palpable consequences of the white settlers coming: the loss of land and food... *Their* parents had friends and family who were killed in the early 1900s by the second influx of settlers who could not distinguish the Maipeke from other, less peaceful tribes."

"I can't imagine. It must have been horrendous."

"Indeed it was, and must never be forgotten, but horrors take place everywhere, daily, monthly, yearly and for centuries, and that is what my studies – taken before I had a clue about my family's history – taught me first and foremost. Atrocities throughout history follow patterns and cycles, and every nation is a guilty party. We can wallow in past pain, or we can work towards an optimistic future as we strive to break those cycles. I am no more responsible for my ancestors' grievances and sacrifices, as you are for your ancestors' invasions and conquests. Bitterness keeps us stuck and the cycle going; education, tolerance, and acceptance changes tomorrow."

Claire sighed with a sense of satisfaction as she scraped the last few crumbs off her plate. "You are so inspiring."

Holly rolled her eyes.

Elky laughed. "I could say the same about you, your fiancé, and your remarkable daughter."

"Remarkable?"

"Well, most children are. I have never had the pleasure of properly meeting her – although I have spoken to your forester friends very briefly before – but your daughter seems wise beyond her years, and when she looks at you, it seems she sees your very soul."

Claire smiled. "Yes, I suppose she does give off that vibe." Talking about Jasmine was a little uncomfortable, despite the ease she felt around Elky. "But she's also like any other child – carefree, fun-loving, and she's been known to throw a strop or two."

He bellowed another laugh, and nodded. "The sun can both bring to life and kill, can it not."

Goosebumps raced down her arms. She wasn't sure how to respond to such a statement because she had no idea if there was some kind of implication twisted up in there somewhere. No malice at all coloured his words, though.

"Do you all like it here among the forests of California?"

"Yes, it's beautiful here. We feel very much at home, but we've travelled a lot. I think many places can feel like home if you adapt, and accept it for what it is."

"I agree. Survivors throughout history have one thing in common – they adapt, like the greatest shapeshifters. The Maipeke are sun worshippers, although the old ceremonies are practised much less nowadays. My great-grandfather was the tribe's shaman, or medicine man, back in the day. When he first dreamed his power, it was the sun's spirit that came to him. He took this spirit on as his own form of personal power as is the way with the shaman – the sun became his 'power spirit'. It is said he was a mighty warrior who could walk through fire, and even *become* fire."

"Become fire?"

"He would shapeshift into fire, so the stories went."

"Wow ... do you believe he could? I mean, in the real sense."

"The real sense?"

"*Literally* changing into fire. Is that even possible?"

He stared at her, still smiling, and raised an eyebrow. "As possible as a man who can change into a wolf, I should imagine."

Holly's back straightened and she took in a breath.

Claire stared back at Elky, refusing to give away how nervous she felt. So ... he knew. That on its own didn't make him dangerous. And if he *was* dangerous, showing any weakness would do her no favours.

"Relax, Claire. I am not a threat to you. When the gray wolves returned a few years back, I suspected something powerful was afoot. And indeed, I found your English friends, Marco and the other one."

"Bill."

"Yes. I can see the power spirit in the man, it is one of my gifts. I saw their wolf spirits straight away. Same for your fiancé."

She glanced around the hotel restaurant. It was as empty as when they'd first walked in. She lowered her voice anyway. "They're not shifters, they're werewolves. I don't know if there's a difference."

"I believe there is. The were-creature is a genetic construct and the human has little control over the beast within. The shapeshifter is fully human and learns to shift through skill and mastery of the art, and has full control of their allied spirit. But in all other ways, they can be treated as the same; there are similarities – no matter the construct, the werewolf and the shapeshifter are both connected to a force of nature that must be mastered, and can be of great benefit to all."

Claire sat back and crossed her legs, her mug of coffee in her hands. Now she knew he knew, she'd had enough of the cryptic. "Why did you want to talk to us here today, Elkoyti?"

"You don't beat around the bush."

"She never has," piped up Holly – the only thing she'd said for half an hour.

"I like knowing where I'm at, and I don't like having to make assumptions," Claire replied.

"Very wise." Elky leaned his elbows on the table. "Tell me, does your daughter ever ... disappear suddenly, or even appear suddenly, unexpectedly. Is she ever 'gone' for a length of time, only for you to find her where you'd never thought she'd be?"

Oh, god. Her heart thudded faster. Whatever he was about to say, she wasn't sure she was ready to hear it. So much for beating that damned bush. "Yes. But I'm guessing you already knew that."

"Your daughter is a shapeshifter, Claire. When she does this – appearing and disappearing – she is teleporting. It is a shapeshifting of sorts, and an ability that almost all shifters have. I doubt she has actually 'shifted' into her spirit ally yet, though. She's very young."

Teleporting? All this time, she'd been *teleporting*?

He remained quiet, perhaps giving her time to let all that sink in.

"Fuck," she whispered, her eyes tearing up.

"No, it's a good thing. A very good thing. But the skill is one she must train so she doesn't end up on the other side of the world, facing battles she's not ready to face."

"We've always known there'd be something, but we never

knew what."

"It's still not clear 'what'. I cannot tell what her power spirit is; I even think she might have more than one – some shapeshifters do – but she is not Maipeke, or of any Native American descent; her shamanic abilities come from somewhere else, and, I suspect, they are beyond what I have encountered. I do sense an enormous power, Claire. A very great spirit indeed. It would be wise to train it now."

"Are you telling me this because you'd like to train her?"

"If you, your wolf, and your daughter, will have me as her teacher, I would be honoured."

She fell silent as her head spun. "Are *you* a shaman?"

"Me? No. I am a permanent student of life. But I have some knowledge learned from my grandfather I'm able to pass on. Take a few days to think on it. I don't need any answers now."

"Tell me something – did you seek us out today? Did you know Holly and I were going to be there at that spot?"

"No. I was advised by Spirit that I needed to stalk bad medicine – bad energy. My 'stalking' led me to the trail of the two men you met earlier who, by the way, I would not trust. I will be informing your English foresters of their whereabouts. Their trail, though, led me to you. Great Spirit works in mysterious ways."

"Do you think they were poachers?"

"I suspect they might be, but as I said earlier, the question is *what* are they poaching."

"Oh, my god." The penny dropped. "If *you* know about Pete and Jasmine..."

He nodded. "Yes. Knowledge has its own energy that cannot be contained. If I know it, others might, too. We need to keep your daughter safe."

Chapter Six

"Can you see her, Jasmine?" Mrs Myers asked as kids and parents alike milled around the school gates.

"Yes, she's there." Jasmine pointed to her mum who waved at her in return with a large smile on her face. She looked a little worried about something, though. Jasmine had no idea what, but hoped it was nothing to do with anything she'd done. She'd felt a little bad about drawing Daddy as a wolf, but they'd still put the picture up on the fridge, so that must have been okay.

"All right, sweetie, off you go. Have a lovely afternoon, and I'll see you tomorrow."

"Thank you." Jasmine said her goodbyes and ran ahead to see her mum who scooped her into a hug around her legs.

"Hi, petal. You had a good day?"

Jasmine nodded.

"What did you do?" Her mum's eyes wandered around the school grounds as she spoke.

"Stuff. I painted another picture, but this one's still drying."

Mummy took her hand and her lunch box. "That's good," she added absent-mindedly. "Will we get to see it next week?"

Jasmine shrugged and went quiet as they made their way to the car. She suddenly wasn't sure if she wanted anyone to see her picture of the dragon, not even Mummy and Daddy – that one was *her* secret.

"Hop on in." Mummy held the car door open as Jasmine climbed into her car seat in the back, shuffling into a comfortable position as her mum leant over her to put her seatbelt on.

"Mummy, are you okay?"

She looked at her, a little surprised. "Of course." Then, she dropped a kiss on her forehead, opened her window and shut the door. "We're going to go straight home. Holly's still here."

"I like Holly."

"You do?" she replied as she got into the driver's seat.

"Yes, she's funny."

"She is?" Mummy didn't sound like she believed her.

"Yes."

They pulled away from the curb. It took fifteen minutes to drive home. Jasmine liked the drive, partly because she loved the feel of the wind on her face as it rushed past her open window, and partly because the scenery was just beautiful – trees, trees and more trees on either side of the road; some that parted a little and you could see the pretty view in between them. It reminded her a little of the woods at Aiden's house, although that had been a lot smaller. She all of a sudden missed Aiden at the memory. "Mummy, when is Holly leaving?"

"Tomorrow morning."

She felt a lump begin to form in her throat. "I won't get to say goodbye."

"You will, honey. You'll see her at breakfast – she's leaving after that – so you can say goodbye then."

"Will I see her again?"

"I'm sure you will someday."

"When?"

"I don't know *exactly* when."

"But soon?"

"Jasmine..."

There was that slight, telltale sound to her voice that told Jasmine she was asking questions that wouldn't be answered. Jasmine sighed and sat back in her seat, resigned to watching the world go by as they drove along the winding road home.

She could see Mummy's eyes in the rear-view mirror. She still had that 'worried' crease, right there between her eyebrows. Jasmine turned away and went back to the view from her window. Mummy was usually quite chatty, but today she didn't seem to be, which usually meant she had something on her mind. Sometimes Jasmine liked the quiet, and sometimes she didn't. Today, it made her feel a little unsettled.

"Honey..."

She looked back at the mirror, to see her mum's gaze flicker to her before looking ahead again.

"Do you remember how sometimes, when you were a bit younger, you'd go off exploring and we wouldn't know where you were?"

Sort of. She frowned, and turned back to the window.

"Even when we asked you not to?"

Was *that* why she was worried and being a bit weird? She hadn't gone exploring like that for a while. Not since being on the aeroplane. And maybe once or twice soon after they'd arrived here, but Mummy and Daddy didn't know about those times – she'd never told them.

"Do you remember why you used to do that?"

Jasmine shrugged, then realised her mum couldn't hear the shrug. "No." It was true. She didn't know exactly why it happened, and because it hadn't happened for a long time, she'd forgotten the feeling of it a bit – she kind of thought it was because she was excited and her body couldn't stay in one place because of it.

Maybe that wasn't the answer her mum had wanted. She fell silent as they drove on, but Jasmine couldn't properly appreciate the view out the window anymore. She was starting to feel like crying again, even though she didn't know why. She looked at her mum in the mirror.

Mummy was staring into it, her frown bigger than ever, but this time her mum wasn't staring at her, she was staring behind her, out the back window. "Honey, is that one of your school friends' parents driving the car behind us?"

Jasmine had to stretch in her car seat to turn around far enough to see, especially over the back dash (which Mummy called a parcel shelf, which was just weird because she'd never seen her put a parcel on it), but she just about managed it.

"No," she replied. She didn't think so anyway. It was a man driving, and another man beside him. Not a lot of dads picked up their kids – just two or three – and these men were not any of them.

Mummy muttered something, then reached over and pulled her phone out of her bag. She put it on loudspeaker, pressed two buttons, and left it lying on the passenger seat. The sound of it trying to connect to a call filled the car. Jasmine recognised Daddy's voice, but he wasn't picking up – it was his voicemail.

Mummy said a bad word under her breath. When the beep came, she spoke fast. "It's me. I'm driving Jasmine home from school; we've gone past those two trees that look like skinny bears" —that was a joke; they always laughed at those trees— "and I think we're being followed. Holly and I saw two men on our walk this morning – we weren't sure if they were poachers – but it looks like it might be the same guys following us. They're in a black sedan; I don't want to lead them home. I think I'm going to—" They both screamed as the car hit them from behind. Everything lurched, hard, the phone and handbag flying off the seat.

Jasmine's seatbelt hurt her chest. "Mummy!"

"Jasmine, stay there!" Her mum fought to keep the wheel straight. "Keep your belt on!"

"The car banged us!"

"I know."

"Why?"

Another *bang* shook their car, this one harder than the first. Jasmine wasn't sure if it was her screaming, or her mummy screaming, but she knew she didn't like hearing Mummy scream. At all. And her mum looked very frightened which made everything feel much worse.

"Fuck. I can't go faster on these bends; there's no space to turn..."

"Mummy..." She was crying, but she couldn't help it. She was more scared than she ever remembered being. "Mummy!" She leaned as far forward as she could and reached for her shoulder with her hand, needing to feel her, but she couldn't manage it.

"Jasmine, no! Sit back!"

She ignored her. Her fear was big, just like her excitement could be big. It was going to make her body do things. She needed to touch her mum – she didn't want to end up somewhere on her own, not this time. She was too scared.

There was a final shunt from behind, this one so hard, her mum lost her grip on the wheel completely. She didn't just scream, she shouted words, panicking, though Jasmine wasn't able to take any of them in. The road wasn't that wide, and the car was flying off it now, to the right, where there was no road, but a drop into the trees below.

"JASMINE!" On that desperate shriek, her mum turned to her, reached back, and finally took her hand.

The contact was a relief – she wasn't going to leave Mummy. But it wasn't her mum she was looking at; it was the sky around them and beyond them as everything seemed to slow right down. They were rushing through mid-air – soon, they'd be falling – and all she could see in her mind was the dragon that had flown above her over two years ago at Aiden's home.

If she could just fly like the dragon...

The wind from the open window whooshed past her. Her fingers gripped her mum's wrist, and she squeezed her eyes shut.

~*~

"There's more right here – see this?" Pete looked over to where Bill stood, pointing at the tree trunk. Marco approached him from the other side.

The alpine trees in this area had contracted some kind of disease – a powdery white-green substance that spread up the trunk. Marco leaned in and sniffed it.

"Same deal?" asked Bill.

"Yep – no smell."

And which kind of tree disease didn't give off a smell? Pete wasn't educated in forestry enough to know the answer, but according the Bill and Marco, none. Which made this an anomaly.

With his spray can, Bill marked the trunk in yellow. "So, it's affecting trees from about a quarter of a mile radius – only alpines – but we can't find the source. It appeared suddenly overnight, and all the affected trees look to be in the same stage of the infection. The disease looks mould-like, but emits no scent as if it isn't even there, and the rest of the tree systems seem as robust as usual – no attack to the roots or branches – just this mid-section of every trunk." Bill dropped his clipboard, from which he'd been relaying his notes, to the ground next to his spray can. "I'm stumped. I haven't got a handle on this."

Marco scratched the back of his neck and looked around, surveying the woods. "You and me both. Any thoughts, Pete?"

"Hmm? Oh … if you guys don't know, there's no hope for me."

"If *we* don't know, we'll take any and all guesses. And you really don't have to worry about Elkoyti."

"Huh?"

"That's why you're distracted, right? Claire's message about having lunch with him?"

Pete tried to shrug off his discomfort. "She's with Holly." He didn't know why he'd said that. Holly was hardly useful if any emergency should arise.

"Elky's family is well known up in the ranchería, although we haven't had any dealings with them ourselves – we've heard of them through word of mouth. We've had no reason to set foot there as it's out of our work zone, but we've spoken to Elky on occasion, and while we don't know him well because he only moved here a couple of years ago, we'd vouch for him. He's good people. Claire's in good hands. Besides, wouldn't she have picked Jasmine up from school already? If anything was wrong, the school would have phoned you by now."

He was right – obviously. It wasn't usual for Pete to dwell on his instincts when his logic was clear, but the niggle in his gut wouldn't let up, and a wolf was a wolf. No matter the lack of reason, his sense of danger had been triggered, and he didn't like it one bit. Before he could reply, Marco's phone went off.

"Hello?" he answered. Then, he looked over at Pete with an 'I told you' written over his face. "Elky – good to hear from you." He gave Pete a thumbs up, and mouthed, '*See?*'.

Pete stuffed his hands in his pockets. He *was* marginally relieved, but he didn't like that he couldn't shake this feeling...

"What's up?"

Pete walked over to Bill as Marco spoke to Elkoyti. He nodded at the damaged trees. "Anything useful I can do to help?"

"Nah. I've got all the samples, measurements and observations I need for now, so I think we might call it a day down here. I need to hit the books and research this stuff 'cause it's nothing I'm familiar with. I'll stick it under a microscope tonight. I *hate* that there's no scent."

That wasn't a surprise. No werewolf liked anything with no scent; it was virtually how their kind communicated first and foremost.

Marco joined them having finished on the phone. "Claire's fine. They had lunch, then she left – said she was going to drop Holly home first, then leave to pick up Jasmine."

"Thank you for checking."

"No problem. But the reason he phoned me – they all ran into a couple of guys earlier by the large boulder near Pilot Peak. He said he got a weird vibe off them; possibly poachers. Said they were heading up to Quincy. I'll radio in and put the feelers out; he gave me a description of them. If any of the foresters come across them, they can dig a little – ask some questions."

"Good plan," said Bill. "Let's get out of here. This alpine disease is frustrating me; I wanna get on top of it right away."

They headed back to the Range Rover. Pete's phone beeped.

"Bloody connection," he mumbled. "Missed call."

"I told you to change your provider. The signal's often a bit temperamental around here."

He grumbled a reply as he dialled his voicemail, deciding to keep the phone on loudspeaker because he hated the way his ear got hot every time he held the phone to it.

After five seconds or so, Claire's voice came through, and it punched his heart rate up a notch 'cause she sounded more than anxious. *"It's me. I'm driving Jasmine home from school; we've gone past those two trees that look like skinny bears and I think we're being followed."*

They all ceased movement and stared at the phone he held.

"Holly and I saw two men on our walk this morning – we weren't sure if they were poachers – but it looks like it might be the same guys following us. They're in a black sedan; I don't want to lead them home. I think I'm going to—"

The horrendous clash of metal and screaming that followed all but ended his life. If he was speaking, he couldn't hear himself. Bill was yanking him forward. He could hear Marco shouting at Bill as they all rushed to their car. Through the speaker, he could hear Jasmine shouting for her mum; he could hear Claire cursing, yelling instructions, more screaming, another horrific grinding BANG, Jasmine's name shrieked from Claire's lungs ... and then nothing.

Chapter Seven

"Mummy, wake up ... Mummy ... I'm sorry. I'm sorry."

The struggle to remain in comforting darkness was a little greater when the voice of everything you lived for so desperately sobbed for you.

"Mummy ... pleeease..."

She was shaking. Something was shaking her. Jasmine was shaking her.

Claire prised her eyes open, her head aching, her vision spinning.

"Mummy," gasped Jasmine.

"Jasmine..." The word came out a whisper. Where were they?

Full memory of her car sailing off the road painted a startling picture in her mind. Feeling nauseous, she slowly pulled herself to sitting.

Jasmine wasted no time catapulting herself against her side, hugging herself to her arm.

Finding her balance, she hugged her back, then took in her surroundings, eyes widening in confusion. "Jasmine – where are we? Where did you bring us?" Because that was what had happened, wasn't it? They had teleported, just as Elky had said – this was what Jasmine did.

"I didn't mean to," she sobbed into her sleeve.

"It's okay." At least, she hoped it was. She brought Jasmine in for a tighter hug, stroking her hair. She hadn't a clue if anything was okay, but at the moment, her assumptions were all she had to go on, and she *assumed* Jasmine had teleported both of them ... here. Where 'here' was, though, was anyone's guess.

The forests were gone. All the trees were gone, bar one. Its branches draped over them so they sat in its shadow out of the afternoon sun – a sun which was much hotter here than where they had been. From under the tree where they sat, and reaching for maybe a quarter of a mile in all directions, the greenest grass rolled out. But, oddly, the grass ended, sloping upwards into nothing but desert and dunes – they were in some kind of basin. And there were no desert and dunes where they lived.

Claire looked up. The single tree wasn't an alpine, or a fir, but some kind of large, wide specimen that did look familiar, though from her past travels in her early twenties to parts of Africa. Was this an acacia tree?

A wooden shelter – if one could call it that – bordered it, forming a triangular, open roof above the leaves, and a bench part way around the trunk, as if people would gather here and sit under its shade. It gave one the impression this was perhaps a sacred tree, and this, a ceremonial spot.

"Jasmine, honey, I need you to be brave. I need you to think really hard about why you brought us here."

She pulled back to look up at her, her eyes streaked with tears. "I don't know. I was scared."

"I know – I was, too. This is what you do, isn't it? When you disappear and we can't find you – this is what happens?"

Jasmine nodded.

"I'm not mad. I think maybe you saved our lives – the car was going to crash. But I need to know where we are so I can get us home."

"I don't know."

God damn it. She had no idea how teleportation worked. "Um … all right – were you thinking of anything before you brought us here?"

"I was so scared."

"I know. But was there anything else besides feeling scared?"

Jasmine looked at her. Her big brown eyes, while teary, also guarded some secret. She'd seen that look before when she'd had to keep silent about birthday and Christmas presents, but never relating to anything as crucial as this.

"Honey, I'm *not* angry, I promise, but this is *really* important, and I need you to tell me."

Her bottom lip quivered with her quiet struggle. She looked down at the grass underneath them, then up again. "I was thinking about the dragon."

Right.

So … that wasn't exactly what she'd expected to hear. "The … dragon?"

She nodded. "The one I saw at Aiden's house when I was chasing dragonflies. The wind took me away then, too."

"The wind? Is that what it feels like when you … disappear?"

"Yes."

"Okay, that's good. Jasmine, that's good." She decided to leave the bit about the dragon to one side for now – she couldn't make head nor tail of that. "Do you think you could try to get us home? Maybe if you *think* about home, or Daddy, or your bedroom – something that makes you happy about home … maybe then we'll be able to get back." Jesus fucking

Christ, what was she *saying*? Jasmine wasn't Peter Pan!

"Maybe," she whispered. But the poor girl looked terrified, and Claire almost put the silly suggestion to bed. It very well *would* sound silly if she didn't know the things she knew.

Nevertheless, her daughter closed her eyes in concentration.

"Wait, wait ... do you need to hold my hand? Is that why I came with you?" She was shooting in the dark, trying to piece together bits from films and books she'd read that had involved teleportation, or time travelling, or the supernatural – those had all been fiction, though. Regardless, they helped to make sense of the reality she now faced.

Jasmine looked unsure, but nodded and took her hand, then closed her eyes again.

Claire's heart panged with guilt. This was far too much to lay at the feet of a five-year-old.

"I can't do it, Mummy." Her voice quivered, once more on the verge of tears.

"It's okay. It's not your fault."

"I think I need a big feeling."

"A big feeling?"

"It always happens when my feelings are big."

Really? Was Jasmine's fright not big enough right now, because her own was shooting through the metaphorical roof. "Never mind. We'll find another way." And she was glad she sounded more certain than she felt about that. They were in the middle of a desert. Despite the strange green grass – so out of place – the arid sand surrounding it was plain to see. But she could see nothing – absolutely *nothing* – beyond the barren horizon. The heat of the sun, beating down upon them, was close to unbearable. If they didn't get out of here, they were going to fry.

Absent-mindedly, she patted her back trouser pocket,

then scanned the ground around her. Nope. Bag and phone – both in the car.

Fucked.

They were fucked.

Swallowing her panic, she squeezed Jasmine's hand, then let go of it and stood up. If they were to attempt a trek, which direction looked the most promising? She could see no paths at all.

Jasmine suddenly jumped to her feet beside her. "Somebody's coming!"

Claire felt like sprinting away as fast as she could; instead she followed Jasmine's pointing finger to face a figure in the distance, over a hundred metres away, striding over a grassy knoll. He (looked like a 'he' anyway, despite being far away) seemed to know where he was going. Everything rested on whether he was going to help them, or hurt them.

"Stay behind me, Jasmine, okay?"

"Why?"

Claire bit her tongue to stop her exasperated sigh. At five, Jasmine simply didn't understand all the dangers present. "Please just stay behind me."

The figure in the distance, waved. She waved back, because there was no chance he was waving to anyone other than them.

"Hi!" he called out.

As he approached, she could see he was of dark hair and tanned skin; he sported a big smile with very white teeth, and was a bit podgy around the middle. *So he gets food from somewhere – he's not a starving hermit living in some sand cave.*

"Hi. We're a bit lost, I'm afraid."

"How lost?" His smile remained on his face; he seemed genuine enough. She hoped her instincts concerning people were as good as ever after her whiz across space. "There's no way you could have walked here."

Which means he likely knew about how they *did* get here. It seemed like she was last to get the teleporting memo. She ignored his statement. "How did *you* know we were here?"

"Guy I work for – he had a vision of visitors to this tree."

"Oh." A vision. Of course he did. She squared her shoulders and raised her chin a bit, pretending all this wasn't totally out of her depth. "Any chance his vision explained how we get home?"

His smile widened into a truly infectious grin. "Same way you got here, I should imagine."

"That ... might not be possible."

His gaze rested on Jasmine, then found its way back to Claire. "I see. Here..." He opened the small satchel he was carrying and pulled out a flask. "Water. Have a drink – both of you."

She took it without dropping her eyes from his, wishing she had Pete's werewolf nose so she could determine if it really was water in the flask.

"It's okay," he said, reading her correctly. "If I wanted you dead, I'd just leave you here. My name is Jerrod, by the way."

Her gut said he was telling the truth, and her gut hadn't let her down in the past. "I'm Claire. This is my daughter, Jasmine." She popped the lid off the flask and took warm water into her mouth, swishing it around. Yeah – it was just water as far as she could tell. "Honey..." She handed the container to Jasmine. Drink was imperative in this blistering sun.

She took it from her and clumsily drank.

"Where is 'here', exactly?" she asked their new companion. This was certainly a day for meeting people under odd circumstances.

"Death Valley, USA. Nevada end – not California end."

"Death Valley?" Well, that sounded cheerful, and not at

all perilous. And they had jumped a state. She eyed the tree above her.

"This whole area was once called the Wastelands. It was hard, arid rock and sand. Then, about nine years ago, there was a change. A change in climate, or environment, or perhaps something else – there's no official explanation as such – but the grass began to grow in this basin, as if the tree gave it life. It's now known as the Birthlands."

"This tree was already here?"

"Indeed it was – and quite a story it has, too, but that's for another day unless you'd like to become human raisins."

"It's not on our to-do list."

He laughed. "I didn't think so."

"How do we get out of here?"

He looked at Jasmine. "I take it you teleported in? There's really no other way out of here if not by air. Even desert trucks can't make it up the dunes. So, we're teleporting back."

Jasmine pressed herself into Claire's thigh. She felt like doing the same to be honest. After meeting Elky, and being run off the road ... it felt like everything they'd tried to keep at bay for Jasmine's sake was converging at once. "Look ... this, erm, teleportation thing is new to us. It's my daughter who can do it. I can't."

He stared at her with genuine surprise. "Your daughter brought you here?"

"She did."

"Goodness..." He spoke directly to Jasmine. "You're young. That's quite a gift you have there. Most as young as you can't teleport, and certainly can't carry others along for the ride."

Jasmine had gone mute. She wasn't saying a damned word.

"Hmm ... well, you have a choice. I can teleport you both

back to my house – it's not too far from here as the crow flies."
He laughed at his little joke. "But you'll need to get a lift home
from there because I won't be able to teleport again. I'm human, you see, so carrying you both will be quite a load and will
tire me out for a while. Or I can teleport you to your own
home straight away – I have a map in my bag; I just need your
address – but I'll need a lift back to my own house for the
same reason: can't teleport twice in such a short space of time.
Which would you prefer?"

Shit. This might be the fastest lesson in teleportation
anyone had ever had. Elky had told her a bit about how it
worked before they'd parted after lunch, but she was still trying to get to grips with what he'd said. And the reference this
guy had just made to being human... She repressed her panic.
He clearly knew Jasmine wasn't.

She could swallow all her fears and believe this Jerrod
guy to be honest, but if his home was near here, in Nevada,
that meant they'd have to be in his company (alone in his
house?) for at least six or seven hours before Pete could reach
them by car. If they chose to go back home, he'd know their
address, which meant he could potentially tell others where
they lived. If the poachers got hold if that information...

She had no idea which decision promised the most safety.

She had no guarantee he'd allow them to use a phone
once in his house – they'd be at his mercy there. At least back
home, she'd know her way around, Holly would be there (shit
– poor Holly was still waiting for her to get back from the
school run); the others might be there, too... There was less
damage Jerrod could do to them, and get away with it, on their
own turf.

Claire hugged Jasmine to her, and took the risk. "I can
give you our address. I'm sure one of the boys will give you a
lift back here, though it may be late by the time you arrive.

Can you please take us home?"

He smiled, nodded, and whipped the map out of his satchel. "I can."

~*~

"Just up ahead," said Bill. They were in the car, having slowed down to thirty miles per hour so they could pick up on the scents around them through the open windows. They'd just passed the trees that looked like bears, and Pete could smell it: burning rubber, and a taint of crushed metal in the air that would be imperceptible to human senses.

His chest tightened, Claire's distressed message replaying in his mind over and fucking over again. He wasn't a male who'd ever taken his family for granted since he'd given up on having one at all, but the mere thought they could be gone from his life in an instant... It was a terror that felt all too real in this moment.

"There!"

Marco pulled over, all their eyes on the skid marks that carved all Pete's fears into manifestation. The tyre marks ended at the side of the road.

"Fuck no." Pete was out of the car first, sprinting to the edge that gave way to a steep drop. Rushing water bubbled somewhere far below. "*Claire!*"

"Look."

Bill pointed at his worst nightmare: silver metal wrapped around two tree trunks, about thirty feet down, the car on its side wedged between the two trees, and utterly wrecked. Its bonnet was smashed; one door swung open.

"CLAIRE!"

Only his own echo replied.

"How do we get down there?"

"Carefully and with ropes. I have some in the trunk." Marco squeezed Pete's arm and ran off to get them. The squeeze said it all: this didn't look good by any stretch of the imagination.

It wouldn't take as long to reach the car on four paws. Pete whipped his T-shirt off. "I'm shifting."

"No." Bill grabbed his shoulder. "Come on, think clearly."

"I need to get there *now*."

"Not even wolves can fly. What will you accomplish injured?"

Unwanted tears stung his eyes. "If I lose them, I lose everything."

His phone rang. He fought the urge to fling the damn thing in the ravine.

The call came from home. Holly?

Because Bill hadn't let go of his shoulder – and because the smidgen of reason he had left knew his friend was right – he answered it instead of leaping into the gorge, battling to keep the suffocating lump in his throat down. "Hello?"

"Pete?"

Fuck! "Claire?"

She started crying at the sound of his voice. "I'm fine. We're both fine."

Jesus Christ! Then he was crying, too. "Claire..." It was fucking stupid he couldn't manage to say anything else – all he wanted to do was hold her.

"We're home. I need you home."

"I'm coming now. I'll be there in ten."

"I love you."

"I love you. So much." He hung up, cursing he hadn't said half of what he'd wanted to, yet thanking every star in the sky they were alive and – he hoped to god – unhurt.

Marco had made it back with the ropes, and had clearly

heard the conversation through the phone. He held out his keys to him. "Take the car. Get home now."

"Thank you."

"I've caught a scent." He looked at Bill. "Can you smell it?"

Bill nodded.

Pete couldn't. But his senses were all in disarray, tears and panic clogging up his nasal passage. "What can you smell?"

"People – here around the same time as Claire and Jasmine. The poachers I'll bet. I want to see how far I can track the bastards."

"I'm with you," said Bill.

"Be careful, both of you."

"We will be. Give Claire and Jasmine a hug from us."

"I will." He made for the car, giving himself a shake to get his head together. *They're alive. They're both fine.*

If only the mangled car around the trees didn't cloud his vision.

Shit. His hands were shaking; *he* was shaking.

He slammed the door shut, and took a couple of breaths behind the wheel before starting the engine. He didn't know what he'd have done if they'd died. He hoped he'd never have to know.

Chapter Eight

"It's a drag. The more you carry, the harder it is. Even for the most seasoned teleporter, managing extra weight while you travel is something best avoided. If it were easy, we'd all be holidaying a hell of a lot more cheaply, you know what I mean?" Jerrod laughed. "Save a huge chunk on air fares. But it's *not* easy, which is why I'm astounded your kid did it – most kids with the ability to teleport or shift don't display it until their teen years at the very least. The mind's a muscle that needs building, and there's only a certain amount of weight it can carry. You could lose your strength half way to your destination and end up god knows where, and you wouldn't be able to get back because the trip would have worn you out for at least twenty-four hours. Witches and demons can handle it a lot better, but they only carry extra in emergencies – such as this was."

"Witches and demons?" Claire's head was spinning, and not just owing to the mind-blowing experience of teleporting. She hadn't passed out this time, but had been able to stay conscious. Though the actual trip was fuzzy, the buzz running through her entire being was clear. And she felt like her brain had been jacked into a new source of energy.

Her neck twinged from the car crash – she'd probably

have whiplash tomorrow – but Jasmine, thank god, seemed to be mainly unscathed apart from some very slight bruising along her chest where her seatbelt had dug into her. There were no broken ribs.

"Yeah, witches and demons. I take it by your tone you haven't been schooled in such things?"

What did she say to that? Werewolves, yes. Crazy old ladies with magical powers, yes. Neither of those had been referred to as witches, though, and ... *demons*? "Demons exist?"

"So many things exist, though usually as whispering shadows and thoughts. Where do you think our imagination gets all its food from? Sometimes, though, those whispering shadows become manifest."

But ... *demons*.

Claire looked over at Holly.

Face pale, she looked back from where she was – perched on the end of the sofa's arm having taken all the news in in silence – and shrugged.

The front door opened.

"Daddy!" Jasmine, who had been silent this entire time, leapt from her position on the floor and practically threw herself into Pete's arms.

He caught her in a bear hug, relief and love all over his features. "Jesus, Jasmine ... god, I was so worried." He kissed her head, then searched her face and body with his eyes, all senses alert, his nostrils flaring. "Are you hurt?"

"No, Daddy."

And then his eyes landed on Jerrod. They narrowed in warning and a growl erupted from his throat.

Claire stood and went to him. "Pete, this is Jerrod. He brought us back. We ended up in the Nevada desert – he saved our lives."

Protectively, he grasped her arm in his large hand, pulling

her to him in a sideways hug, still holding Jasmine in his other arm. His gaze didn't leave their visitor's face; he was prepared for any move. "You'd better start from the beginning."

"We'll fill you in," she assured. "I'll start. But you might want to get a drink and take a seat."

"I'm not thirsty and I'm happy standing." He was rigid, his muscles tense, waiting for an attack, whether likely or not.

"Okay ... it's been a long day." She wasn't sure how Pete would take it all. Where Jasmine was concerned, his defences surrounding her were pretty much impenetrable. He was a wolf guarding his pup. Since the direct approach had always worked best for her, she put her trust in it one more time. "I'll start with this: Jasmine's a shapeshifter, and she can teleport."

~*~

Marco had left with Jerrod two hours ago to take him home. Jasmine had finally fallen asleep thirty minutes ago, and he and Claire were lying on their bed, wiped out, staring at the ceiling, wrapped up in the silence of each other, letting the events of the day sink in.

Elkoyti; now Jerrod. Poachers, too. Bill and Marco had tracked them out of the forest boundary – they'd left the premises – presumably because they hadn't been able to find Claire and Jasmine in the wreckage. Bill had said their scents had been all over the area around the car. It got his blood raging just thinking about them anywhere near his girls. What the fuck would the bastards have done to them if they'd captured them?

Had they wanted to capture them? Or had they wanted them dead? Perhaps running them off the road entirely had been an accident; perhaps they'd been hoping Claire would hit the brakes and give in.

Whatever the answers, one thing seemed obvious: three unrelated incidents in one day, all to do with Jasmine and who she really was, indicated the cat was out of the bag. Someone, somewhere, knew about her heritage; that she was a Trident birth. Regardless of the fact there didn't seem to be a trace of Trident in her blood (at least not under a microscope), the very fact of who her biological father was made her the only Trident offspring to ever exist, and the last to carry the Trident gene.

"We'll get through this." Claire's voice pierced through his thoughts.

He turned his head towards her. "We always knew there'd be something."

"Right. And now we need to help Jasmine deal with it."

"How do we do that when we might not be able to deal with it ourselves?"

"Elky said he'd help. And we have Jerrod's number in case we need him again."

"I'm hoping we'll *never* need him again. He told us very little in case you hadn't noticed."

"He talked a fair bit about shapeshifting, and about himself."

"But not at all about who he works for."

Claire sighed, blinked, and turned to face the ceiling. "We've got to trust someone sometime. We can't keep shielding her. Whatever this thing is, it's begun – it's out in the open now and we *have* to prepare her."

"I know."

"There are people out there trying to kill her."

"Or catch her."

She turned back towards him, eyes lit with fury. "Over my dead body."

"Hey..." He scooped her towards him with his left arm

until her head rested on his chest. "I appreciate the sentiment, but don't ever bloody say that again. For a second today, I thought you *were* dead. It was the longest fucking second of my life; I don't ever want it replayed."

"Neither do I," she mumbled against the beat of his heart.

"How's Holly with it all?"

"I don't know. Her flight was supposed to leave in the morning, but she phoned the airport and managed to switch to one twelve hours later to give us time to sort things out down here. After we arrived back with Jerrod and told her what had happened, she went all quiet and hasn't really spoken about it. I get the feeling if she could redo the past five years of her life, she would."

"Never really jumped aboard the supernatural train, did she?"

"She did – didn't have much of a choice – but she's been travel sick the whole time."

Pete laughed softly.

"She's going home tomorrow. I think it's for the best."

"You two been getting on okay?"

"As well as ever, I suppose, but without Sarah here ... I dunno. It's *so* different. I never realised how influential she was in keeping the three of us together."

Silence fell as Sarah's name bounced around in the air, almost as if it had a life of its own.

Pete was the first to break it. "I guess we'd better go pay this Elkoyti a visit then."

"He gave me his number."

"Marco and Bill have it, too."

"Shall we give him a call after Holly's gone?"

"Yes. The sooner, the better."

Her long fingers stroked his chest all the way down his torso, where they veered off to the right, tickling his side a little as they continued their caress. Her warm mouth found its way to his left nipple, marking it with a kiss, then branding him as hers when she opened that beautiful mouth and sealed it around the projection, pulling a moan from his throat as she sucked and teased it.

She glanced at him, playfully, but that furious fire was still there, gleaming in the blue of her irises; only now, the fire emitted a different kind of heat altogether – one that brought a misty sheen to her eyes. "It was the longest second of my life, too," she said.

God damn it... He fisted her hair and pulled her lips to his, the kiss urgent, battling the day's dangers as his tongue duelled with hers. It wasn't just fear he rode on, or relief, but that innate sense of *possession* that belonged to his wolf.

She was his, he'd almost lost her, and in the far corners of his mind, he could still *smell* that clash of metals he'd picked up on at the crash site. That scent burned him as surely as the flames from his bedroom's fireplace had done so, many moons ago. That scent promised pain, blood, and death, and he wanted it *gone.*

Primal impulse carried a consuming kind of fervour.

With a low growl, he turned and landed on top of her, pinning her to the bed, relishing the feel of her body beneath his.

Her nipples received the same treatment she'd given his through her blue cotton vest, until he couldn't take the thin material blocking his prize any longer. Using his teeth, he yanked the vest down over her mounds, releasing them to the air; then he clamped his lips and teeth around her left breast, his tongue lavishing its nub.

His cock went hard in an instant on her groan of want.

No. It was a groan of *need* that matched his. Love, desire, and unreleased rage coalesced. He pushed up her left thigh, bending her leg at the knee, opening her wide to him. He was going to fuck the day right out of her for both their sakes.

He jerked her knickers to one side, perhaps a little rougher than he should have since he heard elastic tear, and thrust two fingers into her, forcing himself to go steadier so he wouldn't hurt her.

She didn't seem hurt. Wet and hot, she grasped at him anywhere she could, her desperation filling the air and arousing him further; pining whimpers and the furious rock of her hips pulling him too near to the edge. Fuck, this wouldn't take long – for either of them.

His fangs emerged; the new clarity to his vision told him his eyes had turned luminous, his wolf dangerously close to the surface.

Climbing up her body so his mouth met hers, he lined his cock to her entrance, staving off the thrumming ache that demanded he plunge deep into her like the beast he half was – he *wouldn't* hurt her.

She untangled her tongue from his, gasping for air, pulling his hair almost painfully, her grinding hips about to undo all his efforts, and met his eyes. "Don't hold back. I need to feel you."

Jesus ... this woman...

A knock on the door. "Mummy?"

Fuck, no! He buried his head into her neck, exhaling his groan of frustration.

She froze around him, all her muscles tensed, but didn't let go. Or perhaps she couldn't.

He looked up and met her eyes. They were as pained as his.

"Mummy?" Jasmine's voice was teary through the door. "I had a bad dream."

Claire scrunched her face, then took a breath and let it

out.

"We could just tell her to go back to bed," he whispered, even though he knew that wasn't fair. "To wait in her room for five minutes."

Claire blinked away the sheen of need veiling her eyes, and shook her head. "She needs us."

With every morsel of strength he possessed, he pulled himself off her, and lay on his back on his side of the bed, pulling the cover across him, bunching it up to hide his crazed erection.

"Sweetie, come in," she called out as she adjusted her underwear and vest.

Good god, his balls might *actually* bruise.

"At least she knocked this time," whispered Claire – a strained attempt at humour to dull the fire that still tore through them.

Jasmine could reach the door handles now, but it still required some strength to turn them. Her clumsiness gave them an extra few seconds to calm their breathing.

The door finally opened and she stumbled into the dark grey of the room, rubbing her eyes, and sniffling from crying. "I had a bad dream," she repeated.

"Come here, sweetie." Claire held out her arms, and Jasmine climbed into them, lying on her chest.

Where I've just fucking been.

Pete sighed, and told his wolf to get the hell over it.

"What did you dream?" asked Claire, gently.

She sniffed again. "The sun fell out of the sky and burned everything except me. Then I was the only one left, and I was all alone."

A strange silence settled.

The hairs on his arms rose.

"It was just a dream," soothed Claire, though a telltale

waver coloured her tone. "We're all still here, and the sun's still in the sky."

"It's dark."

"Well, it's not in the sky *now*. But it'll rise tomorrow."

"Promise?"

"I promise."

More silence. It was disconcerting that he suddenly wondered if that was a promise they could keep.

"Mummy?"

"Yes?" Claire stroked their daughter's back in comfort.

"What am I?"

The silence thickened. What answer could they give? "Jerrod called you a shapeshifter. You're magical ... a bit like Daddy's magical."

"But I'm not a wolf like Daddy."

"No, you're not a wolf."

Jasmine ran the back of her hand across her nose and sat up, her dark brown eyes seeming to swallow the dark of the room. "Am I a monster?"

Claire sat up against her pillow, concern stealing over her features. "What? No, honey – of course you're not."

There were those goose pimples again, racing up and down his arms, teasing his fine hairs.

Claire took Jasmine in for another hug, calming her with further words, denying any monster exists.

If only he could shake the image of the Trident's slitted yellow eyes and drooling snout that clawed his mind.

~*~

"Thanks for driving me here this late." Holly took her suitcase from Claire. "It was the only other non-stop flight to JFK today – I didn't want to miss it."

Marco and Bill could have driven her here, to Reno-Tahoe International Airport, last night while taking Jerrod home, but Holly had insisted on moving her flight later (Claire suspected she hadn't wanted to get in the car with Jerrod) and Claire had been grateful for the extra time to breathe. She'd always planned to drive Holly to the airport, but she hadn't wanted to get back behind the wheel so soon after the crash – she'd needed time to gather herself.

However, she'd also wanted to get straight back to driving – even if it was in Bill and Marco's Range Rover – and not let the fear settle. As it happened, the six-hour journey to Reno-Tahoe Airport had been fine, and she hadn't felt as panicked as she thought she might.

It was nearly nine o'clock at night – Claire wouldn't be getting home until three in the morning, and Pete was already acting all moody about that since yesterday's run-in with the poachers – or whoever they were.

But she had insisted he stay with Jasmine. In some ways, he could defend her so much better than she could if push came to shove. She swore she'd be careful and check in with him every hour. They couldn't become prisoners in their own home.

He'd conceded, albeit reluctantly.

"Did you pack those photos I gave you?"

Holly's smile was wide and truly grateful. "I wouldn't forget them. Thanks so much for them, Beth." She pulled a face. "I mean Claire. Sorry – force of habit."

"Don't worry about it. And I'm glad I was able to give the photos to you – I have so many of us... Sarah would have wanted you to have them."

They walked into the airport and searched for the check-in desk.

Holly found it first. "There. That's me."

"You got your passport?"

"In my handbag."

"You want me to come to the gate with you?"

"Like an over-protective momma bear?" She laughed. "I'm good." She gave the iPod headphones hanging around her neck a shake. "Besides, I have Evanescence to keep me company."

"Good choice. Well, it was great to see you. Sorry it got all chaotic towards the end."

"Seems it's become a pattern," she joked, although concern was etched in her face. "Promise you'll be careful, okay?"

"We will be. Hey, I've got Pete and the boys, and now two new boys looking out for us."

She smiled a warm, sincere smile that reached her eyes. "You've always been the one who's okay, Beth. If the world collapsed around us, you'd be the last man standing. Keep me posted with any big news."

"Are you sure you'll want to know?"

"No."

Claire laughed.

"But I think I'd rather know than not. For old time's sake."

"Right. For old time's sake. Text me when you arrive at the other end."

"It'll be gone four in the morning over here."

"And I'm not getting home 'til three, so text me anyway, all right?"

"All right. Thanks for putting me up ... and putting up with me." Holly grinned that wide grin she was famous for, and Claire found she couldn't stay too irritated with her for any length of time – never had been able to no matter how great the irritation.

She moved in to give her a hug.

It was returned with affection. "Send me a picture of your engagement ring when you finally get it, okay?"

"I will, but it's not going to be anything fancy – none of your designer brands – so no poking fun at it."

Holly waved away her words. "As if I would."

"Ha."

"You know I never really mean it."

"Uh-huh."

Holly kept waving as she sauntered off in her black Versace skirt and Armani denim jacket, wheeling her suitcase behind her, and Claire found herself smiling – that 'old times sake' thing again. Sarah would probably have sided with Holly about the ring. Claire had never quite leapt onto the fashion bandwagon with equal passion.

Turning, she strode out of the airport, taking her phone out of her small rucksack. She dialled Pete's number. After five rings, he answered. "Claire?"

"Hey, babe. All's good. I've just dropped Holly off – heading back to the car now, and I'll come straight home. I might stop half way, though, for a snack and toilet break."

"Drive safely. Keep your wits about you."

"You know I will."

"I love you."

"I love you, too. Did Jasmine get to bed okay?"

"Fell asleep five minutes ago. She kept asking after you, but she was fine. Marco and Bill are here – full house tonight, apart from you. You're missed."

"I miss you guys, too. I'll check in every hour like we agreed."

"Thanks. Watch the road though."

She rolled her eyes. "You know I will."

"Good. See you soon."

"Don't wait up."

"You know I will."

She laughed. "Good."

"'Bye, honey."

"'Bye." She hung up, and fished her keys out of her bag, quickly scanning the car park without looking like she was scanning the car park.

Everything seemed fine. She wished she could shake the apprehension she felt. Perhaps it was simply because of everything that had happened yesterday – it was stuck in her subconscious now. Maybe she'd be apprehensive every day. It wasn't a good way to live.

She forced herself to block out the vague feeling she was being watched. *If you* think *about the Bogeyman, you're going to* feel *like he's there even if he isn't.*

She'd stay vigilant and keep to the main routes. She wasn't going to let fear cower her.

Chapter Nine

Two weeks later...

"What do you think?" asked Bill. He and Marco, Pete, herself, and Elky, stood in the centre of the diseased alpines. Pete said it didn't look like the disease had spread since they'd first spotted it two weeks ago, but neither had it subsided.

Elky shook his head, frowning. "It's nothing I've seen before, but I can take it to the chief – see what he can uncover."

"You mean ... visionary mojo stuff?"

Elky raised his eyebrows and smiled. "I was thinking more along the lines of, he's been around much longer than me and may have seen something like this before, but failing that, yes, 'visionary mojo stuff' often turns up a few surprising things."

Marco chuckled – *at* Bill – who gave him a shrug back. "It's not my area of expertise."

Elky let out a laugh. "Nor mine to be honest. But I do know that nature works as a unified body throughout the planet: there's a Supermoon and a Blood Moon about to descend upon us."

Bill looked more than surprised, as did Marco and Pete.

"There is? Blood Moon ... you mean a full lunar eclipse?"

"I do."

"How do we not know this?"

"I heard wolves no longer feel the moon's pull as they did."

"True, but if it's a Supermoon it'll be very close to the earth—"

"The eclipse is taking place across the Atlantic – you won't see it here. Perhaps that is also why you feel it less than you might otherwise."

"I guess. I've gotta say, it's taken some getting used to – not feeling the moon's phases over the past five years. Leaves me edgy, and I never thought it would."

"It could be that the coming Supermoon has triggered this mould or disease on the trees – as I mentioned, nature does work as one. The chief might know more. Claire," Elky addressed her, "do you have any thoughts on this?"

She had no bloody idea why she was here – she wasn't a forester, nor a wolf who could sniff things out, nor could she 'feel' the moon. But when Bill and Marco had asked Elky to meet them at the alpines, he had asked them to bring her. "I ... wouldn't know where to start."

"With your instincts. You have some of the finest instincts I've ever come across."

"I do?"

"Mmm-hmm. I don't mean like animal instincts that can smell and hear danger; I mean that human sixth sense of your higher consciousness that can know a person or situation. It comes from a place of wisdom and experience."

She was kind of dumbfounded. "Oh." A refined 'sixth sense' felt a far cry from the brash, heavy-handedness she'd always affiliated with herself.

"You really think so, do you?" Pete asked Elky. His tone

was slightly scathing.

Claire stared at Pete questioningly, and actually, a little hurt. Did he not agree? Did he not think she should be here, either? Feeling that way herself was one thing, but having him confirm it...

"So what do you think?" pressed Elky, ignoring Pete's question. "Don't think with reason; think with that sixth sense."

She pushed away the hurt, determined to at least *try* to be useful. "Um ... well ... you say there's no smell to the mould and the trees seem all right despite it; it's only the alpines that are affected ... why is that?"

"I don't know. But I can tell you that the alpines are energetically and spiritually connected to the tribe that live here. The alpines have always been guardians of the Maipeke people."

A gentle breeze rustled through the narrow path they stood on. *That* carried a scent – the sweet, nutty aroma of pine nuts in early October and a slight spice to the needles that held them aloft. Or perhaps she'd spent far too much time in the company of wolves. Still... "Okay... It appeared overnight – the night before we bumped into those poachers and Jasmine and I were run off the road." Silence fell, but she wasn't concentrating on that. Instead, she'd closed her eyes with an awareness of how the breeze felt a little out of place in this nestled space they stood in, yet meant to be; like it was delivering a...

The image of the other two alpines sprang to mind, quite suddenly – the ones on the side of the road driving home that looked like skinny bears guarding the way, just before they'd been hit.

"It's a message." She opened her eyes, realising she sounded bonkers, but it just made sense. It clicked. It made complete and utter *sense*. "It's not something done *to* the trees, it something the trees have developed to *show* us something – a message; a warning."

"What warning?" asked Pete, his voice now lowered in tone, almost gruff.

"Of what happened that day, but we didn't understand. There's something hidden that needs to come to light."

Bill brushed the side of the mould with his finger and sniffed it, presumably still trying to get a scent out of it. "But it's been two weeks since then; the disease is still here."

"Because the danger is still here," said Elky.

She looked at him.

He was looking back, seemingly impressed, right along with that twinkle in his eye he always exuded. "You're a native at heart. I do believe you may have taken the words out of my chief's mouth and saved him a job."

"I'm a little lost," mumbled Pete.

"My tribe, around this area, have historically looked to the alpines for guidance; their messages can be heard on the wind and in the ground beneath our feet if we are skilled in listening. This is the case for all trees, of course, but alpines dominate this region. There are some tales, handed down, of different ways those messages have protected us over the past few hundred years."

"And this 'mould' is one of those messages?"

"It would appear so. We must be careful because, clearly, the message is still relevant. The disease will go when all is deemed safe."

"Why would the trees protect us?" asked Claire.

"Traditionally, they have always protected the people here. But it seems to me they feel a need to protect your daughter, too. Jasmine is quite unique in her 'supernatural-ness', shall we say."

"Does she have a connection to the trees here?"

"She has a connection to all life; her power seems worldly."

"'Power' seems such a strong word for a five-year-old."

"But we must not deny the truth – it's what she has. Power in itself does not need to be corrupt – it's *people* that abuse it. Many use it for good."

Elky had been 'training' Jasmine for the past week. By his admission, it had been a little harder than he'd thought in that the girl had been quiet and less communicative than usual, as if the events of the past couple of weeks weighed heavily on her mind. Instead of opening up, though, she had retreated into a shell, churning over all her worries in silence.

Claire and Elky had both been trying to encourage her to talk, but she wasn't ready to, for whatever reason. It broke Claire's heart a little. It was a sign of innocence gone. She'd hoped that maybe they'd have at least five more years or so before the shit hit the fan.

Bill sighed and gathered his rucksack and ropes from the ground. "I'm going to have to make up some vague bullshit – I can't write 'the alpines are trying to protect us' on my notes to the board."

Marco slapped him on the back. "We'll think of something. Let's go. I'm hungry as fuck. Elky, you'll speak to your chief?"

"I will."

Claire slipped her arm into Pete's. "I'm picking Jasmine up in two hours."

"Stay alert," he muttered, still in mumbling mode. Unsurprisingly, he didn't seem happy about what they'd just discussed. After the shock of the car crash, they'd only just all started to feel a little more relaxed. Nothing else had rung alarm bells since then.

They had decided not to notify the police because there was no way to explain how they had escaped the vehicle. They might have gotten away with saying Claire had jumped out, but there was no way Jasmine could have done the same belted into her car seat and barely able to reach the door handle. Instead, Marco, Bill and Pete had hauled the wrecked car out of the trees one night, protected from prying eyes by the quiet and safety of the dark. They'd had to write it off and Claire was now driving a Ford Mustang – a bit more flashy than she liked, but Marco had managed to acquire it cheaply.

With the exception of dropping Holly off at the airport that night, she hadn't felt like she'd been followed since – and she'd likely imagined it at the airport anyway. She'd hoped the poachers might have moved on, put off by the fact Jasmine was surrounded by those fully capable of looking after her. Or perhaps they were not 'supernatural' poachers after all. Perhaps they were only here to hunt bears and they suspected Claire had caught onto their intentions when they'd bumped into her and Holly, so they thought they'd play it safe by scaring her into saying nothing.

Holly had texted to say she'd arrived in New York, and everything had slowly started to go back to normal.

Apart from Jasmine.

Claire chewed her lip. What was she going to do about her? She didn't want to push her to talk, but she didn't want to let her retreat into her own bubble either.

"Claire?"

"Hmmm?" Elky had said something. God, she'd been deep in thought.

"Will you consider coming with me tomorrow to speak to the chief?"

"Me?"

Pete stiffened by her side.

Elky laughed, bemused. "Yes, you. You still seem startled about your sensitiveness."

She snorted. "You know, in my entire life, no one has ever referred to me as sensitive."

"That's not true."

"Oh? You know my life?"

"I know that's not true – think harder."

"Maybe later," she brushed away. "I can't do more of this today." And she didn't want Pete to feel any more annoyed, whatever the reason for it. He'd been a bit of a moody arse the past few days.

"Armour is always so comfortable once you get the fit just right, isn't it? Please think about it. And let me know in the morning if you'll come with me to see the chief."

~*~

"So, did you have a good day at school?" Claire had already asked this question three or four times, disguised in different ways, on the drive home, to no avail. Her answers had been monosyllabic words and sounds, accompanied by the odd shrug. Jasmine wasn't talking. Claire had finally decided on the direct question.

"I already said yes, Mummy."

No, she had not said 'yes', but Claire knew if she carried on pushing, her daughter would clam up completely. Her persisted aloofness was slowly driving her insane.

She didn't respond to Jasmine's reply as they pulled into their driveway, but parked the car and carried on as they always did, familiar routine their buffer for the awkwardness.

"I saw Elky today," she said as Jasmine hopped out of the car with her school bag. "He said you're doing so well. He's very pleased."

A small frown creased Jasmine's brow, but that was all she received to her comment. They continued on through the front door.

Claire picked up the mail on the floor, and added it to the growing pile of things yet to be opened – mostly bills, and three packages which were things she'd ordered online for the garden. "Jasmine, do you feel happy training with him? Because if you ever want to stop, or take a break, you know you can."

Jasmine stared at her, giving nothing away bar another shrug. "I'm okay." Then, she turned and headed for the stairs that would lead her to her room.

"Wait ... why don't you stay down here for a bit. Have some juice with me, and I thought maybe we could go see if the salmonberries are ready to be picked." All she did most days on coming home from school was shut herself in her room and read books, or piece together jigsaw puzzles. Claire hadn't thought anything of it at first – they were stimulating activities for the brain, and reading was always encouraged – but in recent weeks, she felt like she was losing her child to a different world.

Jasmine had been pressing to have friends around for the best part of a year. They had put it off, concerned with the risk of exposing Pete, Bill, and Marco, but also with endangering Jasmine if they increased their profile. Guilt had eaten away at her – Jasmine needed a normal childhood; to do the things all other kids did.

She had spoken to Pete about it more in-depth this past week, and they'd agreed on arranging a play date for her two best friends. "Hey, I have good news," she continued when Jasmine failed to jump with excitement at the chance to pick salmonberries. "Daddy and I think it would be a fabulous idea to invite Diego and Molly round – I know you'd love to see them

– so, we were thinking that Tuesday next week after school would be good. They could stay for dinner – what do you think?"

Finally – *finally* – a small smile broke through. "I'd like that, thank you."

Still not the whoop of excitement she'd hoped for, but it was something. "Great! We can write invitations for them tonight, and you can give them out tomorrow."

Her smile grew a bit wider, and she nodded. "Okay."

The pause that followed stretched out, and for the life of her she couldn't think of a way to fill it.

Jasmine looked up the stairs. "May I go to my room now, please?"

Claire bit back a scream. "Of course. Maybe we'll save the salmonberries 'til the weekend, then we can all go pick them."

"Okay, thank you." She spun around and raced up the stairs.

Claire swallowed her still-lodged scream and took in a breath. *Invitations...* She'd concentrate on those – it was something. It would be good to have kids here. Jasmine needed to be running around getting muddy; gaining scrapes and bumps from falling over and climbing trees – anything other than shutting herself in her room.

She fished out paper, felt tips, and glitter from the stash kept in the kitchen sideboard. Hopefully Jasmine would look forward to helping her create these.

~*~

"I think you should speak to her."

Pete had barely walked in through the front door before Claire had started talking about Jasmine. His mood was a little dark. Claire being with them at the alpine trees earlier and the way Elky had taken to both her and Jasmine had rocked him a bit – not that he didn't want both of them to be able to defend themselves and sharpen their skills.

It was more to do with the uncontrollable feeling that he was closer to losing them than ever before due to fate, or forces beyond his comprehension, or whatever the hell liked to keep them all on their toes. While the last five years of his life had been fraught with potential dangers and the need to lie low, they had been some of the best years of his entire life. It was about to go tits up, he could feel it.

Claire was taking food out of the freezer for dinner. "I don't know why she won't talk to me, and I really bloody hope Elky's doing good by her – I hate the way she won't talk to me – but you might have better luck. Maybe she'll open up to you. I'm all for giving her space, but I think it's important we know what's going on with her."

"I agree. Elky's wrong about the moon, though."

"What do you mean?"

"I mean, I *can* feel it. I've been feeling it for days, though admittedly, I wasn't sure what it was – it's a different moon to what we're used to, and the rules changed when the Trident died. But it crossed my mind that if I can feel it, maybe Jasmine can feel it, too. Maybe that's why she's quiet."

Claire stopped what she was doing and looked at him. "You think so?"

"I don't know, but he was wrong."

"You don't like Elky, do you?"

"I don't like the way he puts suggestions in your head."

"He doesn't do that."

"He does."

"Can you hear lies in his voice?"

"No, not *lies* exactly, but ... something's off. There's something he's not saying. Or maybe it's that he knows just what to say – he says all the *right* things."

"That's ridiculous. You don't like him because he's *right*?"

He waved her pending argument away. He knew it sounded unreasonable, and the last thing he wanted was a fight. "You're right about Jasmine, though. I'll talk to her tonight."

After a pause, she pursed her lips and turned back to the dinner prep. "Thank you. Also, we're inviting her two friends from school here on Tuesday."

"All right." No problem. He'd just stay out the way.

She frowned at him as if she'd caught onto his train of thought. "I'd like you here, too."

"Really?" *Bugger.*

"Yes, really. Just in case something happens with Jasmine and I need your help to deal with her."

"What could happen?"

She stopped what she was doing and gave him *that* look that told him he was about to enter shaky ground if he didn't change his tune. "Did you really just ask that?"

He sighed. It was no big deal, right? *Just three excited kids in one house. No problem.* "She hasn't done her disappearing act since the aeroplane over two years ago."

"Teleportation."

"Yes – that." Though the terminology creeped him out. Weird considering he went through his own bone-crunching, muscle-twisting transformation every time he shifted.

Claire gestured into the air with her hands. "But now she's training in it, and with everything that happened two weeks ago ... I just want to make sure everything and everyone is safe, okay? Please be here."

"I'll be here."

"Thank you." She went back to sorting out food.

He took off his coat and slung it over the back of one of the dining chairs. "By the way, did Holly's boyfriend phone you today?"

"Tim? No – why?"

"I'm not sure. I got a missed call on my phone – it was from another cell and it wasn't Holly's number. He left a message – it was a guy – but the sound was grainy and he barely managed a few words before he got cut off. Sounded like he was on the road or something. I swear he said Holly's name, though, so I guessed it might be her boyfriend."

"Can I hear the message?"

He'd already gotten his phone out. He dialled his voicemail to retrieve the message, put the phone on loudspeaker and waited. The guy's voice finally came through.

"*Hi, it-hmmfmt-im … get through to Holly … was wondering if_____*" The line went dead.

Claire stared at him, bewildered. "That's it?"

"That's it."

"I think he said Tim at the beginning."

"He did?"

"It was muffled, but it sounded like '*it's Tim*'."

"Why would he be calling us?"

"I don't know. I've never even met him all the years they've been together. I did give Holly both our numbers though for emergencies." She dried her wet hands and reached for her own phone on the corner of the kitchen counter. "I'll call her now."

He watched Claire dial her friend as he pocketed his own phone. He turned his attention towards the stairs and Jasmine's room at the very top of it, and strained his ears. Not a peep sounded from that direction, not even to his wolf hearing. Claire was right – she *had* been awfully quiet recently.

Claire lowered her phone and shook her head. "It's just gone straight to her voicemail. I guess one of them will call again if it's urgent."

He nodded. "By the way, can we do something about her smell?"

"What do you mean?"

"Holly's scent is still floating around this house."

"It is?"

"Definitely. I'd have thought it would have gone by now, but it's so strong she might as well have popped over this morning."

"I can't smell anything."

"That's definitely her perfume."

Claire sniffed, but clearly couldn't smell what he could.

"It's not *fresh* perfume, it's a couple of weeks old, but it's still permeating the air."

"I've hoovered, I've washed the bedsheets in the guest room, the doors and windows have been opened—"

"I know, I know, but I'm telling you, I can *smell* her."

"Well, I'll ... light some incense."

He stared at her.

She threw her arms up, defeated. "I don't know what else to do. Besides, her perfume probably cost her an arm and a leg – it's not a *bad* smell, is it?"

"As synthetic as any perfume, but..." He took in a breath. "Maybe it's 'cause it's stale on the air, but there's a tang behind the smell that's bothering me."

"A 'tang'? Okay, look, I'll burn candles, incense, make sure there's a breeze through the house, and change the cushion covers. I don't *really* want to wash the sofas, though. Other than that, I'm all out of ideas."

"It'll do, thank you. Sorry I'm being a grumpy sod." He leaned in for a kiss. "That Supermoon eclipse – it's happening now. I think that's why I'm sensitised to everything at the moment."

She pulled back and stared at him. "*Now?*"

"Yeah. And it's a rare one. The moon's closer to the earth than it's been in about thirty years."

"Why didn't you say anything earlier?"

"I just found out an hour ago; thought I'd research it since Elky mentioned it. There's nothing in the newspapers about it here – it's happening over England – and it's not like we've been keeping track of the lunar phases now they don't affect me. We've had bigger things to concentrate on over the years. It didn't occur to me I might be reacting to the full moon, but it's a big and rare alignment, so ... you're stuck with the grumpiness for a few more hours. There's every chance Jasmine might snap out of her mood, too, once it's over."

"I guess..." She gave him a small smile. "I really hope that's all it is." Then, she tugged on his collar until he was against her lips once more. "I fell for your grumpy sod routine, remember?"

He chuckled, but deepened their kiss, delighted and feeling suddenly more relaxed at the gentle groan that escaped her. God, he needed this woman between the damned sheets with no interruptions. *That's* what he'd been bloody missing.

"Mummy?"

"Oh my fucking God," Pete growled, his voice low.

Claire laughed, then pushed him away with one hand on his chest.

"Seriously, her timing is impeccable."

"It's four o'clock in the afternoon."

"It's a dark part of her magic powers. I think we need to have a word with Elky."

"Don't you dare!" But she was still laughing. "Sweetie, we're in the kitchen," she called out.

He heard her footsteps descending the stairs.

"Mummy, do mirrors always show you the truth?" she asked from somewhere near the bottom of the stairs.

"Aah," he whispered to Claire in jest, "it's kid's hour on Question Time."

"Oh, stop it." She nudged him playfully with her shoulder.

Jasmine appeared in the kitchen's doorway looking down and rubbing her eyes.

"Sweetie, what do you mean?"

"Does the mirror show me what I really look like?"

"Well, yes. A mirror just shows you your reflection."

"Even the small mirror in my bedroom?"

"Yes, even that one."

She was still rubbing her eyes, as if trying to get sleep out of them. "I think I *am* a monster, then."

Claire lost her smile in an instant.

Pete crossed his arms, not liking the feeling that flooded him on hearing their daughter's verbal self-caning.

"Honey, I thought we talked about this. Of course you're not a monster. You're special, but *not* a monster."

"But I'm changing."

"You're not."

"I am. The mirror showed me." Now she was crying, though trying not to, her head still hung low.

Pete crouched down and reached for her. "Come here."

With a sob, she walked fast into his arms and grabbed onto him as he hugged her tight, hiding her face in his shoulder.

"You're not a monster, no matter what the mirror showed you."

"Promise?"

"I promise."

"You'll still love me if I change?"

He felt himself tense, even though he didn't mean to. "Jasmine ... what *did* the mirror show you?"

With another watery gulp, she released him, then took a step back. Slowly, she looked up and met his eyes.

He had to tell himself – consciously talk the instruction into his mind – to *not* react to what he saw: two large eyes staring back at him the way they had since he'd sneaked her out of that damned hospital as a baby. Only this time, there was a marked difference. One eye was the very dark brown it had always been; the other was green.

Chapter Ten

“And you did nothing differently?” Pete had taken Jasmine out of the kitchen and to the foot the stairs where they both sat. He was having his 'chat' with her earlier than planned.

Claire was still in the kitchen, gripping the counter so she wouldn't fall over, one ear on what was being said, and the rest of her concentration focused on not submitting to the fast-rising panic punching her chest.

Her eyes. What the hell? Was that change in colour possible? She knew there were people in the world with different coloured eyes, though she couldn't remember the medical term for it. But could it occur *this* way? Without warning and in the space of mere minutes?

When she'd picked her up from school, both her eyes had been dark brown. Now...

“I promise. I was making a jigsaw puzzle and my eyes started to get itchy, so I rubbed them, but the itchy wouldn't stop, so I thought I had something in my eyes. I went to see in the mirror and now my eyes are different.”

“It's okay, we'll find the answers. Jasmine, listen to me, honey. You've been very quiet the past two weeks, and Mummy and I have been wondering if you've been all right. It would be good to know what you're doing when you're with Elky and how you feel about your training and your new powers. Maybe the answers are there somewhere."

"You never talk about being a werewolf."

Pete fell silent.

Claire exhaled and looked up – maybe the answers would be in the ceiling. Damn it! No, they *didn't* talk about Pete being a wolf, and they'd told Jasmine never to talk about it to others. Fuck – no wonder she'd not said a word. *We've been idiots.*

But there was no way around the fact that Pete's wolf needed to be a secret; that Jasmine's birth and genealogy needed to be a secret. However, they should have talked about it more amongst themselves as a family, shouldn't they? Maybe Jasmine had felt isolated by it all, and confused.

She cursed under her breath, thinking about all those werewolf text books she'd seen in Lawrence's house – some in Pete's bookcase when he'd been living on his grounds. There wasn't a fucking text book for what Jasmine was.

"Oh … Jasmine, honey, I… You know, I never really had anyone to talk to, so I learnt to stay quiet because I had no choice, but *you* … you have us. And you'll always have us. So, as long as we're in private, you can talk to us about *anything* whenever you like."

"But I want to be strong like you."

Claire blinked tears out of her eyes. She heard Pete murmur something, and it sounded like he was giving her another hug.

"You *are* strong. And talking about things doesn't make anyone *less* strong. In fact, talking can make you stronger because it's so hard to do sometimes. We just need to make sure we trust the people we talk to. You trust us though, don't you? I hope you know you *can* trust us."

"I do, Daddy."

"Good. I know you talk to Mummy about most things."

"Not about this."

"But you can."

"But she can't help. She's normal – not like you and me."

Fuck.

Anger pushed further tears out. She swiped at them furiously. She'd never felt so fucking useless as she did in that moment, with Jasmine unwittingly voicing all her silent fears.

"Jasmine, Mummy understands so much better than you think, and she *can* help. She's helped me so many times."

Claire grabbed her phone, shut the kitchen door, and strode to the far end of the room. Before she could change her mind, she dialled Elky's number.

Jasmine was right. She couldn't help her without knowing what she was up against – at least knowing as much as she *could* know.

"Hi, Elky?" she said, when she heard him answer.

"Hello, Claire."

"I can come with you tomorrow morning to see your chief. What time's good?"

Dawn crept beyond the window, teasing the bedroom curtains. The curtains won. Dawn could not yet trespass, but Claire knew if she climbed out of bed and peeked through the gap between the material, she'd see the sun turning tufts of grass golden as it sloped gently uphill towards the forest; she knew that the lake she loved to walk to would shimmer the most deep sapphire blue, turning a darker and darker shade until the October sun was overhead. After that, as the sun fell west, the lake would take on a blue-grey haze, both mysterious and majestic.

This was, hands down, one of her favourite places on earth and she'd been to quite a few places.

"I know you're awake," said Pete, softly, his back facing her in the bed they shared. "I can tell by your breathing."

She turned on to her right and shuffled up against him until she spooned him from behind. "I'm not sure I've slept all night."

"You haven't."

"I guess neither have you, then."

"I haven't." He turned to face her, now lying on his left. The bed creaked in protest over his movements.

"Do you think there's something wrong with her?" She'd whispered that, partly conscious she never, ever wanted Jasmine to hear her say such a thing, but also disgusted with herself for even asking such a thing. It wasn't an easy question to speak or hear.

"I don't know. But it was always going to be this. Right or wrong, young or old, this year or in fifteen years ... it doesn't matter. It was always going to be this."

"Can it happen like that? Her eyes changing colour..."

"It happened at the exact moment of the lunar eclipse."

Her throat closed up. What could she say to that? What did that mean?

Pete let out a long breath. "I don't know if it can happen like that. I left a message on Dr Matheson's phone."

She cringed. It must have shown on her face. Dr Matheson was someone they both liked and trusted – he'd pretty much saved their lives – but his name conjured memories and feelings of the first few months without Sarah, bringing up her baby with no instruction and no emotional aid, and that was a painful thing to recollect. Matheson – appointed to them by Lawrence five years ago – was one of the very few people who knew the truth of that night. "He's in England; we're here.

Maybe we should take her to a regular doctor. They don't have to know her history."

"Way too risky, Claire – you know that."

"Her blood is as human as anyone else's."

"So were her eyes. Things change."

She rolled onto her back, exhaling more sharply than she'd intended, her frustration at feeling so useless already sneaking into the day. "I could ask Elky if he knows of a doctor who could help."

"It's a last resort. We spoke to Marco and Bill about all of this when we first arrived, remember? We asked them to say nothing to anyone about Jasmine's history. They've respected our wishes and remained silent – all but lied to Tristan, who they answer to, putting their own livelihoods at stake. Finding a specialist doctor here … it would put us all at risk. Tristan has a reputation of being fair and just, but if he caught a whiff of Trident among us, he'd end it, Claire. He'd take Jasmine's life. We know her, he doesn't, and to protect his pack – to protect all wolves – we'd lose her."

"He'd do that to a child?"

"You know he would. Wolves and Tridents … our bound history is too destructive. He'd be too scared she could herald a rebirth of the Trident in the future – he'd see it as his duty to kill her."

"Bill and Marco really trust you, don't they?"

"They trust *us*. They were there with Lawrence and all of us – they've seen our struggles and what we've overcome. They met Sarah. They've grown a soft spot for Jasmine, too. Tristan wasn't there."

"Maybe Elky's chief will … I don't know … maybe there's some kind of native medicine that could help. Something herbal, or magical, or—"

"Are you sure you want to go over there this morning?"

"How can I not? We need answers."

"I know, it's just that … what the hell is a 'chief' anyway? I mean nowadays. Are we talking like 'medicine man', or what?"

"I don't know. I think it's just a term that's been kept. It's all more political nowadays, isn't it? I'm guessing he's like a chairperson for the tribe or something, or a representative."

"But he'll know about Jasmine's abilities – Elky will have told him."

"I've explained to Elky how imperative it is that no outsiders know of her abilities. He agrees."

"But I know nothing about his tribe as a whole, and their involvement in this comes down to diseased alpine trees. I find it a bit—"

"Pete, we need *answers*. It's the only way we're going to get them. I need to go."

He sighed, then went quiet, though she could see his mind turning.

When he looked back at her, there was a gleam of determination to his eye, and a hitch to his voice which she couldn't decipher. "All right. But I want you to do something for me."

"What?"

He paused, searching her out with his gaze. "Drink my blood."

"*What?*"

"You did before."

"I was dying."

"And it gave you strength. Do you have any idea how fucking lucky that was? Most humans don't even react to wolf blood, but your body just lapped it up like a nutritional boost."

"I don't need it now."

"You might. I know you're not ill, but it'll increase your

strength and senses for a few hours – maybe half a day – just like it did before. Fuck, Claire, with everything going on, don't leave me worried senseless about you while you walk, unarmed and blind, into some lion's den."

She fell silent. That night she'd taken his blood, she'd been brutally attacked and suffering from internal injuries. A Trident invasion on Lawrence and the wolves was imminent and they'd worried she wouldn't be strong enough to survive it. It had been a last resort, but Pete's blood had worked. Her bleeding had stopped, her bruises had healed, and more than that, she'd woken up feeling like her body was ten years younger and ten times stronger. His blood in her had also bonded them in some way – broken down that last self-imposed barrier between them against any potential relationship, despite their attraction for the other. A wolf and human ... it was too impossible in the long run; too ill-fated.

Yet, here they were.

"Please, Claire."

She stared at him, and her heart leapt. His black eyes were even darker than Jasmine's, but they now flashed briefly with gold at his request of her. His love for them both exuded from his every pore. In his silent, private, unwittingly menacing way (menacing to the outside world, anyway) he was the epitome of male protectiveness, and she loved him. There was a point in her life she'd felt incapable of loving a man this much, this deeply.

"Now?" she whispered.

"Yes, now."

She nodded her consent. "Yes."

Her breath caught as his irises turned fully golden on his next blink. His fangs elongated, every muscle in him bulged with tension and anticipation, and even before he tore the flesh on his wrist with his razor-sharp teeth, a wanton rush of need carved a path through her.

Lust and love enmeshed, the scent of his blood reached her just before he did. He moulded his full length on top of her, naked – because that's how he slept – every contour of his body fitting into every curve of hers.

She remembered it now: the sweet spice to his blood – not quite like human blood, but denser; almost ambrosial, as if all its power could be found in its smell and taste. Her mouth watered for it.

"You don't need much," he reminded her, his voice guttural with need.

What a sly little lie. She needed everything he gave.

But he held off, his bleeding wrist inches from her hungry tongue. At this moment, just as it was five years ago, she found herself wondering if a wolf lay hidden deep within her having skipped generations, because her humanity slipped a little. No human could crave anything with such fervour on scent alone, surely.

Instead of placing his blood against her lips, he slipped his other hand down the seat of her backside, pushing her underwear down.

Her senses were heading towards overdrive. She let out a moan of impatience. But she knew what he wanted – she wanted it, too. His cock nested in the entrance of her sex, every rigid inch of him telling her he craved her as much as she did him.

His stubble grazed her cheek. "Are you ready?" he panted into her ear, the force of the question making it pretty damned clear another interruption from anyone or anything would pretty much end him.

But she'd been ready for years. She'd *always* been ready for this male.

"Yes," she hissed, angling for his wrist, the need for his

blood drowning out all else.

One stroke and he was fully inside her.

Her soul screamed her love for him; what came out of her mouth was a '*fuck*' she never completed as his blood laved her tongue with his flavour.

She drank.

Not enough. He wouldn't let her have too much for her sake, but he gave her the rest of him, thrust after thrust, his moans of ecstasy chasing hers.

It was a rapid rise to the top of that crest, but she wanted more. She wanted a crucial togetherness she couldn't frame with words. Before she tumbled over the edge, she grabbed his hair and tore her mouth from his wrist. She could feel his blood coating her lips. "Bite me."

God ... she almost came just saying it.

His eyes burned with desire, but a wariness persisted, even if his pace didn't slow. He shook his head. "What if I turn you?"

"Women can't be turned."

He wavered at that truth. "I'll hurt you."

"No you fucking won't." His blood in her would heal any wound.

Before he could protest further, she grabbed his lips with hers.

The taste of his own blood damn near did it, she could tell – his cock became steel; his relentless rhythm became a life line. She almost felt bad for pushing him so, but she couldn't hold out too much longer – she was too close, and she *wanted* to feel her skin break under his urge.

Christ! Too late!

She cried out as she came, unable to contain it, her climax intense; crushing. "I love you, I love you..."

His growl wasn't one she'd heard before in all their

shared moments. Deep and positively dangerous, it rumbled through her, heightening her sensitivity; prolonging her release.

In a flash, she saw his werewolf in complete potency, his head flung back, teeth fully bared, the bridge of his nose almost muzzle; his dilated pupils, his iridescent irises... What a stunning, stunning vision.

Then, he did as she asked, and she felt every second like it was her last.

Teeth didn't rip through flesh, but *slid* in like flint through the heart. Her pulse beat in her ears. His suck on her blood moved her like the moon moved tides; she felt every lap against her shore; liquid and body merged. Where she ended and he began, she had no clue.

It was over in an instant; his tongue now bathed her wound to seal it shut.

She wanted more, wanted to protest, but couldn't because his blood was her blood and both effervesced inside her, dragging her fathoms deep.

"*Jesus Christ ... Jesus Christ...*" Pete's bewildered mantra tugged her core, but even that wasn't enough to shift the veil that drugged her.

Her eyes closed. Darkness invaded.

"Sleep, Claire," Pete whispered. "I love you so fucking much. Sleep. I'll wake you up for the school run. I'll always wake you up ... I'll always wake you up."

Chapter Eleven

"Are you going to be all right to drive?"

Claire looked at Pete, Jasmine's lunch box in her hands, both bemused and slightly irritated. He'd been a right mother hen ever since she'd woken up with wolf in her veins.

"Go slow. It'll take five minutes to get used to how all the sounds are louder, and how anything that moves becomes a distraction because you're so sensitised to it. Even your own movements are—"

"Pete," she sighed, then leaned into him for a kiss, "I'll be fine. I feel *fine*." And she really did. Just like five years go, she'd woken as if this was who she was all along, hidden from sight. It was as if life itself became … *more*. Colours were, indeed, sharper; objects were more defined. All movement – anything that ran, walked, crawled, scurried, fluttered – was something she tried not to openly marvel at, but she was thrown by how much she *didn't* see with human senses. The difference was astounding.

Smells, quite literally, assaulted her – this was possibly the worst part of the change. Some were so pleasant, some were repugnant, but in any case, most scents spiked her brain and planted images there of what the aroma belonged to and how it got there – a story within a story within a story that humans simply didn't see. Having Pete's blood in her was like experiencing the world in 4D.

"Glad to hear it. Text me when you get there."

She refrained from rolling her eyes. It was better to have a partner who cared about her than one who didn't give a flying fuck. He was behaving in an over-protective fashion (and she suspected he knew it), but it was understandable given the circumstances. It was also a bloody turn on most of the time. "I will – promise."

"Stay vigilant all the time; make sure you—"

"Pete – go." She all but pushed him out the front door.

Jasmine came bounding down the stairs in that moment.

"Hey, squirt," Pete called out. "Have a good day at school; I'll see you tonight."

"Okay, Daddy. Bye-bye."

His attention turned back to Claire, and she all a sudden found herself caught within two hands and by a searing kiss, which she'd have sunk into with abandon had she not felt Jasmine's stare burning a hole in her back.

She gently untangled herself from her lover's hold. "I love you," she whispered. "And I'll be fine. I'll see you later."

"Okay. 'Bye." He smiled, but thankfully left – finally. He was already running a little late, and soon, they would be, too.

She turned to Jasmine who was staring at her with a funny expression on her face, one eye still green instead of the brown it should be. She was still just a little too young to be put off by lovey-dovey grown-up kisses. In a couple of years, there'd probably be outright disgust – at least, Claire remembered herself behaving that way as a child.

Her mind laughed at her. *And right up to early adulthood – you couldn't stand anything remotely mushy. Look at you now.*

She hid a smile, and held out Jasmine's lunch box for her to take. "Do you have everything? Do you need your rucksack today?"

She shook her head and took her lunch. "Everyone's going to laugh at me."

Claire bit her lip, not really knowing what to say, so she just repeated what she'd said earlier, even if it might not be true. "No one's going to laugh. If anyone says anything about your eyes, just say it doesn't hurt and you're not worried, but you're going to see the doctor about it tomorrow."

"Are we seeing the doctor?"

She bit her lip harder. No, they fucking weren't. What doctor? "I'm speaking to someone about your eyes today, and we'll see what they say."

Jasmine stared at her a beat too long, as if she knew she wasn't telling the whole truth. She probably did, but it was the best Claire could do.

"Come on, sweetie. You'll be fine. Be brave."

Be brave, be brave, be brave... It seemed like that was all she said to Jasmine sometimes, and it wasn't fair. How would it feel as a five-year-old if all you heard most of your life was 'be brave'? They asked too much of her, too often.

Regardless, she nodded, her face sullen, and walked out the front door to wait by the car.

Claire repressed a sigh that was part grief. She hated seeing Jasmine sad; she hated seeing her sullen. They needed to do something to cheer her up – maybe they'd go to an amusement park this coming weekend, or something like that; something 'ordinary' that all kids did.

And if she teleports off a ride because she gets too scared or excited?

She ignored her thoughts and grabbed her car keys from the hook by the coats. She froze ... sniffed.

Shit, Pete was right: she could smell Holly.

Taken aback, she stood still and breathed in again,

concentrating on that hint of her perfume, stale on the air, but definitely 'Holly' nonetheless. She *was* going to have to wash the damned sofa. How could her smell still be lingering?

"Mummy, can we go now?" Jasmine called from the car, still looking as sombre as ever.

She snapped out of where Holly's musk had taken her. Pete was also right about the weird 'tang' to it. It must be due to the fact it was old and not fresh. But maybe she was making too much out of it – as a human, she couldn't smell it. *No* human could smell it. "Yep, let's go."

Not thinking further on it for now, she shut and locked the front door, trying not to be swayed by every god-damned scent and sound that invaded her as she walked towards the car. She had to take care when opening and closing things too; when turning things and using any kind of force – she was quite a bit stronger than she was used to.

Despite the unfamiliarity of this new state of being, it was not a bad feeling at all. It wouldn't take her too long to get used to – she could live like this. Shame the effects never lasted.

~*~

With Claire having taken their Mustang, and Marco and Bill driving the Range Rover, Pete had shifted and, as a wolf, made his way on foot (or paws) to where they'd arranged to meet. The trot through the forest was soothing for his senses, and he found himself more relaxed than he'd been in days when he finally arrived at his destination.

It looked like he'd missed out on quite a bit, though. Bill and Marco were packing up.

Pete transformed into his human self, not paying any mind to his lack of clothing – no one was about. "Sorry I'm late. I wanted to make sure the girls were properly sorted before I left."

"Not a problem. There's nothing new to report – not about the alpines anyway."

"Oh?" That sounded a little ominous.

"Tristan's called me and Bill in for a meeting. I suspect he's heard about 'happenings' along the grapevine – probably thinks they're not more than rumours for now, but he's gonna want to check in with us. If he asks outright about Jasmine..." Marco let that sentence sit unfinished.

He didn't have to finish it. Pete knew the score, even if it was the worst possible outcome. "You won't be able to lie, I know. Nor should you."

Looked like they might be packing up and moving on. *Fuck.* He tried to hide how much of a blow that was.

Marco looked almost as crushed as he felt. "Tristan's put a lot of trust in us. We could say we knew nothing about Jasmine up until now – that we feel as duped as he. He might pick up on the lie, but if we both stand our ground, I reckon he'll concede to our version of events – he's not a bad guy, he just wants future packs safe. Coming clean would protect our hides, though he'll never take our word at face value again. Not for a long time – we'd have to earn that from scratch. We're good – we knew this might happen. But it doesn't help you, Claire and Jasmine. I wish I had better news."

"There's no chance he's calling you in to talk about something else?"

He shrugged. "It's possible. But with those poachers knowing about Jasmine, Elky knowing about her – and by the end of today, his whole tribe will know – we'd be fools to assume it's anything else. Hell, even that Jerrod guy knows and *we* don't know shit about him. For all we know, he's told an army of people and word's got back to Tristan."

"Jerrod knows about Jasmine, but we never told him we're wolves. There's no reason he'd connect us with Tristan."

"Jerrod walks in the supernatural world, just like us. You know that. What we don't say, he'll find out eventually. The good news is, the same goes for us. We've got a couple of contacts on Jerrod's case."

"You do?"

"Yep – we need to find out exactly who he works for and how he's gained all his knowledge about teleporting and shapeshifting and the like. We'll keep you posted with what we find. In the meantime, we need a contingency plan for Jasmine. After our meeting with Tristan, depending on how it goes, we might have orders to bring her in. If we refuse, he'll come get her with his pack."

Pete blinked and looked away. His chest felt gripped by giant pincers. "She's innocent. Fuck it, she's a *child* with feelings and thoughts and ... she doesn't know a damned thing."

"Not the point – you know that. No wolf across the globe will ever risk a Trident uprising again. I hate to say it, but you need to make plans to leave. Sneak out when no one's looking."

It was over. The safe zone they'd built for Jasmine and for themselves ... maybe it had all been an illusion to begin with. Maybe he'd been an idiot to hope otherwise.

"I'm really, really sorry." Marco's voice broke, though he caught it and looked the other way, his shades hiding his remorse.

Pete knew if there was any chance to keep them here, he and Bill would take it. Regardless, if Tristan came for them ... his pack was strong in numbers. But they were just three wolves, a human, and a child. Disturbing the ambience Bill and Marco had forged this side of the ocean was not anything Pete wanted to do – they needed allies, not enemies. "We'll make sure it looks like you never knew we were leaving. We won't tell you when, we'll just go." They could then answer to Tristan with truth to their tone – Pete owed them that.

Marco nodded. "Our meeting with Tristan is on Tuesday. Assuming the news is what we expect, we'll do our best to delay things as much as possible for you. Take your time planning – you need to be safe from other things out there, not just Tristan's pack."

Other things. Christ, it would be good to know exactly what those other things were. This was going to break Claire's heart.

Bill, who had been silent this whole time, handed Pete the clothes they'd brought for his change, nothing but apology in his eyes.

Pete took the clothes and got dressed. "It's all right. You've both stuck your necks out for us. We always knew staying here might be a temporary thing." If only Jasmine hadn't settled in so well. *Damn.* "I'll speak to Claire tonight; we'll figure it out."

"Is she at the ranchería?"

"Yep." He tightened his jaw. Her reasons for going there made complete and utter sense, but he didn't like it, and he especially didn't like it now this curve ball had been thrown at them. What was supposed to have been 'training Jasmine' seemed to be getting more and more complicated. Embroiling Claire in it, too, made it feel like he ... hell, it felt like they were being separated from him; like they were being herded in opposite directions. He'd told himself over and over again it was his wolf feeling territorial and overprotective, but the feeling hadn't gone. His sole comfort – and it was only a small one – was that he'd given Claire his blood this morning. Nevertheless, she was human, no matter how much of his blood she drank. If the shit hit the fan, and it now seemed likely it would, he *couldn't* be separated from her.

~*~

Elky was waiting for her on the corner of the road that led into the ranchería, and it was beyond weird how she could smell him before she could see him.

She pulled over and he made his way to her car, waving. "Good morning, Claire," he called out towards her open window.

"Morning." She had no plans on telling anyone about the 'wolf' in her, but she found herself wondering if he could see it or sense it since it was one of his gifts. Would it work if she was fundamentally still human? If Pete's blood only had a temporary effect on her?

If Elky picked up on anything different about her, he showed no signs of it. "Chief wants to meet us at the edge of the woods half a mile out of the ranchería."

"Why?" Her skin prickled. Pete was right – fucking hell. She could hear it now. It wasn't a lie exactly, it was … something hidden in his voice. Or something veiled.

"There's a place we use for ceremonies and sweat lodges – he's set up a sweat lodge, and although women are traditionally not permitted to sit in on them, he is making an exception and would like you to join us."

She felt pensive about it. This new 'thing' in Elky's voice that the wolf in her was picking up, threw her. At the ranchería there would at least be others within shouting distance, but in the forest? "Did you know that's what we'd be doing?"

"No. It's not my place to question the chief – I simply wait for his instruction."

"And then just do as he says?"

"If there's no good reason not to, then yes."

She sighed, reached over and opened the passenger door

for Elky. Beggars couldn't be choosers. There was no outright lie from him that she could sense, and she needed this information. "Hop in. I take it I'm driving us there."

"That would be helpful, thank you." He shut the door once inside.

"I know what a sweat lodge is – at least in theory – and I've got to say, I'm not kitted out for one." Unless they did it differently, she assumed she'd be sitting in some kind of yurt, breathing in herbal steam from water poured onto scorching hot stones. Her clothes were going to get drenched unless she stripped.

"I've brought you a loose dress to wear. The rest of us will be in our smalls."

"In your underwear?"

"We have ceremonial 'underwear' shall we say, but we are used to only men participating, so additional modesty is something we have never thought about."

"Why am I being invited to participate?"

"I don't know the answer I'm afraid – the chief will have to tell you himself – but it's a privileged position. As well as forbidding women to take part, no outsiders have ever been permitted within the lodge."

She started the engine. "Can you direct me there?"

"Of course. It's straight up this road for most of the way. I'll tell you when to veer left."

She pulled on to the road again. "Does your chief have a name? How do I address him?"

"He has never been one for too many formalities. Bob will do."

"Bob? His name's Bob?"

"No. But that's how he's known to outsiders. Or you could call him Chief. Again, it tends to be only tribe members who use that title, but I should imagine he'd make an exception for you given you'll be in the lodge with us."

Chief sounded better than Bob at any rate – Bob sounded too informal for what she was about to step into.

And what the hell is that, Claire? Do you know what you're doing?

Anxiety – even if just a hint of it at any time – was a permanent state within her now she was a mother. It always festered under the layers of every other emotion, playing on all her insecurities. Damn, she'd never paid any mind to *any* insecurities before – she'd just gotten on with things, that was her nature. She wanted to feel more carefree like she'd been in her younger years. "Hey," she smiled, attempting to lighten the mood. "You never told me what your name means."

"Elkoyti?" he asked.

She nodded.

He laughed. "It means 'hidden bear leaps out and eats man's intestines'."

"*What?*"

He laughed louder. "It's not as bad as it sounds. Its meaning is bravery and strength. The bear protects his territory."

"So, the man in question is the enemy?"

"Of course – the poacher if you like."

She fell silent. Unease rippled through her belly and doubt crept in, overshadowing her determination. Regardless, she kept her foot on the gas and continued on. She needed answers for Jasmine's sake; she had no idea how else to get them.

~*~

Diego was staring at her; Molly hadn't noticed – most of the other kids hadn't. She knew Mrs Myers knew because Mummy had told her she would speak to her to confirm they were taking her to the doctor, but Jasmine caught her staring at her anyway every now and then, looking anxious and confused.

Mummy told her to be brave. She was trying, but she really just wanted to hide. She let her hair fall over her face whenever she could. What if *they* thought she was a monster?

Daddy was picking her up from school today, which made her feel a bit better. Everyone stared at him, too.

It was morning recess. She wasn't sure who to play with. Usually, she'd run off with Diego and Molly and they always knew which games to play and no one got bored. Fifteen minutes went by really fast. Today, she stood alone in the bottom corner of the playground because Molly had been dragged to the climbing frames by Cindy, and Diego had disappeared. She couldn't see him anywhere.

"Sweetheart?"

Jasmine turned to see Mrs Myers looking at her with a slightly sad smile.

Her teacher knelt down so they were the same height. "Your mom told me you have an appointment with the doctor soon."

She nodded because Mummy had told her to let people know she'd be seeing the doctor if they asked. Or 'Mommy'. She loved her teacher's accent and the way everyone spoke here in America. It sounded nice to her ears, and sometimes she tried to copy the sound of it when she spoke back.

"Good. Are you feeling okay today? Do you have a sore head, or are you feeling too hot or anything?"

"I feel fine, thank you."

"That's good." Her teacher smiled again, but still looked worried. It made her feel a bit guilty. She didn't want to make people worry, but she didn't know how to fix it. "And you can see okay? I mean, nothing's blurry, or looks strange?"

"No, Mrs Myers. I can see okay."

"Good ... good." Mrs Myers stood up, wringing her hands,

as if she didn't know what else to say.

There was a tug on her arm.

She turned to find Diego smiling at her and pulling her towards their favourite tree in the playground.

Mrs Myers smiled a less sad smile now. "Hello, Diego. I'll leave you two to play – there's ten more minutes of recess." She walked away, looking back a couple of times.

Jasmine decided to ignore the guilty feeling, happy that Diego was here. She took his hand and they ran to the oak tree. They loved it because it was so huge and the only one here on this side of the play area. For some reason, it made her think about the other tree in the desert with the roof thing over it. That tree stood on its own, too.

When they reached the oak tree, Diego turned to her, and his smile looked a little more weird. His eyes sparkled, full of mischief. "What's wrong with your eyes?" he asked.

Her own smile faded. She didn't really want to talk about it. "Mommy's taking me to the doctor," she said (because that's what she was supposed to say) and copying his accent so she stood out a little less.

"Are you sick?"

"No."

"Do your eyes hurt?"

"No."

"I know a dog that has one brown eye and one blue eye."

"You do?"

"Yeah." Then he laughed. "You're like a dog."

She frowned, then cautiously smiled. She didn't think he meant that in a mean way – Diego had never been mean before. He probably just meant it as a joke. "Maybe I'm like a wolf."

"You're not scary enough to be a wolf."

"Wolves aren't scary."

"Yes, they are. Can I catch what you have?"

Her smile wavered. "What do you mean?"

"If I touch you, or touch your eyes, or if I stare at your eyes too long, will I catch it? Will my eyes go weird?"

"No." But she didn't actually know if that was true. *Could* he catch it?

"It's kinda cool."

"It is?" She raised her eyebrows in surprise.

"Is the doctor going to fix it?"

"I don't know." But she suddenly felt a bit better. If Diego thought it was cool, maybe other kids would, too, and no one would think she was a monster. Would he think the 'teleporting' thing she could do was cool, too? She wasn't supposed to talk about that. There was a lot she was never supposed to talk about. But it occurred to her that if she could take Mummy on her flying trips, she could probably take Diego, too. He would *definitely* think that was cool!

"Do you think it's like a super power? Maybe you're like Spiderman – he's got awesome webs that come out of his wrists, and you've got weird eyes! Do your eyes do anything?"

"I don't think so." She looked at her wrists – she didn't have webs. She could fly though. Well, it was *sort* of like flying. "Would you rather be like Spiderman, or Superman?" she asked. She was testing him – she wanted to know his answer. It meant he might still like her once he knew just how strange she really was. She also felt a bit guilty again, though, because this was *almost* like telling him her secret, which she wasn't supposed to do.

He scrunched his face up, hard, thinking about her question. Finally, he came to a decision. "Superman. He can fly *and* he's super strong *and* he has x-ray vision." He gasped and looked at her, sharply. "Maybe you have x-ray vision!"

She giggled. "Would you think it was cool if I did?"

"Yeah!"

She felt elated, her giggles like bubbles that lifted her higher. Mummy and Daddy always made it seem like the secret things they had were bad things and could get them in trouble; that people wouldn't understand. But Diego wasn't acting like that, and he'd definitely understand because he was into all those superhero films. The idea of being able to share her secret – something she'd never really thought possible before – made her feel lighter and happier than she ever had. "Diego, if I tell you something will you *swear* on your life never to tell anyone, ever, ever, ever?"

"Is it a secret? I swear."

She hesitated, her heart thumping wildly in her chest. She *really* wasn't supposed to tell anyone. But Diego was different, wasn't he? He was her best friend, and he'd think it was cool; he wouldn't be scared at all.

The bell sounded, signalling the end of recess.

Her face fell. She'd missed her chance. All the other kids were yelling and laughing, and running back towards their classrooms. She couldn't tell him now because the teachers would look for them if they didn't go back straight away.

She chewed her lip, feeling determined. "I'll tell you at lunch. As long as you *swear* never to tell anyone, not even Molly."

He nodded without hesitation. "I swear."

~*~

"It's a tricky situation," said Elky as they walked up the trail towards a destination she was completely unfamiliar with.

Claire had left the car – now at least four hundred feet away – just off the road in a layby. Here, in America, there didn't seem to be an official term for a layby. She'd heard it called a pullout by some, and a 'scenic area' by others, the difference in language not one she normally gave any mind to except that, in this second, it highlighted the discomfort she felt at being in a strange place, about to take part in something she was unversed in. She wondered if Jasmine felt this way all the time.

She focused on her heightened senses – smell, sound, sight, and even the taste of things in the air – and wrapped the ability around her like a security blanket. It was like Pete was with her even though he wasn't.

"Her skill is beyond any I've encountered in anyone, even adults, and yet, she's so young that her emotional maturity is not sufficient enough to cope with that skill. If anything, it seems that emotional coaching might be of more benefit to her at this stage. If Jasmine can understand how to *emotionally* carry this gift of hers, she will be able to handle herself exquisitely."

"That's a lot to ask of a five-year-old."

"I agree. And there lies the problem. The issue is not one to do with her supernatural talents, it's one to do with her humanness, and only time can ease that."

"Are you saying you can't train her after all?"

"Oh, I can train her in her abilities: teleporting, shapeshifting when the time comes – in truth, she'll need very little training in those areas. Her instinct for her natural gift is extraordinary, as if she's been doing it for centuries and it is only her small physical body – her incarnation – that stops her from being fully fledged... But understand that those I have trained in such things have been adults who comprehend the way of the world and have had two decades or more to refine their feelings and senses when it comes to that world."

"She has five-year-old feelings, in a five-year-old body, but some kind of ancient, capable soul – is that what you're saying?"

"That's exactly what I'm saying. I'll do what I can to pre-pare her, but her human years will be her greatest teacher, as it is with all children. In that respect, she is no different to any-one else. We're here." Elky slowed to a stop.

Claire stepped in beside him and looked upon a stone hut with a cone-shaped roof made out of sticks that didn't look like it quite met at its tip.

"The sweat lodge. The steam eventually travels out the top, but very slowly. The stones keep most of the heat and steam in."

She found herself taking in a breath.

"They will be inside. I can see a flicker of the flames from their torches."

And she could smell the paraffin from those torches. She could also hear their voices, though couldn't quite make out what was being said behind the stones. "I take it there's no electrical wiring in that hut, then."

Elky laughed, as he shook his head and made his way for-ward.

She followed, hoping to god she wasn't about to end up as kindling.

The chief, it turned out, was a man of few words, and the few words he did speak, she did not understand. Nearing what could have been seventy or a hundred – it was hard to tell – he was of slight build, but held himself tall. He was also, appar-ently, of a serious disposition, the two attempts at light jokes she had made earlier doing nothing to break the man's stern features.

Claire sat beside him, to his right, as they all – ten men and one woman – convened in a circle on thick, wooden planks that had been turned into benches. It was like a Stone Age steam room, which was *exactly* what it was, she supposed.

But she was none the wiser as to what she was doing here. Having changed into the thin, loose, linen dress that was given to her, Elky had introduced her to his chief who had barely looked at her but continued on, speaking to Elky in their own language.

Elky had translated some of it, and asked her to sit where she was. He had also told her his chief had said "she would come to know" why she was there.

Such detachment, after having been 'invited' here would have earned a curt word from her as she turned on her heel, but she reminded herself she was here for Jasmine. The days of impetuous retorts and rash decisions were over when you were responsible for a life more precious than yours.

Her werewolf senses (as well as her usual human ones) detected no lie from the chief, or any of the men – they detected nothing at all, actually – and that was what she held on to as the ceremony began with the thrum of hard cloth on a bear-skinned drum, and a dash of herb-infused water thrown onto red-hot stones which lay bundled in a firepit at the centre of the lodge.

Steam rose, wrapping its pearly tendrils around each of them as a pipe was passed around. Each person inhaled from the pipe, just once, before passing it on. Claire did the same when it reached her, her nose picking up various spices she couldn't fully name, although she thought she smelled cedar and sage, perhaps even lavender, among the mix.

The temporary wolf in her veins did not recoil. In fact, as she began to relax (an effect of the herbs?) the unfamiliar began to feel somewhat familiar, as if *many* wolves ran through her veins now, and had done for a long time.

More water lashed the stones; the steam vapours

thickened.

Padding paws and the beat of the drum merged; became one entity.

Sweat tickled her cheek as it fell from her forehead, bringing her awareness to the surface for a brief second, and she realised she was already drenched, her dress soaked, her breathing deep, yet tight, her lungs searching for oxygen with every breath it took. Fear would claw up her throat until she realised she *could* breathe – she was just left of suffocation, but nowhere near death.

The constant beating drum, growing louder and faster, kept her from crying out or complaining – its relentless rhythm demanded respect, creating an invisible barrier between herself and the mundane weaknesses of the human mind. To cry for help would be a sin because her cry would be based on fear alone – fear was the sin.

Her next breath fought for yet more air, but she could say nothing and do nothing except rock to the beat of the drum.

She briefly opened her eyes ... at least she thought she did, but when she tried to close them, she realised they were already closed. All she saw was fog. All she felt was heat against the wind that rushed past a thousand wolves tearing through her blood. She wondered if they would have always been there, of if it was her lover's blood that fuelled their arrival. Whichever the answer, she welcomed them. They felt like her guardians; her protectors.

Who knew how many minutes passed. Had she been asked, she might have said five minutes only, yet would not have been surprised if hours had flown by.

The chief was chanting, and she was disconcerted to realise he had been chanting for a while, yet she had not taken note.

Something was happening – she didn't know what.

The drum raced ahead, but swept in its trance she was racing with it.

Water splashed. Stones crackled.

She looked down at the pit and could make out sparks of light – fire – racing across the surface of each rock. *Bizarre.* Her foggy mind tried to tell her that simply couldn't be – it was too wet in here for fire, despite the redness of the heat still trapped within the stones.

They crackled further, and more sparks flew.

She would have gasped had her lungs not needed wringing out. The air had never felt heavier.

The chief's chants grew furious as did the beat of the bear-drum. She suddenly understood: this was a summoning. *Something was being summoned.*

Far too deep in the trance, she could not fathom whether she was afraid or ... other ... but it didn't matter. It was too late.

"Demons exist?"

"So many things exist, though usually as whispering shadows and thoughts ... sometimes, though, those whispering shadows become manifest."

They were summoning a *demon.* She wasn't sure how she knew it, but she did.

She felt she should scream, run, throw herself out of the hut, but she was caught in the rhythm of the ceremony, rocking to its sway and unable to move.

The sparks across the rocks lit up and grew.

Oh, no!

Flame became a living thing that twisted and danced itself wider and higher until it was no longer flame but fire, spiring; as tall as a man, towering...

Demon.

Caught between fear and fascination, and a humbling sense of calm engineered by the chanting and drumming, she watched as the mass of fire took form. Muscled limbs became visible – two legs, two arms – black vacuums near its top became sockets for eyes. Broad shoulders sloped down from a strong neck to create a rippling torso of not fire at all, but dark skin that bulged with tenacity and brawn.

Claire gulped, amazed oxygen could even be found anymore in the mist-filled lodge. This demon's fire cut through all the fog – absorbed it, even – and then, his flames dimmed, revealing the manifestation before them. It seemed some demons were not dissimilar to dark-skinned gods because *this* six-foot specimen of masculinity would have had her drooling in her younger years.

Who was she kidding – there might have been a bit of drool now. She'd just tell herself it was sweat.

Not an inch of him wasn't muscle, though she – thankfully, perhaps – could not make out anything beneath his underwear ... which kind of looked like a loin cloth, and that was *all* he wore apart from a necklace of ... oh, were they *bones* around his neck?

Claire still owned enough of herself to know lust was blinding. She was wary. This demon did *not* look best pleased and those muscles used in anger would be fatal to all in its path.

"I was asleep," he growled, his eyes flashing yellow like a cat's, but his voice held some kind of familiar humanity. Or maybe that was because he sounded more British than American, though there was a lilt to his accent ... a demon living in England for a while?

And why wouldn't demons live in England? her brain asked

her, rhetorically.

The chief said something she didn't understand, and for the first time she'd heard, he sounded meek – even apologetic – his sternness gone.

The demon's eyes narrowed as they roamed around the lodge, menacingly. "In nearly four hundred years I have *never* been summoned by anyone – *not once*. Until now. You've ripped me from my family." His gaze landed on her – the only female in the room. "This had better be good."

Chapter Twelve

"Claire." All eyes were on her. Elky, sitting to her right, nudged her with his knee.

She jumped, coming to, though she wasn't altogether sure where she'd gone.

"Ask him." He nodded to the demon standing before them with his arms crossed and looking more pissed off by the second.

"Me?" she whispered.

"Yes. You came for answers, didn't you? And your answers will likely provide us with ours."

Eh? Was *that* the plan? Use her as a guinea pig in case the demon wasn't feeling too cooperative?

"Your need to know was greater than ours; the energy of your desperation, here among us, was able to summon him." He'd answered her unspoken question. It didn't make her feel any less of a guinea pig. She swallowed hard, and looked back at the demon. He looked just like a man, really.

He's just a tall, muscular man. That's it. No need to be scared.

The demon's jaw twitched, and his eyes flashed yellow again.

Right. So not scary. "Um ... hi," she began.

His gaze landed on her face and stayed there.

"So ... er ... sorry to wake you up and everything ... um ... we have a situation here ... well, *I* have a situation with my daughter—"

"For the love of all that's holy, spit it out," the demon ground out.

An *impatient* demon. Wonderful.

Annoyance flashed through her. She held onto it – it was much more comforting than uncertainty.

Claire pulled herself to standing, and crossed her own arms, mirroring him. "People are trying to kill my daughter because she has supernatural abilities, and I need to know who they are and how to protect her."

Apart from a small crease in his brow, his expression didn't change.

"She can teleport and she's only five; her birth was ... not normal. We always knew she'd harbour some kind of ... power or something ... we just didn't know what or when."

No fucking change of facial features at all. Shit. Maybe demons didn't care for people much; maybe his thing was nature and the planet.

"Also, the trees are going mouldy." There. That was all she had with regards to nature.

Both his eyebrows shot up in what might actually have been amusement.

She looked at Elky.

He looked back up at her, seeming a little lost for words, and offered a small shrug.

No one moved or made a sound for the next few seconds, and then the demon let out a chuckle. Just a small one, but it was definitely a chuckle.

Or maybe that's the sound demons make before they kill – you really don't know.

He stepped off the hot rocks.

A couple of people gasped, there was some shuffling; it seemed some of the tribe were ready to attack if they had to. "Elky?" Claire turned to him, still on his seat.

"Yes?"

"Has the chief ever summoned a demon before?"

"Not to my knowledge. This could be the first time."

Fucking fantastic. They had no idea what might happen next. *Men! They never read the instructions first.*

The chief spoke. His sentences were fast and sharp. If only she could understand a word.

"What's he saying?" she asked Elky.

"He says he did not know which brand of magic you would bring to the lodge, but the strength of your 'prayer' made it necessary for you to be here."

"Prayer?"

"Your need to keep your daughter safe."

"And it turned out my brand of magic was ... summoning a demon?"

The demon cleared his throat, not looking too pleased about being ignored. In fact, his frown was quite a thing – it had a life of its own. He looked, not just pissed off, but confused.

Well, wouldn't you be if you were summoned?

"I'm sorry," said Claire, "I'm just trying to—"

"I'm here. You called and I'm here. I'm assuming because I may have some answers you seek. It would help to know the questions, though. You and I are going for a walk – I can't breathe in here." The demon glanced around the lodge suspiciously.

She was going for a *walk* with a *demon*. If Pete was here, he'd have a fit over this.

"I smell wolf in you."

"Erm ... yes."

His gaze softened, taking on some curiosity. "But you're human."

Claire held her head higher. She *wasn't* going to talk about drinking Pete's blood – it was private. "Yes, I am."

He nodded, a small smile turning the corners of his full lips up. They looked as formidable as the rest of him, and she'd never thought lips could look anything other than lips. "I'm glad you have someone who cares for you so much, they would share such an intimate part of themselves to protect you."

She went red. He knew. And he probably knew everything that sharing had entailed.

"It's a sign of your character. Makes me feel better about taking a walk alone with you in the woods, anyway."

What the... She might actually have gaped. *Alone with* me?

He grinned. It was real and infectious, and he even had a bloody dimple set into his left cheek, but none of that dampened his ability to call the shots one bit. "Come," he said. It wasn't a request.

He led the way out of the lodge, and she followed, her wet linen dress sticking to her legs uncomfortably; nine pairs of eyes burning into her as she stepped into the fresh, cool air.

"Is it true what you said about having never been summoned before in your life?" Claire was having trouble keeping up with his long strides, and she was tall and fit, so that was saying something.

"Yes. Took me a while to figure out what the hell was going on when I started to disappear, against my will, right in front of my girlfriend. The look on her face wasn't pretty."

"You have a girlfriend?" She didn't know why she felt so shocked about that. Stereotypically, maybe she'd thought demons kept prisoners and slaves rather than girlfriends. Still, he was a *demon*. By all accounts, he was supposed to be evil, so it wasn't such a huge leap to make, surely.

He nodded. "She's the mother of my child."

She stopped and stared at him as he strode off before she realised she'd have to run a marathon to catch up with him if she continued to stand there like part of the foliage. *He has a child.*

"My son," he continued. "So I do know the worry of a parent, believe me."

She did believe him. Whether that was wise or not, she didn't have a clue. Should one believe what demons said? "Where are we going?"

"Not much further."

"Do you know the forests around here?"

"Not that well, no. I'm better acquainted with the desert further south in Nevada."

Should she tell him that's where she'd ended up with Jasmine and that they'd met a guy called Jerrod who knew about shapeshifting and things of such ilk? Perhaps he would know who Jerrod worked for.

The demon came to a halt before she could translate her thoughts into words. "Through there – look."

"I don't see anything."

"Then, listen."

She did as instructed and heard… "Water. I can hear rushing water."

He nodded, then led the way onwards, towards it.

Ten minutes later saw the forest lead out into a clearing; the brightness of the sun that beat down on it – unfettered by the canopy of trees – was startling. And magnificent.

A few more steps into the open space had her gasping.

They were at the bottom of a large cliff from which the water tumbled – a ferocious cascade that put all things man-made to shame. Yet, amid the devastation such a force could cause, lay unmatched beauty. The sun danced with the water, bouncing gleaming bows of golden and rainbow light off the flowing liquid. The grass on the banks of the river was a true green; the vegetation and flowers that grew, lush. The rock of the cliff stood proudly in the midst of it all, a vivid reddish-brown where it was dry, a deep chocolate where wet. "This is..." She lost her words. There were no words.

"Stunning," finished the demon for her. "And all four elements shine. This is where you ask me your questions; this is where I'll seek the answers."

She suddenly felt dwarfed by everything, a crippling case of imposter's syndrome shadowing the landscape of her vision. Her – in wolf's clothing. "I'm ... I don't even know if..." Her throat closed up.

He sighed and softened his tone. "You're important. So is your daughter. It's notoriously difficult to summon a demon – any demon – and I'm not any demon, I'm a king among them. My name is Pueblo. And yours is...?"

"Claire." That darned imposter's syndrome reared its head once more at the name that wasn't hers.

"It's also next to impossible to take a demon from under a witch's nose, yet here I am."

"A witch's nose?"

"My girlfriend's a witch, and a bloody good one. But no spell she belted out when I began to disappear could compete with your need to have me here, so ... ask me your questions. What's going on?"

~*~

Jasmine's heart thumped so loudly she was sure Diego must be able to hear it.

They were at the oak tree again, only this time, behind it, hidden from the view of anyone not also behind the oak tree, which was no one else. This wasn't the exciting area of the playground.

Her lunch box sat at her feet. She hadn't eaten anything. Her tummy felt in knots and it made her not hungry. She was a bit worried she might throw up.

"Are you going to tell me, or not?" Diego was impatient now. He leaned against the tree and shuffled his feet, looking a little bored, and worse – like he didn't believe her anymore. That was a horrible feeling.

She'd wanted to tell him, but her throat had closed up around her secret and she hadn't been able to get the words out. Guilt washed over her like the waves over pebbles on a beach. She couldn't figure out if she felt more guilty for wanting to tell the secret, or for telling Diego she would, then finding she couldn't. Whichever it was, she just felt bad.

Jasmine blinked back tears that she knew would fall far too easily if she wasn't careful. She ducked her head, and reached into the front pocket of her lunch box where Mummy had placed the invitations for Molly and Diego.

Standing back up, she attempted a smile as she handed his to him.

Diego perked up a bit, curious, and took it from her, hurriedly opening it. But then, his face fell in disappointment. "Is this the secret?"

"Well ... no. It's an invitation for dinner at my house on Tuesday. Molly's got one, too. You can come to play." She grinned at that last sentence. They'd been asking for *months* if they could come to her house, and now they could.

Diego didn't seem as happy about it, though. "Great," he said, his tone sounding all bored again. And that's all he said while he folded the invite up, small, and put it in the pocket of his trousers. He stared at her. "You don't have a secret, do you?"

Her grin disappeared, replaced by a purse of her lips as the tears threatened again.

Bad – you're bad for saying you'll tell him. Now you have *to.*

Half of her wanted to and half of her didn't. "I do! It's just ... I shouldn't tell anyone."

"It's to do with your eyes, right?"

She nodded. "I think so."

"Aren't we friends?"

"We are." She nodded in earnest.

"Tell me, then."

She took a breath and looked up at the sky, wondering if the dragon would save her. If it just *appeared* then she wouldn't have to use words to tell her secret – he would just know. Then it wouldn't be her fault. Nothing would be her fault.

The sky remained blue and empty.

Diego kicked a stone, suddenly annoyed. He'd had enough. "You don't have a secret," he snapped, then he turned and walked off fast.

Panic snared her. She felt torn. Tell, don't tell; be normal, be different; be cool, be friendless; be the weird kid with strange eyes, or be a superhero who's *supposed* to be strange. "I can fly!" she blurted out, and for a second, she thought she'd disappear in front of his eyes because her feelings were definitely big and the main big feeling was fear. Fear at what he'd say. But also, excitement. There was another odd sensation, too, which she didn't have a name for – she'd *said* it.

It was the first time she'd said it to anyone, ever. And it made her feel light like a bubble, but heavy like a stone, all at the same time.

Diego had stopped in his tracks and was just staring at her. His lips twisted into a smirk of incredulity. "You can't fly!"

"I can. I'll show you." She bit her tongue, but it was too late to take that back. *Could* she show him? Should she?

He wouldn't believe her if she didn't, and she thought she maybe *could* do it because the bigness of her feelings was kind of all over the place. She pushed away Elky's voice in her head that told her it was better to shift when the feelings were calm. She couldn't do it when she was calm anyway, so maybe the lessons should be different for her. She'd been able to carry her mum, after all – she could carry Diego, too.

Diego crossed his arms. "Go on, then."

She was shaking. "I need to hold your hand to do it. It's sort of like flying, but a little different, but you need to try and stay awake when it happens."

Something she'd said made him frown, and then, his expression changed to genuine intrigue. He took a couple of steps towards her. He was starting to believe her again.

Relief washed all the other horrible emotions away. She smiled at him and held out her hand for him to take.

Elky had said that when she felt herself start to teleport (she didn't like that word – she preferred 'fly') she had to take a deep breath and try to be confident even if she didn't feel confident. It would help her to stay strong, because sometimes, if you practised being the thing you wanted to be enough, you *became* that thing in the end. So, that's what she did. She took in a deep breath when Diego placed his hand in hers.

His hand was sweaty like hers got sometimes when she was either nervous or excited. She didn't know which one he was. Maybe he was just feeling hot.

She kept her smile on her face, pretending she felt confident. *It won't be hard,* she told herself. After all, she *knew* she could do it, so the confidence should just be there, right?

Looking around, she wondered where to fly him to. She decided it should be to the other side of the school building because she didn't think anyone would be there. She couldn't exactly 'land' in the middle of the playground where everyone would see.

Her decision made, she closed her eyes and thought about where she wanted to go; she searched inside herself for the big feelings. Her confidence slipped – the big feelings weren't there. Gripping Diego's hand harder, she tried again. She'd been all excited and nervous, hadn't she? Where had those feelings gone?

Panic started to rise again, but even that wasn't enough for her to latch on to. Or was it?

As it rose more and more, she focused on the feeling, even though she didn't want to because panicking was a *horrible* thing to feel. She started to get a little dizzy … was that it? Did the dizziness mean something?

She opened her eyes, dismayed to find herself exactly where she'd been: behind the oak tree holding Diego's hand.

He looked at her, unimpressed and annoyed. "Liar." There was disgust in the way he'd said that, and a bit of hurt, too.

"No … I *can* do it."

"Liar! Stop *lying*."

"But I'm not, I promise!" There was a big feeling right there – quite a few in fact. Embarrassment, anxiety, anger … all wrapped up in the still-growing panic. But before she could grab onto it, Diego had yanked his hand from hers.

"You're not my friend if you're a liar." He stormed off.

"Wait!" She had no idea what happened next – not really. It was like something in her snapped; like all the feelings got *too* big, and since she couldn't fly with them, they exploded instead. Fear and anger were the biggest, but it was as if they no longer belonged to her, but became this beast *outside* her.

She reached for Diego, calling him back, but all she could see in front of her was fire. Her hands were on fire.

But not burning. *She* didn't hurt. All the hurt was in the fire, and before she knew it, she could feel it leave her body – *want* to leave her body – so that's what it did: the fire left her hands, making a beeline for Diego.

"NO!" The fire would hit him. It was going to burn him. She yelled again and pulled it back, not knowing if she could or couldn't, but running purely on instinct.

The flames seemed to hover mid-air, and in the struggle between her and it, the ground began to shake. Was *she* making the ground shake? It felt like it. It felt like it was caused by the strength it took to make the fire stop.

Diego came to a halt when the ground started to move. He was looking down at his feet, holding his arms out for balance, oblivious to the hazardous flames floating behind him.

All of a sudden, faster than anything she'd seen, the fireball swirled and *dove* at her. She couldn't move and she couldn't stop it as it hit her full force. But not burning her.

Not burning.

It soaked into her instead as if she was paper and it was water. The flames rushed straight to her head, swamping her mind; engulfing her brain in their blaze. The only thing she was aware of before the world faded away was Diego's scream.

Chapter Thirteen

"She's not the only one. Over the past decade, many humans have awoken to their innate abilities."

"No," pressed Claire. They were sitting in the middle of the clearing, the sound of the waterfall, soothing, yet stirring a sense of huge things to come. "She's different, I promise. Her birth was..." She sighed. How did she even begin to explain it? "Her birth was out of this world – the timing of it, the circumstances, who her parents were... There's something big at play here."

The demon – Pueblo – focused on her intently as she spoke. It was almost uncomfortable, but she'd come to understand in the very short space of time they'd communicated, he was a pretty intense kind of guy.

"The full moon last night – it was an eclipse and a Supermoon – I think it's triggered her changes."

He nodded. "And whatever's to come. I'm not unfamiliar with deific births," he said, his voice holding some kind of emotion she couldn't reach.

"Deific?"

"When old gods die, new gods step into the space they leave. Often, unusual or rare planetary alignments are portents of their movements on earth."

She paused, unsure of how to proceed. "I never said anything about gods."

"Think, Claire. Was there any mention of gods surrounding your daughter's birth, or even during the time period from her conception to her birth, even if you didn't connect the gods with her at all?"

"Um ... I don't know, I... No."

"Nothing at all?"

She sighed as she racked her brain. "The only thing I can think of is that once – just once – Sarah said something about Amil – that was Jasmine's father – having a very religious mother. But that's *all* she said. This was in the early days when she was trying to talk herself out of being with him. She said he never talked about his mother; they had a bad relationship or something. But he wasn't exactly the responsible, committed type. He bolted to Egypt as soon as he knocked up Sarah."

"Egypt?"

"Sarah said that's where he was from."

"So, his mother was a religious Egyptian?"

"Yes, I think she was Egyptian. I'm struggling to remember everything Sarah said. It feels like a long time ago now in some ways. She did say that Amil used the term 'religious nutter' to describe his mother." She pinched her brow, trying to recall those conversations with her best friend. "I think Sarah said his mum was involved in a cult, or led a cult – some kind of Egyptian cult. God, I told her 'so what, every family has problems'. I'm such an idiot. I pushed her into giving it a go with him because she hadn't had a relationship for so long. Or so I thought." She sighed. Reliving it all was hard. "She said Amil told her his mother had all but disowned him, and that he wanted nothing to do with her." She pulled herself out of the past and sat up straighter, stretching her spine. "Mind you, if my son was a mutant werewolf, I'd probably disown him, too."

"Mutant werewolf." He looked intrigued. "Four hundred years in this existence and I still don't know everything."

"Well, I can't say I knew about demons – not like you, anyway."

He smiled. "If it helps your belief, I'm only half demon. My father was a human."

"Oh, I *believe*, don't worry about that."

"Full-bloodied demons are less—"

"Human looking?"

"To an extent. Back to the mutant werewolf – he was your daughter's biological father?"

Now she grew uncomfortable. It was *the* secret they never liked to think about, let alone talk about. She looked away. "There was a whole species of mutant werewolves called Tridents. Five years ago, they became extinct. Yes – her father, Amil, was one of them. She has no idea."

He stared at her. And said nothing.

Fuck, it was too much to bear. "Say something."

"Her father was an irresponsible and uncommitted mutant werewolf, whose mother was a religious nutter involved with – and possibly the leader of – an Egyptian cult."

When he put it like that... "Yeah, Sarah picked a right one there."

"But don't you see the connection?"

No, she didn't.

"A religious Egyptian cult is going to worship some kind of deity."

"So?"

"So? This woman is her *grandmother*."

She shut up. Hell, she *hadn't* thought it through to that extent.

"Did these Tridents display the same powers your

daughter has?"

"No. They were just … beasts. Huge, monstrous, violent, strong beasts. But they had no abilities outside of what a normal werewolf has." A 'normal werewolf'. Sheesh, she never thought she'd hear herself say that in her lifetime.

"So her powers don't come from them. Again, I say your daughter is displaying *deific* abilities, not Trident abilities. Her biological paternal grandmother is the connection. Find out about her. Blood ties might count for a lot in this case."

Jesus … she'd wanted answers, but this seemed far too surreal. Gods? She couldn't get her head around that at all. "Isn't that a massive leap to make – from werewolves to *gods.*"

"Not to me. The connection is there. Find out *how* it's there."

"I wouldn't know where to start."

"Start with what you know: her father and her mother. Just talking about them now in the way we have has unearthed things. Speak to people who knew them both."

"No one knew Sarah better than me."

"Claire…" Pueblo crossed his hands over his knees and leaned back where he sat, hesitating over something. He frowned. "Everything's connected in some way or another."

"Why do you look so concerned about it?"

He raised his eyebrows, perhaps at her trademark bluntness, then his featured warmed. "You know, you remind me a little of my girlfriend – she doesn't take any crap either. My concern is for myself and my family. Everything *is* connected, and I don't fully understand the reason *I'm* here – why your need summoned *me*. But that isn't anything you need to let worry you. At least not yet. You wanted answers from me, and they are this: your daughter is much more than anyone knows – not a shapeshifter, not a teleporter, not a 'mutant werewolf' – you've only touched the tip of the iceberg where her powers are concerned. Who she is and her future lies in divine forces. While this is yet to be proven, for I cannot fully see the future, I will say that I am one hundred percent certain of it and I'd rather not go into the reasons why, suffice to say ... a few years ago, I witnessed another deific birth. I can feel the ripples between each one, I just don't know what they mean. Seek further answers from those willing to talk about gods."

"That's not you, then?"

"I ... cannot talk about it."

"Because you're a demon? Is it a heaven and hell thing?"

"No." He smiled. "That's so last decade."

She was the one who raised her eyebrows at that.

"Come on." He stood. "I need to return home."

"Wait ... what about those two men I told you about who chased us off the road? We think they were trying to get at Jasmine."

"Yes, there'll be a lot of that now, I'm afraid." His mouth turned downwards as if affronted. "Look out for evil shamans, by the way."

"What?"

"Never mind – my issue. Protect your daughter. Shield her. If those around here know of her true existence, leave."

Leave here? But she loved it here, and more importantly, so did Jasmine. "No. You're saying run away?"

"I'm saying buy her time. She needs to grow. If she *is* godly in some way, she has the power to change fate to an extent. It's tremendous, Claire, you can't comprehend it. Human enemies? Pfft. They'll be nothing but dust to be flicked away, but she can't fight them as a child. As an adult, she'll be a force to be reckoned with. She'll move the god-damned earth."

Claire followed him to standing, willing threatening tears away. Hearing Jasmine talked about like this... "I feel so powerless next to her." And then she couldn't hold them back

– a tear slipped. What a thing to have to admit as the parent of your own child.

"Bollocks."

She snorted. She'd just heard a demon say bollocks – she'd add it onto her growing list of crazy life experiences.

"You *summoned* me. A mother's love is probably the most powerful force on this planet; perhaps even in the known universe. Use it."

They walked back towards the forest. She wondered if she'd be able to find the waterfall on her own again.

Suddenly, the ground rocked.

Claire yelped and stopped; automatically held her arms out for balance.

Pueblo grabbed her wrist, probably more for her safety than his. "It's not an earthquake." He frowned. "I don't think."

"Is it one of those aftershocks? My fiancé talks about those. I can't usually feel them."

He mumbled something she didn't quite catch – it sounded like a curse. "No. This feels different." He seemed to come to a decision about something. "Where's your daughter?"

"At school."

He nodded, still looking concerned. "Take my hand. I'm going to teleport us out of here. Then, you need to go get your daughter."

Pueblo had teleported her back to the lodge and left straight away. That had been half an hour ago, but 'going to get her daughter' was proving a more difficult task than she'd anticipated. The chief wanted a word-by-word recount of everything Pueblo had told her. She had dutifully given him this using Elky as her translator – she'd felt duty-bound to do so since none of it would have been possible without the chief's invitation and ceremony – but by the time she had answered further questions, said her thank yous and goodbyes, and changed out of her borrowed dress into her clothes, she was running later than planned and her worry for Jasmine was growing. She couldn't place why, though. The aftershock, or earthquake, or whatever it was, had been a minor tremor. Certainly not big enough to cause any damage to anything. But the chief had asked about the tremble, too, and more and more people acting like it was an unusual phenomenon was getting her back up.

She double-checked her car keys were in her jeans pocket. "Do you need a lift back?" she asked Elky who had just said his own goodbyes.

He shook his head. "No, thank you. I'm heading in a different direction this afternoon. I'll walk back to the ranchería this evening."

"All right. Thanks again for inviting me."

"The chief requested it, not me. But you're welcome. If anything further comes to light, I'll let you know."

"Thanks. I'll catch you later." She waved and headed to her car, reaching for her phone from inside her jacket so she could call Pete.

The screen showed three missed calls and a text from Pete which read: **URGENT. Call me.**

The two missed calls were from the school. *Fuck!*

They'd all arrived on her phone just minutes apart.

The last missed call was from a cell number she recognised but hadn't logged in her address book. It looked like it might belong to Holly's boyfriend, Tim. *He's just going to have to wait.*

She opened the car door, got in, and rammed the key into the ignition. Her heart thudding, she rang her voicemail before phoning Pete – without a doubt his text must have something to do with the school's phone calls. The first message on her voicemail was blank, even though the call had definitely come from the school. For whatever reason, they'd hung up.

She started the engine and pulled away as the end-of-message 'beep' sounded in her ear.

The second voice message had come in two minutes later, also from the school. This time, they'd left a message.

By the time she was half way through it, she was gripping the wheel so tightly, it was all she could do to keep the car on the road.

~*~

For five years they'd managed to avoid it – the dreaded hospital. After stealing Jasmine from the maternity ward that stormy night, he'd sworn he'd do whatever it took to make sure she'd never have to set foot in a damned hospital again.

The white walls of the emergency room glared back at him, screaming his failure. The call he'd received from the school was just as fear-inducing as the one he'd received over two weeks ago from Claire in a state of terror.

Add to everything, the curious but wary glances he received from every single member of staff as he waited for the doctor, and it was all he could do to keep his feet planted where they were instead of sprinting out the door. He needed Claire here – she'd phoned while driving to say she was on her way.

The school teacher who had ridden in the ambulance with Jasmine was nowhere to be seen, although the reception nurse had told him she thought she was still around. The doctor seeing to Jasmine had not come out of her room yet, and no one else could offer any further information.

Waiting was torture.

"Pete!"

Thank god. "Claire." He turned towards her voice.

She jogged across the waiting area into his arms, not paying any mind to the many eyes following her movements. "What the hell is going on?"

He kissed her forehead, not ready to let her go. "All I know is what the reception nurse told me: Jasmine had some kind of convulsion at school. The doctor's seeing to her now."

"Convulsion?"

He shrugged, helpless, then finally pulled back and let her go. "She wasn't conscious when the paramedics reached her. That's all they'll tell me. I'm waiting for the doctor."

"Oh, god." Claire scanned the room. Wandering eyes looked away quickly, back towards their magazines or to the television on the wall, or to the wall itself. "I'll go tell the reception I'm here."

"I'll come with you."

"Pete," she lowered her voice to a whisper, "if they take her blood…"

"I know. She might still show as human though – we just don't know. But we'll need to stay vigilant and think on our feet if the worst comes to the worst."

She nodded, and they made their way to the desk. Before she could say a word, though, the doctor emerged from Jasmine's room. "Peter Cryer?"

"Yes." Pete swiftly turned towards him; Claire followed. "I'm Jasmine's father; this is Claire, her mother."

"Adoptive parents, yes?"

He clenched his jaw – hated that that was the case, but it was what it was. "Yes."

"All right. My name is Dr Galvinson. Could you both come with me, please?"

Pete looked at Claire to find her looking back, his worry reflected across her face. They followed the doctor into a small room a few doors down from where he was told Jasmine had been taken. "Can we see our daughter?"

"Of course you can, but I'd like to first run through with you what her condition is and ask some questions that will determine any aftercare and subsequent treatment."

He heard Claire's sharp intake of breath. "Subsequent … treatment?"

He gestured to the two chairs opposite the small computer desk. "Please, Mr and Mrs Cryer, take a seat."

They didn't bother correcting him on their names, and though Pete certainly didn't feel like sitting (he felt like punching the stark walls), they both did as instructed.

"Your daughter had a seizure in the playground. She was witnessed to be trembling and she lost consciousness for a time. She's since woken up."

Claire went to speak, but the doctor cut her off. "She's fine. She wasn't responsive to stimuli at first, but she's functioning fully now. Hasn't said a word, but appears to understand everything we say to her. I told her I was coming out to speak to you and that you would be in to see her soon." He smiled. "Quite a serious little thing, isn't she?"

Pete sensed Claire's ire stoked. How did the doctor expect a five-year-old waking up in a strange hospital to act? Laughingly and jokingly?

"There was a quake – just a small one – at the same time she fell unconscious."

"Yes, I felt it," said Claire.

"So did we," muttered Dr Galvinson. "Very small compared to what we used to get, but I'm not yet clear if she fell due to the quake or due to her seizure. I'm not sure which came first. Did she fall because of the quake, hit her head, and then have a seizure? Or did she have a seizure first and *that* caused her to fall – not the quake. I'm trying to see if I can decipher which way around it happened. Due to her state when she was brought in, we treated this as life-threatening. We've carried out blood tests, and conducted both a CT scan and an MRI. We're hoping those will determine some answers. They've been sent off to their respective labs, but we won't get the results for a few hours. From her EEG readings and from what I can tell through examining her, it's possible your daughter might have epilepsy. If this is her first seizure, though, we can't diagnose it as epilepsy yet."

It took a while before Pete realised the doctor had stopped talking. He was looking at them as if waiting for an answer. Had he asked a question? His own head was spinning. He'd felt the quake, too. Were the quake and her seizure linked somehow? "Um ... yes, this is her first seizure. She's never shown any signs of..." *shapeshifting, teleporting...* "having anything like this before."

"Has there been any trauma to the head recently? Has she been in any kind of accident?"

Did disappearing, mid-air, from a car crash count? "No."

Claire cleared her throat. "Her biological mother ... she was in a car crash when she was pregnant with her – in fact, Jasmine was born that night."

"An induced labour to save the baby?"

"Yes – a caesarean. Her mother was in a coma. But Jasmine was tested after birth straight away for any abnormalities and everything came back fine."

"While the seizure is unlikely to be related to the birth trauma, it's not completely impossible that it could be a delayed development from the trauma. What about any genetic medical conditions? Are you aware of any?"

Oh, boy.

He heard the falter of Claire's breath before she answered. "Her mother didn't have epilepsy or any condition that I was aware of. I knew her well – we were very close. Her biological father, though, I wouldn't have a clue about I'm afraid."

The doctor nodded. "Can you tell me about her heterochromia?"

"Her...?"

He raised a brow. "Her different coloured eyes."

Claire looked at Pete; he squeezed her hand and nodded.

"I was in the middle of trying to make a doctor's appointment for that when the messages from the school came through. Her eyes..." She hesitated, but carried on. "They changed colour very suddenly. Nothing led up to it – everything was completely normal until yesterday at about four o'clock in the afternoon. She came down the stairs and her eyes were different. She said they were a bit itchy just before it happened. I *have* heard of hetero ... er..."

"Heterochromia iridis."

"Yes. But I have no idea if it can come on like that – so suddenly and without warning."

"Actually, it can. What your daughter has is *complete* heterochromia – each eye is a solid colour and is a totally different colour from the other. In her case, brown and green. It's rarely associated with any genetic inheritance, and it's rare that someone with heterochromia is born with it unless there's some kind of underlying condition, which, as you have said, was never found from her post-natal tests. Most cases of heterochromia are isolated and sporadic. However, it *can* appear after a trauma of some kind. My logic is telling me that yesterday, her heterochromia manifested, and today, she had a seizure. A natural conclusion at this point is that they must be linked, but until we have all the test results back, there's not a lot more we can say or do other than keep an eye on her.

"Physically, since waking up, she's as fit as a fiddle. But I would like to make sure she can actually talk to rule out any mutism as a result of the convulsion. Perhaps if I could hear her talk with you two."

"Of course."

"I spoke with the teacher who arrived with her – Mrs Myers?"

"Oh – that's her class teacher. I didn't realise she came, too."

"Yes. It's school policy for a teacher to travel in the ambulance with any student who needs to be brought in. She did actually fill me in on the change to her eyes."

Pete frowned. So, all those questions about it were to probe them to make sure they weren't lying.

"She also told me that Jasmine was with a boy in the playground when the seizure happened."

"She has a friend called Diego," said Claire.

"Yes, I think that might have been his name. Diego was brought in, too."

"He was?"

Pete shifted in his seat.

Claire gripped his hand. "My god, is he okay?"

"Yes, yes, yes. He was quite traumatised by her collapsing in front of him as any five-year-old might be, and perhaps a bit frightened by the quake, but he's fine. Mrs Myers thought it may be best if he also came to the hospital so he could be checked over and offered any counselling. He might also be able to tell us what took place in the moments leading up to Jasmine's seizure."

"Has he said anything about it?" asked Pete, dreading the answer.

"I'll need to check in with my colleague about that; the

boy is being treated in a different section of the ward, and we're waiting for his parents. Last I heard though, he had the same muteness Jasmine seems to have come down with." He chuckled as if that was somehow funny. Then, the doctor stood from his chair so fast, Claire jumped in her seat.

He smiled. "Come. Let's take you to your daughter."

Chapter Fourteen

She was frightened. But she'd balled the fear up into a tiny dot and stuffed it deep inside herself because she'd had no choice. She was stuck here in this bed – they wouldn't let her out. The nurse had just left saying she'd be back soon. There were a couple of pads stuck to her chest, and although she could probably pull them off if she wanted to, Jasmine was sure that wasn't allowed and that she'd get into a whole heap of trouble. She wasn't sure she wanted to be in trouble in a place she didn't know.

Before the nurse had come in, the doctor had been here. He'd told her he was going to see if her parents were here yet. She hoped they were, although she didn't know how to explain to Mummy or Daddy what had happened. And she'd have to tell them about telling Diego her secret. They'd be really mad. *Really* mad. But she hoped at least it would make them feel better to know she hadn't said a word about Daddy being a werewolf.

The doctor had asked her lots and lots of questions. She'd said nothing at all because she didn't know what was the right and wrong thing to say – anything could get her into trouble, so she'd kept her mouth closed tight.

Voices sounded outside her door – she recognised

Mummy's one straight away and tears filled her eyes with relief.

The door opened and they all walked in: Mummy, Daddy and the doctor.

"Baby," said Mummy, also crying. Then, she rushed over to her.

Jasmine reached up, longing to be in the safest place she knew: her mother's arms. Her wish granted, her mum placed herself on the edge of her bed and scooped her into her chest, holding her tight and kissing her head.

"Mummy ... I'm sorry," she managed to get out, then she started to cry, unable to keep her fear inside that small dot anymore.

"Sshhh. Honey, there's nothing to be sorry about."

She felt a large, strong hand on her head, and knew it was her dad. "Hey, pumpkin."

She reached her left hand out to touch his arm, the familiar hairs around his wrists somehow making everything feel ten times better.

Her mum pulled back a little. "Honey, are you in any pain?"

She shook her head. "No." Not in her body anyway; her heart hurt quite a bit.

"Can you tell us what happened?"

She looked at her mum, then her gaze flittered to where the doctor stood behind her.

Maybe she was too obvious, but he seemed to understand. "I've heard enough for now, Mr and Mrs Cryer – why don't I leave you both to speak with your daughter for a while. I'll come back in fifteen minutes."

"Thank you," said her mummy.

"Yes," her dad also turned to the doctor. "Thanks for everything."

The doctor smiled. "Don't thank me yet – let's wait for the test results first." Then, he chuckled. Jasmine didn't know what was funny.

Maybe her parents didn't either because they both looked at each other, worried, and neither of them were laughing.

The doctor left the room and Daddy went to shut the door behind him.

"Sweetie," Mummy kissed her forehead, "what happened?"

She knew she had to be brave and tell the truth even though she really didn't want to. Being in the hospital made everything very serious, didn't it? "I'm really sorry. I wanted to tell Diego that I could fly, so I did."

Her mum closed her eyes and pulled a face that showed her disappointment.

Jasmine's lip trembled in an effort not to cry any more tears. "But I couldn't do it – I couldn't make it happen – so, he didn't believe me and called me a liar, so I got really scared he wouldn't be friends with me anymore and tell everyone I was lying, and I was really angry he didn't believe me because he was the one who asked about my eyes and wanted to know."

Her dad sighed, but placed his hand on her shoulder and stroked it in comfort. "Then what happened, Jasmine?"

She looked down, trying to piece it all together. "I don't know. My feelings got really big with being angry at him, but instead of flying, I..."

"You what, darling?"

"I don't know how it happened."

Mummy squeezed her hand. "Please try to tell us – even if it doesn't make sense."

She sighed, then closed her eyes, and took a breath in as she locked onto the memory of what had happened. "I didn't fly, but it was like I made fire with my hands and the fire was angry too, and it went straight for Diego. I know it wanted to burn him, so I made it come back to me and then ... I think it went inside my body. I don't remember what happened next." She risked a glance up. She almost wished she hadn't. Her father looked horrified. *You're a monster, see? Even he thinks so.*

"Fire?" whispered her mum. "Was it like ... shapeshifting? I mean the way that Elky taught us about?"

She shrugged. "I don't know. I don't know what it was – it was my anger. But I *didn't* burn Diego, I didn't." That was a good thing. She did one good thing at least.

"No, you didn't. That was very good of you, Jasmine, and very quick thinking. Well done. Listen," her voice dropped very low, "we can't tell the doctor this, okay?"

More secrets. She nodded. "I didn't."

"I know you didn't."

"Jasmine," her dad spoke, but his voice was very tight and sounded a way she'd never heard it before. "Do you remember feeling an earthquake while all of this was happening?"

She frowned, trying to focus on her memory. All she saw was Diego's face as he called her a liar which made her feel awful. "I can't remember. Maybe? I ... just remember feeling really angry."

Her mum looked at her dad. It was like they were speaking to each other in their heads, although she didn't think they were *really* doing that.

Mummy turned back towards her and pulled her in for another hug. "You're very brave, sweetie. Thank you for telling us. We need to go and find the doctor and ask him when we can take you home, okay? Is that all right if we leave the room for five minutes? We'll be right back."

"It's fine, Mummy."

She gave her a small smile. "Good. We'll do everything we can to keep you safe – you don't need to worry."

Jasmine nodded. "Have you got Marlo in your bag, Mummy?" Marlo was her favourite soft toy: a lion she remembered choosing from a funfair when she'd been just two years old. She used to carry it everywhere, but she never took him to school in case he got lost.

"Oh, I'm sorry, honey, I don't. I came straight here and didn't have the chance to go home first."

She hid her disappointment. "That's okay."

"But we're going to get you out of here as soon as we can. Before you know it, you'll be home cuddling Marlo."

"Okay."

With a last kiss to her cheek from both parents, her mum and dad stood and left the room. This time, they left the door open. She guessed it was so they could hear her or see her if she needed anything, but it left her feeling a little vulnerable – like anyone or anything could walk in.

With a shiver, she pulled the bed sheet up higher. It felt scratchy – not soft like the one on her own bed.

She looked down at the pads on her chest again and wondered if she *should* pull them off. She felt a little braver now, and a little stronger. She stroked the edge of it with a finger, wondering if it would hurt to pull it off. Was it super sticky?

Before she'd made a decision about it, she was aware of that prickly feeling she sometimes felt when someone was staring at her. She looked up at the open door to find a woman she recognised from the playground looking back at her, eyes shining with anger. Her dark hair was pulled back into a tight bun, like it always was; her face was very stern – sterner than usual. This was Diego's mum.

Diego, she finally noticed, stood a little bit behind her, also staring at her. He looked more frightened than angry.

His mother walked in.

Her heart beat fast.

And then her dad entered the room, too. "Hello. Can I help you?"

Diego's mum turned to her dad and blinked sharply at his features. He got that a lot with his burnt face. It wasn't fair.

Diego was also staring at him, his mouth dropping open in what might have been terror.

Jasmine realised they'd probably never met him before – it was always Mummy who took her to school and picked her up. If he got stared at like this, she understood why.

"I'm Peter. I'm Jasmine's father. Can I help you?" he repeated.

Jasmine heard what sounded like water splashing the ground. Following the noise, she focused on a growing wet patch on Diego's pants. He was weeing himself. Her eyes widened in surprise, but also sympathy. "Diego, it's okay," she said. She didn't want him to be scared.

He jumped at her calling his name, then looked at her, his expression still terrified. "You did it to his face, didn't you?" he squeaked – almost screamed it – his fear clearly leading his tone.

"Diego!" At that moment, his mum noticed him wetting himself. She then looked angrier than ever and turned on her dad. "Your daughter is a liability; you need to keep her under control. Playing with matches – my god! I'll be reporting everything Diego's told me to the school."

"Not matches, Mommy," said Diego.

"Diego, be quiet. What you saw has a very clear explanation."

"*She* did it!"

"Diego!"

Her dad held out his hands, trying to calm everyone down. "Mrs...?"

"Don't you *dare* get aggressive with me."

"No, that's not what—"

"My name is Mrs Alvo and I will *not* have your daughter in the same school as my son, do you hear me? She's dangerous. Come on, Diego." She spun away and grabbed Diego's arm, ignoring the fact he was covered in wee and there was a puddle on the floor.

Diego looked angry as well as frightened now. He pulled away from his mum and shouted in frustration, "It wasn't matches!"

Diego then looked at Jasmine, his face red, his eyes also red and puffy with tears. "You're not a superhero – you're a *monster*."

He turned and ran out of the room, his mother on his tail, shouting after him to 'get back here now'.

Hands on hips, her dad shook his head, grabbed a towel from the trolley next to her bed and threw it over Diego's urine. "It's all right, Jasmine. He'll calm down. It'll be fine."

But she knew it wasn't all right, and so did her dad. It wouldn't be fine. He was just saying what all parents said, but both of them knew the truth.

Diego knew the truth, too – he'd said it. She'd hear it forever now: You're a *monster*.

~*~

The CT and MRI scans had all come back normal. The blood results they would have to wait at least twenty-four hours for, but Claire was increasingly getting the feeling they would not be stepping foot in that hospital again. Their taking her blood was a trail that tied Jasmine back to her birth – the only other time she'd had blood taken. Anyone who suspected anything supernatural about her would be able to find the trail.

What the demon had said about leaving here...

Claire shut the front door behind all three of them, her heart heavy. The doctor had let Jasmine come home, but they had made an appointment for the following week to discuss her bloods and her aftercare. On the face of it, there was nothing wrong with Jasmine at all, so they hadn't wanted to keep her in. On paper, there was no *reason* to keep her in. Ultimately, that was a good thing, but every unanswered question lay at their feet like a yawning hole that kept growing.

"Marlo's on your bed upstairs, honey."

Jasmine let out a small sigh with a smile, clearly glad to be home.

Claire's sense of dread grew as the demon's voice replayed in her mind. *"Protect your daughter. Shield her. If those around here know of her true existence, leave."*

Jesus ... they were going to have to leave. And it would break Jasmine's heart. They'd failed. What a waste – settling down, making roots ... it had all been for nothing. She wanted to scream her despair.

Jasmine headed for the stairs.

"Jasmine, honey, do you promise you're feeling all right?"

She nodded from the bottom step. "I feel good, Mummy. Can I go see Marlo?"

"Sure. Please call us if you need us – for *any* reason, okay?"

"Okay." She raced up the stairs to her room. They heard her bedroom door shut.

Pete turned to Claire on an intake of breath and spoke, his tone low. "Tristan's on to Jasmine. Marco told me this morning. And now with her being at the hospital... There's a chance we may need to pack up and go."

Claire sniffed to hold tears in. "I know."

"How do you know?"

"Not about Tristan. I mean I know about leaving. I ... er ... shit." Where did she start? "It's been a crazy day, and this morning was just as crazy."

"How was the meeting with the chief?"

"It was a ceremony – I was part of it. We summoned a de-mon."

"*What?*"

"It's all right ... I think. He was ... nice, actually. But he said the same thing; he said if people know about Jasmine, we need to leave to protect her."

"You told a *demon* about Jasmine?"

"Well, that was the reason he was summoned – for an-swers."

"But a *demon*?"

"That's what I thought, too, at first, but ... you know, maybe demons aren't all as evil as they make out in books and films. Seriously, there was this good vibe about him – even the wolf in your blood thought so."

His features softened at that. He looked down and stud-ied the ground, then he sighed. "I'm sorry. I'm so sorry. I thought we could have a life here. I thought..."

"Hey." She went to him and placed her arms around his waist. "Don't do that. We *both* wanted this, we *both* thought it would be the best thing for Jasmine ... things change – you said so yourself. If we need to leave, we leave. I'm just not sure where to go. I guess we could pick up sticks again and travel like we used to."

Pete shook his head. "Jasmine needs help and support." He tightened his lips, but his gaze was sure. "You might not like the idea of this, but I think we need to go back to Surrey."

She took a step back, out of his arms. Her short time spent there rushed back, ferocious ghosts refusing to stay down, determined to haunt her. "You mean back to

Lawrence's."

"I know the memories are bad." That was an understatement. Sarah was the reason they'd found Lawrence's home at all; Lawrence's home was the last place she'd seen Sarah alive. "But they can help Jasmine. Her anger – if it's that uncontrollable... Claire, there's no one I know who can master his anger better than Lawrence. And the fire she manifested – Lydia had to learn how to manage something similar. They can help her."

"And the teleporting? The shapeshifting?"

"We'll find a way. Lawrence has books and contacts ... he knows a hell of a lot of people in the human world who made *his* world possible. He can do the same for Jasmine."

"But why would he, Pete? If Tristan would see Jasmine dead, why would Lawrence not want the same after he learns everything about what she's capable of? He's the king of wolves – his priority will be to eliminate any threat to his species."

"He helped us escape with her; he gave you a car; he gave you your identity. His loyalty has always been to those on his land, and to his *mates*. He risked everything to protect *them*. Taylor was Sarah's husband, and he has a bond with Taylor. He'll not see Jasmine dead; he'll not see her harmed. The hardest part will be getting him to accept us back as part of his pack, especially if his own family's growing and other pack members already have their place – they'll come first. Let's face it, we took off and never kept in touch. We even asked Marco and Bill not to say a word about our existence to them. We believed it was the best way to keep Jasmine safe. I'll have some explaining to do, but if we can gain Lawrence's acceptance – if he offers us his home and his pack – you can bet everything he'll do whatever it takes to protect us. To protect *Jasmine*. And we're going to need that protection, Claire. If there are those that know of her birth, we'll *need* that protection."

She blinked, taking in his words. He was right. She just wished... Fuck, she wished Sarah wasn't dead. To call that place home without her there... "What about Tristan?"

"Marco and Bill said they'll try and throw him off our scent. If we leave, we won't let them know when or to where. We'll just go silently. That'll make it easier for them to lie to Tristan."

"And if he doesn't buy it? If he comes looking for Jasmine? What if he comes all the way to England and hunts her down?"

"Lawrence is the king of wolves. Tristan can come after Jasmine if he likes, but he'll fall at Lawrence." He spoke with such certainty, such unwavering loyalty for Lawrence Gunvald, even after everything. Only the same loyalty received could muster its like in return.

And that was what made up her mind for her. She nodded. "Okay. Okay. We'll go to Surrey."

Tears shone in his eyes, mirroring hers. "We'll make it work, Claire. If you're with me, we can make anything work."

"I'm with you forever, so I'm going to hold you to that, mister."

He smiled.

God, she loved him.

Brrrriiiiiing...

"Shit!" She jumped, then hurried for the landline telephone, the ringing to her ears, painful, because she still had a bit of wolf left in her – Pete's blood hadn't quite been diluted by her human gene yet. "Hello?"

"Hi! Er ... is this Beth?"

She froze. What the *hell...* "Who is this?"

The male voice, stuttered, unsure. "Oh, it's Tim. I'm Holly's boyfriend. I've been trying to call..."

"Ooohh." She almost collapsed with relief. Of course Holly would have told him her *real* name. "I'm so sorry, Tim, yes, I know who you are. I haven't had time to listen to your message yet I'm afraid – it's been a manic day."

"Hey, that's cool, no worries. Listen, I'm calling because Holly won't pick up, and I know what a ditz she is – her battery will die and she'll realise she's forgotten her charger... Is she there? I really need a word."

Confused, she looked at Pete. His ears were twitching – he was listening. "I'm ... er ... I don't understand why you'd think Holly's here?"

"Oh, has she left already? When she texted to say she was staying on with you guys for a bit longer, she didn't say when she'd be leaving, but I've been in Rome anyway until a couple of days ago."

Frowning, and growing rapidly alarmed, Claire met Pete's eyes.

He shrugged.

"Tim, Holly left here just over two weeks ago – Monday night. I dropped her off at the airport myself and she texted me to say she'd arrived at JFK."

A pause... "That can't be. That's around the same time she told me she was staying on."

And then it hit her. Like a ton of bricks.

She felt all the blood drain from her face.

The phone slipped from her ear as she looked around the room. "Holly's perfume ... Pete – *Holly's perfume*."

"Fuck," he cursed. Then he moved around, sniffing, tracking the scent.

She could smell it right now because of his blood.

Not new. Old. Stale.

No.

"Beth?"

She brought the phone back up to her ear. "Tim, I'll call you back." Not waiting for an answer, she hung up. Then, she closed her eyes and breathed in.

Holly...

She turned her head towards the scent – towards that 'tang' that smelled so weird. But now that her mind had pieced the puzzle together, it gave a name to the tang. Metallic. *Blood.*

Not stale perfume – the perfume was coating it. Stale *blood.*

She opened her eyes and found herself staring at the pile of envelopes and three packages by the front door that she had yet to open. The packages were things she'd ordered for the garden, except ... *I only ordered two things.* She remembered that now.

Taking strides that showed less trepidation than she felt, she walked up to the packages, Holly's scent getting stronger.

She went cold inside; sound faded into the distance. An image of Bill came to mind – him scraping some of the mould off an alpine tree and sniffing it.

"But it's been two weeks since then; the disease is still here."
"Because the danger is still here."

The poachers never left. Had she really thought they would? That they'd go to all that effort to find Jasmine, then disappear into the night never to be seen again?

"You want me to come to the gate with you?"
"Like an over-protective momma bear?" She laughed. "I'm good." She gave the iPod headphones hanging around her neck a shake. "Besides, I have Evanescence to keep me company."

Evanescence.

"Pete," she croaked.

He was there in a heartbeat.

"The packages."

He saw them, went to pick them up, his nostrils flaring, his face as pale as hers felt. And then, he froze. His back straightened and he looked back at her.

"Just do it," she said, her voice monotone. Because she knew exactly what he'd find.

Evanescence.

Nothing ever really vanished, did it? Nothing ever left no trace. Even memories never truly faded, even those you thought long gone.

"This one," said Pete, grimly, picking out the sealed box on the bottom of the pile.

She had thought she'd been slowly forgetting Sarah's eyes, Sarah's smile, Sarah's laugh, especially over the past year. It had been like losing her all over again in some ways, only it was a lie. Nothing ever really disappeared.

Right now, for example, as Pete ripped into the sealed box, Sarah's face blasted her mind as clear as day. And Holly's. Both of their faces over the years they'd spent lunches and din-ners, and some breakfasts together.

She smiled a warm, sincere smile that reached her eyes. "You've always been the one who's okay, Beth. If the world collapsed around us, you'd be the last man standing…"

The lid of the box was ripped open. Pete looked away, gagging.

"Tip it out."

"Claire."

"Tip it *out* or I'll do it myself."

With a quick glance towards the stairs to make sure the coast was clear, Pete knelt down and turned the box upside down. "I'm sorry," he said, his voice breaking as he removed the cardboard so she could see the contents.

She didn't scream.

She didn't blink.

She didn't move an inch.

Holly's head lay among packaging – shredded newspaper and polystyrene – stuffed into a large, air-vacuum storage bag, the suction and seal clearly having worked for the most part because the scent of decay had been suppressed.

Apart from just a tang.

Holly's mouth gaped open in a silent scream. Her eyes bulged in terror. It looked like she might have been suffocated before they'd decapitated her.

Her murderer hadn't bothered to remove her head-phones. They were rammed in the bag with her head, hanging off nothing now, but tresses of flesh where her neck should be.

It was the photos that got to Claire, though – three of them, loose in the box with the bag. They were among the photos she'd given to Holly at the airport, but whoever had done this had copied them and blown them up to A3 size. The one lying on the top was the boldest. It was of Sarah, sitting on a beach in Thailand, her smile big and wide, her eyes sparkling. That had been the best trip – a true adventure for all three of them. It was one of her favourite pictures of Sarah. Holly had loved it, too.

The scribbling across Sarah's face, in red marker pen, ruined it somewhat:

WE ARE COMING FOR HER DAUGHTER

Vomit surged before she could stop it, the last five years

regurgitated.

Pete held her as she collapsed, retching on the floor.

Chapter Fifteen

Pete had seen a few decapitated Tridents in his time; he'd lobbed the head off a couple himself. He'd even had the displeasure of seeing wolves that had lost their heads by human hands – hunters.

But nothing came close to the horror this mustered. Somehow, seeing a human – and one he'd known – mutilated in such a way made everything more ... *real*.

The front door swung open, pulling him out of his dark thoughts.

Claire still shook in his arms, her puke inches from his knees.

Marco and Bill strode in, laughing about something he couldn't quite catch. Their laughter stopped in an instant, shocked silence falling in its place as their eyes took in the scene at their feet. Marco's sharp intake of breath told him he'd seen the head.

"Fucking hell." That was Bill.

The words knocked Pete into action. He hauled Claire up. "We're leaving tonight."

Bill and Marco looked at him, stunned, but nodding.

"That's all you know; that's all I'll tell you."

More nodding. Because there were no fucking words

when a sawn-off head greeted your return home.

"Claire, honey, look at me."

She seemed to be holding herself up even though her pallor was a little more green than normal.

He took her face in both hands and turned her head. "We're leaving *tonight*," he repeated. "I need you to pack Jasmine's things and get the passports. We're on a deadline. We have no idea what Holly told them before they killed her." Hell, Claire looked bewildered. The reality of her friend, brutally murdered, must be starting to take hold, but he didn't think she'd quite grasped the immense and immediate danger they were all in now. "Claire," he pressed, then gave her a gentle shake.

She blinked. "Yes ... yes."

"We don't know what Holly told them before she died," he said again, speaking more slowly and biting out each word. "They could have our address, our daily schedule, the name of Jasmine's class teacher... They could have the *exact circumstances* of Jasmine's birth. As much as Holly knew, anyway."

She was nodding robotically, taking in his words.

"She could have told them about Dr Matheson; she could have told them your real name. We make no phone calls, we tell no one what we're doing or where we're going – nothing's safe. Her head's been here for well over a week, perhaps longer. Who knows who's been watching us all this time and who's been in and out of this place. If they know we're wolves they'll know to cover their scent. We talk in whispers from now on, and Marco ... Bill..."

They stared at him, their gazes holding all the regret he was feeling.

"That's *all* you know from now. Make yourselves scarce. Come back tomorrow after we've gone."

"Pete," whispered Claire.

He hugged her tighter to him.

"We can't leave her here." She was talking about Holly; staring at her head.

He cupped her cheek and turned them both around a little, then pressed her face into his shoulder. She didn't resist. She turned away from Holly and shuddered into his side. She'd see Holly like that for the rest of her fucking life now.

"Leave it with us," said Bill.

"What are you..." began Claire, then caught herself. Perhaps she was wondering if she really wanted to know the answer.

Bill offered it anyway. "Wood chipper."

They fell into sombre silence.

A creak from upstairs broke it. *Jasmine.*

Claire snapped out of her daze. "I'll get her packed."

Pete let her go. "I'll make arrangements."

Marco and Bill started to clear up the mess on the floor.

Claire stopped half way to the stairs. "Should we tell Elky?"

Pete met her eyes. There was no one they could trust – not anymore. "No. Tell no one."

They had avoided phoning Tim back, and luckily, he hadn't called them either. There was nothing they could say if they were to pretend they'd never seen Holly. Claire said she'd send him a text later to confirm Holly had made no contact with them since she'd left two weeks ago. The rest would be down to the inevitable police investigation that would follow. Poor Tim. Pete wished there was a way he could lessen the man's future pain, but it was out of his hands.

Pete had said nothing to Bill and Marco about travelling back to England and to Lawrence's, and he had decided he wouldn't be informing Lawrence either. Whoever had done this to Holly held all the cards right now. There was a chance they were watching – and listening to – their every move. It made the thought of getting on an aeroplane something close to a phobia for him – if they were cornered on an aeroplane, they were as good as dead. But he couldn't see a way around that except to fucking pray.

He'd called the airport to book tickets earlier, then had put the phone down as soon as someone had answered. If anyone was trailing them, their names on a booking record would certainly flag up; if the police were called because Jasmine's blood rang alarm bells at the hospital, the airports might be alerted. They'd have to turn up and take a chance on buying the tickets at the desk – he'd know by the look they received from the person behind the desk if something was up. He'd be able to smell the increase in their sweat and hear the jump in their heart rate. If that happened, they'd have to get the hell out of there bloody fast.

"It's done," said Bill, walking through the back door.

Pete nodded. He was talking about disposing of Holly. "Thank you. The photos, too?"

"All gone – not a trace left. I'm sorry it's come to this."

"It was a matter of time. We were banking on a few more years, that's all."

There was a pause, and then Bill's hand fell on his shoulder and squeezed it. "I'm outta here, mate. I'm meeting Marco at the car." The catch to this voice was painful to hear.

"That's it, then," replied Pete, softly.

"That's it, then."

He swivelled in his chair, stood, and flung his arms around his friend. The hug was returned threefold. No goodbyes were said.

"Wherever you're going, you're going to get there. I know

you will. You always see things through to the end somehow."

Pete nodded, too choked up to say anything.

Bill clapped him once on the back. "I'll be seeing you."

He turned and left.

Fuck.

He closed his eyes and gathered himself. Leaving a home – a territory – behind – was never an easy thing, let alone leaving those who'd become your pack.

"Pete!" Claire's distressed voice pulled him out of his grief.

"Claire?"

She came racing down the stairs in a panic. "Jasmine's gone!"

"Gone?" Dread settled deep.

"I told her we had to leave – tried to explain the danger we were in the best I could without scaring her. I didn't tell her about Holly – how could I? She didn't want to leave. Threw up a fuss about it, but I began to pack and said we had no choice; it had to be this way. I told her to get three of her favourite toys for now while I sorted through her clothes... Ten seconds, that was all. *Ten seconds.* I turned and she was gone."

Gone... "Teleported?"

"She must have."

"Where would she go?"

"I have no idea."

"Jesus..." The fear was blinding. *Think.* "She can only go places she knows, right?"

"I don't know – I guess. That's what Elky implied, although there was that time we ended up in the desert by that tree. I don't know *why* she took us there."

"There must have been a draw to it – some kind of tie. Phone Jerrod. Don't tell him anything other than she's gone on a teleporting adventure like five-year-olds might, and you're worried she might have ended up at the tree again. Get him to check."

"But what if Jerrod's one of the bad guys? What if telling him puts her in danger?"

Fuck it all to hell! "We have no choice. It'll take us at least six hours to get there and she might not even *be* there when we arrive. It'll start getting dark in an hour. He's our only option."

"Okay," she nodded. She was crying.

He had to pull himself back from hugging her tight – they didn't have time.

"What are *we* going to do?" she asked as she picked up her phone.

"The only other place I can think of that she'd go is to Elky."

"The ranchería where he trains her."

"Yes. But we'll stop by the school first to make sure she's not there. There's a breeze today – I'll be able to smell her if we're within half a mile or so of her."

She brought the phone to her ear. "What about Marco and Bill?"

Pete shook his head. "They've left and we *can't* involve them anymore – not with Tristan breathing smoke down their necks."

Claire nodded in agreement. He heard her phone make a connection at the other end.

"Claire."

She looked at him.

"Forget the packing, just get all the passports, any ID for England, your wallet, phone and charger. Everything else can be bought. We're out of time – we need to leave as soon as we find Jasmine." He swallowed the hard lump in his throat. "We won't be coming back."

Chapter Sixteen

This was bad. *Really* bad. She'd done it again, but she hadn't meant to. She'd been angry and sad and scared – very, very scared – not just because of what Mummy had said about leaving, but because there a weird feeling in the house, like something bad and secret had happened, but no one would tell her because she was a child.

And she *didn't* want to leave. Mummy hadn't said where they were going to live instead, so it could be a really bad place that she might not like. It had been horrible realising she'd never see Aiden again; she didn't want to never see Marco or Bill or Elky or her friends again. She'd even miss Mrs Myers. It wasn't okay.

All her desperate feelings had become one huge one she couldn't make small, so *it* had happened – she'd gone flying again. At least she knew where she'd landed this time.

She'd also brought Marlo with her because she'd been cuddling him tight at the time. She hugged him now, for comfort, then looked at her surroundings. This was the town where Elky lived, only for some reason, it looked empty. Usually, there were a few people walking about along the one row of small shops, but there was nothing and no one today – only silence. The shops looked closed and not just empty, but ...

broken. Old and broken. Some of the windows were smashed, and a couple of the doors were either swinging open, or dangling off their hinges.

"I've got a bad feeling about this, Marlo," she whispered to her lion, and even her whisper seemed to echo up and down the deserted street. The slight breeze in the air seemed too loud.

"Jasmine?"

Gasping, she turned and saw Diego standing behind her.

"What are you doing here?" he asked. He didn't seem angry and disgusted with her like he'd been at the hospital, just curious and confused. Nevertheless, she decided not to say anything about flying, or her superhero powers.

"I came to see Elky."

"Who?"

"He's my friend. He lives here."

Diego shook his head. "No one lives here."

"Yes, they do."

"No, they don't. It's a ghost town."

"What's a ghost town?"

He shrugged. "Where ghosts live? I'm not sure, but Mom says it's empty and no one has lived here for at least fifty years."

"Then, what are *you* doing here?"

He pointed to a small dirt road that forked off the main one and trailed up into the woods. "My granddaddy's buried up there. Mom went to the grave, but told me to stay here. She always goes to the grave by herself."

"Oh." She didn't know his granddaddy had died. "I don't have granddaddy. I don't have any grandparents." That suddenly made her feel sad.

"Where's *your* mom?"

She looked around, feeling guilty. She didn't know what

to say, but didn't want to talk about her flying powers anymore. "She's here somewhere," she lied.

"Is she talking to the friend you came to see?"

"Elky?" She frowned, her confusion growing. Why wasn't anyone here? And why were the buildings all old and broken when they weren't before? It couldn't have been ghosts she'd seen all the times she'd come here, could it? Daddy and Mummy had never mentioned ghosts – not once. She didn't know if she believed in them, though if dragons could be real, she supposed ghosts could be, too.

"Jasmine."

Both herself and Diego jumped at the voice calling her name. They turned towards it.

"Elky!" she exclaimed. He *was* here. But she stopped short of running to him to give him a hug. He looked ... different.

"I was not expecting you this afternoon," he said.

Her words got stuck in her throat. She didn't want to talk about flying with Diego here, but ... Elky looked ... not as friendly as usual. His face, normally cheery, was serious and stern, and something else she couldn't name. "Are you mad at me?" she asked, quietly. She didn't want him to be mad at her, too.

"Of course not, Jasmine." But he didn't look like he meant it. "I just haven't had time to prepare for visitors." His hard gaze landed on Diego. "And who is your friend?"

"I'm Diego," he offered, in his usual sure manner. It was one of the reasons she liked him – he never seemed to be afraid of anything. It was why she'd thought she could tell him her secret.

"Jasmine, did *you* bring Diego here?" Elky speared her with his dark stare.

She shook her head, feeling awful he thought that. "No, I promise. Diego was already here."

Elky looked back at him.

"My mom is visiting my granddaddy's grave," he said, not sounding so sure this time. Maybe he was picking up on Elky's unfriendliness, too.

"Aah, up in the burial ground in the woods."

Diego nodded, then said, proudly, "He was half Cherokee, but he married a Maidu lady and moved here. That's why he's buried here."

"Your granddaddy was Maipeke?" Jasmine asked. Her mum had talked a little about the Maipeke people when she'd started studying with Elky because that's what he was.

Diego looked at her like she'd said something stupid. "What's 'Maipeke'?"

"The people that live here."

"I said Cherokee and Maidu." He scrunched his face. "There's no tribe called Maipeke."

"Yes, there is." Her confusion was stoking her annoyance now, despite the fear still swirling in her tummy. Nothing looked or sounded the same anymore. "Elky is Maipeke."

"Jasmine." Elky knelt down so he was eye level with her. Usually this made her feel a little better, but right now, it made her feel like he was about to pounce on her and eat her, the way a cat pounces on a mouse. "Do you remember what I told you I was when we first started our lessons?"

She thought hard. There was a word … it was on the tip of her tongue.

"I told you not to mention it to your mom because she wouldn't understand. She's not like you and me."

Yes – she did remember that. It had made her feel guilty. Everyone had so many secrets. Why did *she* have to keep them all when they weren't even her secrets? "A … shoe man?"

Elky smiled, but it was devoid of the kindness she was used to. "A shaman."

Yes, that was it, although she didn't really know what a shaman was – something to do with magic. He'd said that if her mummy knew of his magic she might get too scared to let him teach her.

"Wow," whispered Diego. "You're a real shaman? My granddaddy taught me a little about them before he died last year."

Elky threw him a look, but otherwise ignored him. "Do you have any idea how *long* some shamans wait to find a student as powerful as you, Jasmine? Most never find them. We could do amazing things. We could change the world."

Did the world need changing? She didn't know.

"But in order to do that, we need *proper* training – daily training. A true shaman is a shaman all the time – the magic runs through him constantly without a break in the flow. You should come with me. I can teach you so much."

But he was already teaching her. She didn't understand. "Where would we go?"

"Somewhere beautiful, where everyone can do magic, and amazing creatures, like dragons, are real."

Her eyes widened. She'd *never* told Elky about the dragon. "Dragons are real?"

"They most certainly are."

She *knew* it! "Then I can tell Mummy about the dragons."

"No," he snapped.

She hopped back a step at his change in tone.

"No, Jasmine, you must never, ever tell."

"But she'll see the dragon," she said quietly, unable to keep the waver out of her voice over his telling her off.

"Your mom can't come to this place, Jasmine. She's not magical. This is a place only for those like you and me. But if you come with me, you *will* see the dragon, I promise."

Tears filled her eyes. She'd never felt so torn. "Can Daddy

come?"

"No."

Her tears spilled. She couldn't leave them – she *couldn't*. But ... the dragon – it was important. She knew it was. The dragon *meant* something.

"And I'm afraid time is up. You need to decide now. Dragons have a habit of disappearing if you're not in the right place at the right time."

"Can I come, too?" Diego piped up, excitement colouring every note.

Elky gave him that irritated look again, and smiled tightly. "Are you magical?"

Diego's face fell. "Maybe."

"Maybe's not good enough, kid."

A car drove up the road, slowed down, and pulled to a stop a few feet from where they stood.

Jasmine felt a sense of relief at this little interruption. She couldn't give Elky an answer; she couldn't make this decision.

Her relief, though, was short-lived. Her breath hitched in terror when two men stepped out of the car. The last time she'd seen them it had only been for a second, but she still recognised them.

"Hey, boss," said the shorter one.

"You're late."

The taller one had his eyes on her. He looked both surprised, and like he was about to receive a big prize. "Fuck, it's *her*."

"Jasmine, these two are ... friends of mine." The way he'd said 'friends' didn't make it sound like they were friends. "This is Steve, and this is Liall."

Her legs started to shake, and she felt nothing but cold inside as she stared at the faces of the two men who had hit

Mummy's car off the road.

~*~

The passenger door opened and Claire got in.

Pete had kept the ignition running.

"She's not here."

"I can't smell her here either, but are you sure? Is the school closed?"

"No, some of the teachers have stayed behind for a meeting, though not Mrs Myers. I spoke to one of them and to one of the cleaning staff. No one's seen her, and ... I don't know. I just don't *feel* like she's here."

Pete nodded and pulled back onto the road.

"But something feels wrong ... really wrong."

"We'll find her. It's just over ten minutes to Gregstown."

"You know, I mentioned to the teacher I was talking to we were heading to Gregstown next and she gave me the strangest look. 'The old ranchería?' she said, and then she asked me why I was going to that ghost town."

"Ghost town?"

"I have no idea what she meant. But the wolf blood's out of my system now. I couldn't read anything between her words."

"I was with you the first time we dropped Jasmine off there – it was far from a ghost town."

"That's what I thought." He saw her chew her lip out of the corner of his eye. "Pete, how long have Marco and Bill known Elky?"

"Um ... I think one of them said something about him moving here two years ago."

"So, just *after* we moved here with Jasmine?"

"I guess." He paused, then looked at her, questioningly,

before looking back at the road. "You don't think that's coincidence?"

"I don't know. I just … the disease on the alpine trees – it's still there."

"You said you felt it was a warning."

"I still think it is, but disease is caused by an infection. It happens when a dangerous foreign body invades a healthy system which is already there. If the trees represent the native tribe that are home to this land, maybe they're trying to tell us they're being invaded by a foreign body."

"Invaded? What are you getting at?"

"I don't *know*," she said again, the desperation in her voice coming through. "I just know something feels wrong, and I have no idea what it is. We need to find Jasmine *now*."

~*~

Elky was not her friend.

If he was friends with these two men, he was *not* her friend. That was starting to become clearer and clearer. The other thing that was also clear now, was that she was in big danger.

With her eyes fixed firmly on all three men, she took a step back.

Elky noticed her movements and let out a small sigh. "Jasmine…" He shook his head.

She thought about running, but didn't know where to run to.

She thought about flying, but she'd never really made it happen on purpose, just by accident, and she didn't know if she could do it now on demand.

She'd also have to leave Diego behind, and she didn't want to do that. They might hurt him.

"Look, Jasmine. Look at the town."

She didn't want to take her eyes off Elky just in case he did something bad, but she couldn't help looking at his outstretched hand after he closed his eyes and started to chant using words from his language that she didn't understand.

A door belonging to one of the houses on the street banged shut.

She jumped at the sound, then lost herself in awe as some kind of magic seemed to take hold of the entire street. All the houses *moved* as if they were alive somehow. They didn't move a lot, but a little – enough to straighten doors and shutters. Windows that had been broken grew new glass. Lawns that had overgrown or turned brown became lush and green. She watched, amazed and startled, as someone walked out of a house with their bag and continued on their daily business. Then, someone else walked out of another house. The grocer appeared to load some fruit into the empty boxes outside his shop. More and more bodies emerged, and the town was once more bustling and alive. People talked to each other; waved cheery hellos.

Elky clicked his fingers and dropped his hand, and the image froze for a second before fading away like wisps of smoke in the wind. Broken, empty, old houses replaced the scene once more.

Diego stood next to her, open-mouthed.

"Shamans are masters of creation, Jasmine – we can manifest whole realities. The most powerful among us can, anyway. You just saw what I created; what I *wanted* you to see."

"It's not real," she whispered, trying to understand this big truth he'd just shown her. It was hard, but she did understand. At least, she thought she did. She didn't understand why, though.

"What's not real? What you just saw, or what you see

now? What is 'real'? Real to me is a different real to you – most people have no tolerance of that fact, let alone understand it. But we, Jasmine, *we* understand, which means we can become masters of our realities. But we don't need to stop there. I can teach you how to do what I just did – you have it in you, I know you do. I can teach you to be a god."

Sudden and stark, the image hit her. She'd had it once before – when she'd seen the dragon for the first time at Aiden's house: a giant sun setting between two pyramids that dominated an expanse of arid desert, yet it was lush grass she stood on as she watched the winged beast silhouetted against the red sun.

With the vision came a whisper, rippling across the sand; rippling across time...

Gods must fall at the feet of men.

"You're not real," she whispered again, to Elky this time, and she had no idea why she'd said it, or even what she really meant. Maybe something big inside her – something bigger than five-year-old Jasmine – had said it. Whatever the reason, he didn't like it. Not one bit.

His eyes narrowed in anger, but before he could say a word, Diego's mother traipsed out of the woods. "Diego," she called, sounding just as irritated with him as she had at the hospital. "Who are you speaking to? I told you to stay where you were."

"I am where I was, Mom."

She didn't seem to hear him or care. She looked at the three men suspiciously, just like she'd looked at Daddy suspiciously at the hospital.

A car motor could be heard behind them all, down the road. They all turned towards it and Jasmine's heart leapt when she recognised her mum's car.

"Well," said Elky. "I guess we're having ourselves a party."

He smiled.

She didn't like that smile at all.

"Jasmine ... I'm going to show you just how real I am."

Chapter Seventeen

"Slow down," said Claire, her voice barely working, as they entered Gregstown. It was *not* the Gregstown she remembered. At all.

Pete did as she requested, looking out the window, just as perplexed. "What the *hell* is this?" he muttered.

"A ghost town," whispered Claire, her fear rising by the second.

"But ... *how*? I can *smell* it, Claire. I can smell the emptiness. I can smell no one's lived here for decades – how could I not smell it before?"

"Not just smell ... sight, too. We both saw a different town; we saw a busy, live town. Look," she pointed at the house on the right as they drove past. "Look at *all* of them. The houses are derelict."

"Shit," said Pete, a growl colouring the cuss. "We have a bigger problem."

She saw the problem dead ahead. Her veins turned to ice. "Those are the two men who ran us off the road."

"Standing next to Elky," he added.

"It's a lie," she found herself whispering as she stared at the road and houses again.

Pete pulled to a stop a few yards away. She could sense

the wolf in him wanting to shift.

Her gaze fixed on Elky. "It's all a lie." She felt dumbfounded, but more than that, somewhere deep inside, she felt wounded. It was fear that won this contest though – it prevailed in this instance because there was Jasmine standing, helpless – trapped – between all three men, looking just as scared as she felt.

"A fucking good lie since I couldn't smell a god-damned thing about it. Elusive lies. *Magic* lies." Pete gripped the steering wheel as his gaze flittered between each person surrounding their daughter. Wolves really didn't like magic.

"Isn't that Diego's mother? The woman who went berserk at you at the hospital?"

"Yep, and there's Diego behind that shorter guy – see?"

She could now he'd mentioned it, though all she could see of Diego from this angle was his arm. He was standing next to Jasmine. "What are they doing here? Are they involved?"

"No idea. The only thing I know is there's no way to do this without outing my wolf completely."

Claire sucked in a breath as the taller of the two poacher men pulled out a rifle and pointed it straight at their car.

"You can bet your ass there's a silver bullet in here," the man called out. "So take it nice and slow getting out of the car, okay?"

"I think you're already outed, Pete. They know about Sarah and Jasmine – they killed Holly. What the fuck do we do?"

His eyes were on Jasmine. "We get out just like he said, and we play it by ear. Jasmine's all that matters. They won't hurt her, she's too important."

Claire nodded. Then, shaking like a leaf and wishing she was still wired on wolf blood, she opened her door and got out.

Pete followed suit.

"Hands up!"

They both raised their arms slowly.

"Keep them up and come this way."

They walked towards the small gathering, her heart just about breaking over Jasmine's tear-streaked face. "Honey, it's okay," she called to her. Clearly it was *not* okay, but she'd needed to say something; she'd needed to make contact.

Jasmine nodded, eyes wide and pale as a sheet, but she stayed in her spot.

Claire's anger flared over the panic within. She fixed her eyes on Elky and she gritted her teeth. "You lying arsehole."

The man with the gun raised it higher, pointing it straight at Pete. "*Bang*," he said, then he grinned. "I could do it now, boss. One second is all it'll take for her to regret speaking to you like that."

"Steve," sighed Elky, "put the gun down."

"I came here for a wolf; I want my wolf."

"You came here under my instruction, so you'll do as you're told."

So it was true. He *was* behind all of this. "You piece of shit," she bit out, unable to help herself, her anger white hot at the realisation *she'd* put her daughter in danger by entrusting her to this scumbag. All because she'd *believed* him. "All this time... *You're* the mould; you're the infection – the foreign body invading the land. You're what the trees were trying to show us."

"As we discussed when we first met, Claire, the blame game really helps no one step into the future. There will always be those who invade and conquer, that's the way the world is."

"No, that's the way people like you have made the world."

"It's the way the world *is*." He smiled as if patiently schooling a child. "Gods come and gods go, and you, my dear, have no idea of the great future before us. Your daughter is going to build grand things."

"You don't even *talk* about her. You've lost that right."

"And who are you to think you have any more right to her than I, given the circumstances of her birth?"

That made her stop. She looked at Jasmine.

"Being adopted myself – I didn't lie about that, by the way – I hold the belief it is much better to tell our children the truth from the beginning."

"*Shut up.*" Jasmine knowing the truth would damage her further at this stage – it wasn't something she'd be able to wrap her head around. Now was the wrong time. "It's not for you to decide."

"And nor is the decision yours. That piece of paper stating parental responsibility – *that's* a lie, isn't it? Who's the liar again?"

"Who the hell do you think you are, to think you have any claim on *my* daughter?"

"Someone who knows so much more than you about the way of things. You see, she's not your daughter – you're hers. We're all hers. *You have no idea what she is.*"

A whimper from Jasmine had her stalling. She had her hands over her ears, still holding her stuffed lion, his mane between her clenched fingers.

"Jasmine?"

She was crying softly, her eyes squeezed shut.

"Let me go to her," she directed to Elky.

He shook his head. "No."

Unable to resist Jasmine's cries, she took a step towards her anyway.

"Uh, uh, uh." The shorter man standing near Jasmine pulled his own gun out, this one pointing at Claire.

Shit. "Liall, isn't it?" she addressed him.

"Yes, ma'am."

"Is this really how you want to be known? As the guy who scared a five-year-old girl and wouldn't let her be comforted by her mother?"

"I follow the money, lady. I need to get paid. Though, from what your pretty friend said before we took her head off, your daughter might not be a 'five-year-old girl' at all."

"Stop it!" That was Jasmine.

They all looked at her. Diego put his hand on her shoulder by way of comfort.

His mother (Mrs Alvo, wasn't it?) who looked shocked as well as terrified, and had said nothing all this time, now jumped into action. "Diego, come to me now, please. Sir," she said to Elky, "we appear to be here by accident and clearly this is some kind of family matter we're simply not a part of. We would be more than happy to get out of your way."

"There are no accidents in life."

Mrs Alvo seemed stumped as to how to respond to that.

Claire wanted to calm Jasmine down ... perhaps talking about anything *other* than Jasmine; get the focus off her. *Right, as if you're having a normal conversation with friends over coffee. Jesus, Claire...* "What happened to this town, Elky?" She gestured to the houses. "This isn't what I saw before."

"You saw what I wanted you to see. As I explained to Jasmine earlier, I wasn't expecting visitors today, so didn't have time to prepare."

"Prepare?"

"He can change it with magic." That was Diego.

His mother went positively pale at his joining in the conversation.

Pete hadn't moved a muscle where he stood, clearly fearing he'd lose control of his wolf if he did.

Claire turned back to Elky. "You can change it? Like ... a

spell to make people see what isn't there?"

"Not quite. A veil coats everything in this world. If you can shift the veil, you can alter reality; change someone's vision of it."

"So, you altered reality so we'd see a busy, used town instead of this ghost town?"

"Exactly."

"Why?"

"So you would let me have time with Jasmine. So you'd entrust her to me."

Her blood boiled over her carelessness. Some mistakes were too costly. What a fool she'd been. "And what about the sweat lodge? What about the Maipeke tribe? The chief I spoke to?"

Elky's eyes lit up. "One of my finer accomplishments. I wasn't sure I could do it." Then, his eyes darkened. "As it happens, I didn't. People were getting wind of Jasmine – the werewolves up north for example. My magic is strong, but battling many wolves in a whole pack as strong as that one... No. I came to the realisation time had run out. I needed you gone, Claire. I needed to dispose of you."

Pete growled; his fangs protruded and his eyes shone.

Mrs Alvo's mouth opened in a near scream; she looked close to fainting.

Steve realigned his rifle.

Elky held up his hand to stop him. "No, let the wolf hear it – let him know his weakness before we end his world." His gaze fixed on Claire. "You're the matriarch. If – when – you're gone, your wolf will fall apart – everything will fall apart. And Jasmine will turn to me. My plan has always been to take Jasmine away to teach her properly; to teach her *better*."

"To groom her." She felt sick.

"To be my protégé, yes. She's unrivalled in what she can

do – I never lied about that either. There is no Maipeke tribe, Claire, there never has been. I planted the seed of their existence in everyone's minds from the moment I arrived here two years ago, on your tail, of course."

"You knew we were moving here. You followed us."

"Magic has its uses – vision, prophecy... I've never minded playing the long game. I *am* a shaman of Native American descent, though not of this region. It's irrelevant – cultural identity is not why I'm here. The tribe you met, including the chief, were images I conjured which you were susceptible to because they were what you were *expecting* to find. And it was so easy, Claire," he smiled. "You wanted so much to fit in to your new surroundings – to accept the new land and everything that lives on it – your mind wasn't hard to manipulate."

Bastard. The violation felt heinous. To play on her insecurities like that...

"The sweat lodge was real enough, but it was I who was chanting throughout the ceremony; I who poured water on the stones. I have to say, what happened next really was quite unexpected and I still don't know how you did it. *I* was the one who was supposed to conjure a demon to take you away."

"To dispose of me." She felt vulnerable and ashamed; light-headed, too. *Don't pass out.*

"Yes. But it was *you* who conjured a demon instead, so my plan was disrupted to say the least. My moment was gone. I lost control of my magic at that point, and all I could do was hold the space and wait for your return as you walked off with the demon. I could not follow. I could not change that reality. How *did* you do it, Claire? Curious minds want to know."

"I don't know," she replied, though her mind conjured up the feel of her blood pounding in her veins as the drumming had filled the sweat lodge, as if she'd been a thousand wolves stampeding... *It was the wolf blood in you*, it whispered.

Another whisper caught her attention – Jasmine's. With hands still clamped over her ears and her face scrunched up, she seemed a slave to the words she kept spouting. *"It's too big, it's too big, it's too big, it's too big, it's too big..."* Whatever was happening to her, it clearly pained her greatly.

Claire's vision blurred as tears fell for her daughter. She wanted nothing more than to hold her and she hoped Jasmine knew that somewhere deep down. "I have no idea how I did it."

"Hmmm," muttered Elky. "Perhaps there's a bit of magic in you after all."

"I don't understand. All of this ... *all of this* ... for what? So you can have Jasmine? Why not just abduct her the old-fashioned way when our backs were turned? You had plenty of opportunity."

"Because, as with all magic, for it to work its best there must be an element of free will. If she does not come freely, she will refuse me her powers. And I need those powers, Claire. I *need* them."

She could *not* believe her ears. *What* had she just heard.

She laughed. It wasn't funny at all, but the ludicrousness dug under her skin. "You call *this* her coming *freely*?"

Elky shrugged. "Let me rephrase: it's *best* if those who train in magic come of their own free will." He smiled. "But not *necessary*. And I think, Claire, we've said all we're going to say. Jasmine will be coming with me now."

Her attempts at stalling were over, but it was over far too fast. She didn't even have time to blink, let alone think.

Elky waved a hand out in front of him – that's all he did – and the ground came alive, rumbling and shaking, breaking itself into shards of grit that puffed up in a rapid swell of dust that clawed her eyes.

Claire fell, shouting, unable to keep her balance. To her

left, she heard Pete's bones crack as his wolf raged forth.

A gunshot sounded, freezing her heart. But it was Jasmine's scream that pierced it. Shrill, deafening, it may as well have been what split the ground.

"JASMINE!" Springing from hands and feet, she leapt forward into the plume of rusty-brown haze towards where Jasmine had been standing. Or she tried to – she didn't get far.

Pete's black and white werewolf attacked her; lifted her right off the ground and catapulted her through the air *away* from Jasmine, and she had no idea why – WHY – he would do such a thing, until she saw what chased him.

Fire.

A *huge* wall of unfurling flames, twelve-foot high and stretching even wider, rushed at them like a tsunami from the pits of hell. It consumed everything and everyone in its path – Liall, Steve, Elky – and that's all she saw.

She landed on the ground with a painful jar to her back, Pete's weight on top of her. They were on the other side of her car, using it as a shield, Pete having sailed them right over its roof.

The heat of the fireball melted paint. God, she could *feel* it like they'd been thrown in an oven.

Pete was nudging her, roughly, with his entire body, teeth nipping her neck, his desperate message clear: *MOVE!*

She scrambled to her feet and ran with him, away from the road, towards the grass and trees.

Five seconds later, her car exploded.

~*~

Fire had been his silent captor for damned near thirty years, quietly torturing him since his then-mate had burned his flesh in a fit of mindlessness. Three decades ago felt like another life ago – not here and now at all; he'd changed so much – but his pyrophobia had taken root that night and not let go.

It was possible to feel torn asunder in a split second, it really was. Ripping both himself and Claire away from Jasmine, knowing he was sealing her a deadly fate, would be his new captor; that decision, made on the fracture of his heart, his new torturer for the rest of his life.

But he couldn't let the fire take Claire. He just couldn't.

When he had come to on the grass, his body had felt battered and bloody and human. He had shifted back into a man and now sat up, naked. His skin had been scraped and pelted with grit, but it had escaped a scorching, thank god. In his ears, he could hear nothing but a high-pitched, never-ending, sonar-like screech from the explosion, and even that was muffled as if he were wrapped feet deep in cotton wool.

Until Claire's cry broke through everything. It was the loss in her cry he heard most.

Six metres or so away from himself, she was sitting up, bleeding, clothes torn, skin smudged black, wailing Jasmine's name as she took in the scene.

The scene was one he'd never wipe from his mind: the town was ablaze from its outer reaches to the new crater that marked the ground where Jasmine had stood.

His eyes widened in shock. "Fuck me," he whispered, though he couldn't hear his own words due to his damaged eardrums. Where Jasmine *still* stood.

He blinked sweat, tears, and dirt out of his eyes, but his vision didn't change. Jasmine *was* standing in the middle of the crater, her back to them. Her clothes were gone – they'd been burnt away. Clutched in her right hand which hung by her hip, was a wispy string with small clumps of melted, synthetic fur attached: Marlo had not survived the explosion.

"Claire," he pulled himself to standing and hobbled over

to her.

She reached for him, and he hauled her up. Her eyes were fixed on Jasmine; she'd stopped crying out her name though. She stared in shock, and he was sure he mirrored it.

"Pete." She clutched at him.

He held her tight, unable to do much else.

Together, they took in the rest of the scene. To Jasmine's left, two blackened skeletons littered the ground: Steve and Li-all. To her right...

Claire gasped – he felt it rather than heard it – and pulled her hands up to her mouth.

A much smaller, charred body lay to her right. *Diego.* "Oh, no..."

Pete's skin crawled, his own ancient burn, tight on his face and itching as if new. His phobia was piqued, but also somewhat numbed by shock.

Claire pointed somewhere further out from the other bodies. Mrs Alvo, Diego's mother, had met the same fate as the others. Some skin, red and charred, remained on her frame.

Pete looked away, gulping for air, and pulled Claire closer.

She squirmed out of his grasp though and gripped his shoulders.

He looked at her, focusing on her lips, her words very faint through the ringing in his ears, but just about audible. "Where's Elky?"

Unwillingly, he turned back to the horrific scene. He shook his head. He couldn't see the man's remains.

"Jasmine?" he heard Claire call.

It was a cold, indescribable unsettlement – being afraid of your own child.

But she was still theirs, and love burned just as hard as the destruction surrounding them. They made their way towards her.

"Jasmine?"

Her back still facing them, she didn't move a muscle, as if in a stupor.

A bullet ricocheted inches from Pete's feet. Claire screamed and they both jumped, spinning around to find Elky behind them, the barrel of a shotgun staring back at him. The shaman looked out of breath and a little worse for wear, but other than that, untouched by the explosion.

"Do you see?" he grunted, his words taking some effort. "See her power? She's mine. You can't handle what she has. She's *mine*."

~*~

"Jasmine, we can leave now to the place I told you about. The magical place."

Still, she didn't stir.

Claire forced her gaze away from her daughter and focused on Elky. All wasn't yet lost, but her body felt bruised to the point of brokenness. If she had to run, she wasn't sure she could. Her hip shot pain through her abdomen and up her spine, her knees locked with every step, and she hoped her hearing wasn't permanently ruined.

"You're *not* taking her," Pete growled.

Elky aimed his gun at Claire instead.

Pete bristled.

The wind blew.

They all stilled.

An odd interruption to be sure, but it was a *strange* wind that made the hairs on the back of her neck stand on end. Claire certainly felt it. She knew Elky felt it, too.

He frowned, his gaze flittering to the sky before landing

back on her and straightening his gun.

It was just like the wind she'd tapped into when intuiting the alpine trees, and suddenly she knew: *that* had not been some conjuration of Elky's. The breeze, the messages – those had been for *her*. "Your time's up," she said, and honest-to-god, she felt that was what the wind was here to say. The certainty of it she felt deep in her bones even amid the devastation she stood in.

Elky looked at her, both irritated and confused, but yes, there was fear there. "More magic, Claire? What secrets have *you* been keeping? Is there witchcraft in your veins?"

She hadn't a damned clue – her family background was as normal and boring as family backgrounds came – but she'd take that fear of his and play on it, just like the bastard had played on hers for weeks. "You have no idea what you're dealing with."

He tightened his grip on the gun, his finger on the trigger whitening with the added pressure. "Jasmine!" snapped Elky. "It's time for us to go."

Another, much stronger gust of wind brought a shadow which cast over them. The shadow was gone in an instant.

They all looked up, but nothing was there – no cloud hovered over them.

A growl sounded, and it wasn't from Pete.

Startled, the three of them looked towards the woods from where the sound had come.

A rustle.

Yellow eyes gleamed.

Claire took in a sharp breath. Pete pulled her closer to him; Elky took a step back.

A large panther emerged from the dark gaps between the trees, coat black and glistening. Its eyes were fixed on Elky.

"Jesus fucking Christ," muttered Pete as he clutched at

her, tugging her further back.

"Wait," she said. *Its neck*. A wreath of bones hung around it; bones she'd seen before.

The panther roared, baring its sharp, white teeth; its eyes never left its target.

Elky swung his gun towards the panther.

"Mummy?"

Everything froze at Jasmine's clear voice slicing through the chaos.

All of them, including Elky, glanced at her.

"Honey?" Claire made to go to her.

Pete held her back. "Wait ... something's wrong."

Jasmine turned around.

Pete's grip on her arm tightened.

The odd colours of Jasmine's irises could not be seen, for in their place small flames leapt and sparked. Fire consumed her sockets. "Mummy?"

With struggle, Claire found her voice, her heart racing so fast, she was sure it might suddenly stop beating altogether. "Yes, darling?"

"I want to go home now."

A strange sound from above them broke the reverie caused by Jasmine's resurgence, and they found themselves looking up again.

Elky breathed hard behind her. He was panicking, his gaze flitting between Jasmine, the panther, and the sky.

The panther's stare remained, unflinching, on Elky.

Again – *that sound*. A giant 'flapping'. Birds? No bird sounded like that, did they?

This time, the wind that followed was the sharpest of blusters, like a prelude to a hurricane. Claire had to look down to hide her eyes from the grit blowing up, and suddenly there it was. *There it was*. Just a distant outline in the sky behind

Jasmine, but coming in *so* very fast. It was clear it was of a monstrous size.

Damned if she could say *what* it was though, although her mind did conjure a word she didn't have the strength to accept right now.

Pete shouted, and for the second time, took her into his embrace as he threw them both to the ground.

'It' flew at them, over Jasmine's head, her eyes still alight. Its wings spanned god knew how many metres. It upturned dust and stones as it soared. The remains of Claire's car rattled in the turbulence it created.

Elky suddenly screamed, his fate realised. His gun forgotten – all magic forgotten – he turned to run and got nowhere at all, for it was far too fast for him.

"Claire!" Pete pulled her down flat along the grass.

He was right to do so – it flew only feet from the ground and it wasn't slowing down. She had to dig her fingers into the dirt so she wouldn't get swept away.

Elky's scream crescendoed as the beast took him in its mouth, each tooth inside it the size of a grown man.

His scream ended on a high-pitched note. The only sound that remained was the whoosh of wings and wind as it raced over the trees faster than anything she'd seen.

Seconds later, the wind became a breeze, trying to soothe the shocked silence.

The panther was the first to move. It seemed to blur in front of their eyes, but Claire knew what was happening because she'd seen Pete do this many times. It looked less painful when the panther did it though, and there was no crack of bones that she could detect.

In mere seconds, the demon from the sweat lodge stood where the panther had been.

Another figure emerged from the woods, looking a little

put out. "I missed it?" he asked Pueblo. "Again? Why do I always miss it?"

"Jerrod," exclaimed Claire, and though it was only a bewildered whisper, he heard her.

He tentatively smiled at her, then waved.

A wail arrested any further greeting. It quickly ascended to pained sobbing. "*Mummyyyy!*"

"Jasmine!" That was her daughter – *that* was her. *Her* cry, *her* pain – from grazed knees to dropped ice creams – she'd know it in a crowd of a hundred wailing children. "Jasmine!"

She got up and it turned out, she *could* run. She ran to her.

Jasmine's gaze met hers, tear-filled and fire-free; one green eye and one brown pleading for comfort amid her fear and confusion. "I couldn't stop it!" she screamed.

Claire ran faster.

Jasmine held her arms up for her, and it was a miracle really, how the whole world could fall into a hug. She was in her arms – *she was in her arms*.

And the sobbing was tumbling from Claire's lips, not Jasmine's. "I'm here ... I've got you. I'm here." She lifted her up off the ground; Jasmine's legs twined around her waist.

Travelling from one end of the earth to the other to find the right home ... and all the time, it was right here, entwined with her. No matter where they went, *this* was home.

Chapter Eighteen

"You scared the bejesus out of him, you know," chuckled Jerrod, and although the chuckling should have seemed out of place amid the quiet crackling of the town in embers, it didn't. She was quickly learning it was this man's M.O. – a chatty, dark humour which made the unbearable, bearable. "Summoning him like that. He came straight to me, alarmed, asking me to repeat the description of the mother and child I'd found in the desert."

It turned out Jerrod worked for the demon. Small world. But perhaps it was true that there were no coincidences.

They both sat on a fallen tree trunk at the edge of the woods, watching Pueblo and Pete clear up any and all things that would identify them. Claire wanted to help them, but couldn't bear the thought of letting Jasmine go – not yet – so she'd wrapped her little naked body up in what was left of her own coat and rocked her in her arms instead, thankful she'd cried herself to sleep.

Jerrod continued. "Pueblo told me to keep an eye on you; keep my ear to the ground. He had no idea – still doesn't know – why he's involved, but his suspicious nature was roused after you summoned him, especially as a woman alone."

She shook her head. "I wasn't alone."

"But you were. Pueblo saw only you – not the tribe you claimed to be with, and not Elky."

Hot tears of anger blurred her vision. "Because Elky's tribe was an illusion he cast, and he probably veiled himself in that illusion, too."

"Yes."

"God, now that you're saying this, I can remember that Pueblo didn't even address anyone else at the lodge. He looked around it and I assumed he was seeing the other men, but he wasn't. He must have just been assessing his surroundings. And when we went for our walk, he didn't mention them at all; neither did I for some reason."

"But he did suspect you were not alone from the way you were acting. He told me you seemed to be looking to someone or something for guidance. It made him suspect trickery."

"'Look out for evil shamans.' He said that to me before he left that day. I can't believe it," she shook her head, feeling like the world's biggest idiot. "It was staring me right in the face."

"Hey, don't beat yourself up. Pueblo didn't see it either, and he's experienced in shamanic magic. This Elkoyti guy was a good trickster."

"He saw my weaknesses; played with them and twisted them for his own gain, making me believe they were my strengths."

"That's what tricksters do. And we all have weaknesses – you *are* strong."

"Then I need to be stronger, fast," she mumbled.

"When I got that call from you a couple of hours ago about your daughter going missing, Pueblo was the first person I phoned. He sensed something big was about to happen and told me to get to you as soon as I could; he'd follow."

Claire looked at Jerrod, questioningly. "He *was* the panther, right?"

Jerrod nodded. "It's one of his guises as a shapeshifter; the other is fire."

"Is that what happened to Jasmine?" Her heart hurt just talking about it. "Did she shift into fire?"

"More than that, Claire, she *directed* the fire. Elkoyti was not wrong when he said she was powerful – unfortunately, without any mastery of it, poor thing."

Claire looked upon her daughter's face – peaceful now, bar a slight frown creasing her brow. "She didn't seem to re-member any of it just now."

"She might not. It's a large power for a young mind to take in. She will need training."

"I know. We need to go back to England. There's a wolf pack there – they helped save her during her birth; they helped us escape with her."

"It sounds like the best place for her."

"I don't know if they can train her, but … the she-wolf who leads the pack, she's had to deal with her own kind of power. Maybe … I don't know. It might work."

"Wolves are good at protecting their kind, I hear."

"Pete's their kind. But me and Jasmine?" She wasn't so sure.

"Sometimes soul bonds are stronger than blood bonds. Have faith in that."

She let a small smile pass her lips. "I'll try. They have a doctor there, too, who knows all about wolves. He helped Jas-mine when she was born."

"Why did you leave the pack in the first place?"

"We had no choice. We needed to disappear so she wouldn't be hunted – so no one would find out about her birth – and the pack was being invaded by their enemy. It was all-out war. We were already at the hospital when it started. We escaped with Jasmine and then, time did its thing and we just thought it would be better for her to keep on moving; to keep hiding."

"And now you're outed."

"Yeah."

"No more hiding. Elkoyti won't be the last threat to come after her – he's just the first." Jerrod sighed. "Secrets never stay secrets for long, believe me. It's okay to go home now."

She nodded with another smile and hugged Jasmine a little tighter. "I finally know where home is."

~*~

"You don't have to keep staring at me."

Pete glanced at the demon, before looking away.

"I realise cats and dogs aren't the best of friends, but if we're rummaging through human carcasses together, I'd appreciate some leeway."

Pete grunted, but didn't say anything. His nasal passage burned from the acrid smell of charred human flesh and bones. His chest hurt with grief. It also hurt from keeping his terror of fire in check – some of the town still glowed red, though the flames had mostly died, leaving a trail of thick, black smoke billowing into the sky. It wouldn't be long before the authorities arrived.

But it wasn't the fire that stoked his terror now, it was his own daughter. And that was probably the greatest pain he'd ever felt. He didn't know what to do with that.

Jasmine's eyes, alight, was an image he'd never erase.

"I have a son."

Jesus, this demon never shut up. Pete clenched his jaw and rummaged through Claire's handbag which had survived the car's wreckage. Jasmine's passport was missing.

"He turned nine just a few days ago. He's the best bloody

thing that's ever happened to me – well, sharing equal first place of greatness with finding the love of my life – but some days, he's like someone I don't know at all. He's far away, drifting, and when he comes back there's something different in his eyes. Maybe he's just growing fast; or maybe he enters worlds I have no business entering. Gotta tell you, there's no feeling as shitty as knowing you can't help your own kid. Or as terrifying."

Pete spied the passport a few feet away, to the left of the car. He straightened up and placed his hands on his hips, glad he'd been able to cover himself up to some extent with what was left of his trousers. Sorting through the dead, butt naked, didn't appeal one bit.

And he didn't want to fucking talk. He couldn't even get the story straight in his head. *What had even happened?*

"This yours?" The demon held up a wallet. "Half the stuff in it's missing."

He shook his head. "Must have belonged to one of the men."

The demon nodded, and placed it back on the ground where he'd found it. "Something changed with my boy about five months ago after a huge festival that took place at that sacred tree at the Birthlands. I'm assuming Claire told you about her and Jasmine ending up there. When Jerrod told *me* about it – and this was before Claire summoned me – that's when my senses went into overdrive. I knew something big was about to happen, but I didn't know what."

Pete sighed. He just wanted to get out of here. "Look, I don't know what's going on. This," he waved his arms at the destroyed town, "is so far out of my league, I don't even know if I'm awake. But whatever big thing is happening, it ends here. We're going back to England."

"Right." The demon stared at him.

Pete didn't want to look at him, so focused on something else – anything else – then wished he hadn't. His gaze had landed on small bones. They belonged to the boy.

Shit. If Jasmine remembered what she did to him, it would fuck her up, if not now, then in years to come. He turned away from them and went to pick up her passport. "The Surrey Hills – that's where we're going. We'll be out of your way, and you can get back to your family, just like I can get back to mine."

Pueblo continued to stare at him. "I heard dogs like to bury their shit, but this shit won't stay down."

Pete growled, anger rising – *delayed* anger he'd had to cage for the last few hours.

"Hey," the demon snapped, flashing his own feline fangs. "I'm not your enemy, here. I've been through some fucked-up crap, just like you have; I've stood at the end of the god-damned world. I'm telling you what I know: this isn't something you can bury. I don't have a clue why I'm involved; why Claire summoned me; why she even *could*, but if I walk away from this with my eyes closed, I'm a fool. And I was done being anyone's fool a long time ago. Go to England, find yourselves there, but when that girl of yours grows and changes and needs your help, don't let your fear blind you into turning away from her."

Pete squared himself against the demon, chest to chest, standing a couple of inches taller than him. "I would *never* turn away from her."

"Good." He didn't retaliate; didn't respond any threat.

Pete suddenly felt tired. His shoulders sagged, and he stepped away.

"Hey." Claire's voice filled the cold in his chest with its warmth. Fuck, he needed her. *Just* her.

When he turned to her, he saw she was still carrying Jasmine asleep in her arms. She wasn't a toddler anymore though. He went to offer to take her to give her arms a rest, but found the words lodged in his throat. Instead, the image of eyes lit with fire invaded his space. Fear rose sharply. He pulled back. "Hi."

She looked at him, questioningly, then at Pueblo, and then back at him. Thankfully, she held back on the third degree. "I think we're almost done."

"We are," confirmed Pueblo.

Jerrod had his phone to his ear, a small disc attached to its back. He stood inches behind Claire. "Good. The police will be here soon." He gestured at his phone. "I've hacked into their radio system. The report of the explosion has reached them. We need to leave now."

Pete held up her bag. "Everything important is still in here. Most of it undamaged."

"Our phones?"

"Got them."

"Can we make it back to the house first and get ourselves cleaned up."

"Nope. I had a text from who I assume was Marco or Bill – they used a new number and didn't leave their name. They said Tristan had just arrived at the house – a surprise visit. No doubt trying to catch us out. That was about ten minutes ago."

"Oh no. If they're there... As wolves, would they have heard the explosion?"

He nodded. "And felt it."

"Our car's gone. We can't drive to the airport."

"Hello?" piped in Jerrod. "Missing the obvious, aren't we?"

They both stared at him, blankly.

He laughed at their expressions. "You have your own

private airline right here." He held his arms out.

Pueblo smiled. "We can take you to England."

"You can?" asked Claire. "All three of us?"

"Whoa, hang on a second." Pete took a step back. Flying through the fucking air with nothing to stand on was not on his life plan.

"Pete, I've done it, with both Jasmine and Jerrod. It'll be okay."

"I ... er ... I don't know."

"Better get to knowing, pup."

Pete stared daggers at the demon. This guy was irritating to say the least.

"In five minutes, we're going to be overrun with either police, or werewolves – whichever get here first. Well, *you'll* be overrun – Jerrod and I will teleport outta here. We can take you with us, or leave you to them."

Yeah, it wasn't really a choice and the demon knew it. Pete growled his frustration.

"We'll have you in the Surrey Hills in two minutes. All I need is an address."

Jerrod whipped his fingers across his phone. "I'm ready for the co-ords."

"Pete, please," said Claire. "None of us have had time to think – this hasn't sunk in for anyone – but we need to get out of here."

"I know. Fine." He gave Jerrod Lawrence's postcode. "That's it. There's no house number."

Jerrod whistled as the map showed him where they needed to go. "That is one nice piece of land."

Pueblo looked over his shoulder at the screen. "That's where we're going?"

"Yep."

"Zoom out."

"There you go."

"Okay, got it."

"Boss, I won't be able to teleport back for a couple of days."

"Use the business account – get a hotel for a couple of nights."

"I'm going for five-star, nothing less."

Pueblo snorted.

"And you?" Claire asked him. "Will you be teleporting back?"

He shook his head. "Jerrod lives in Nevada and my demon tribe is from this region originally, but I live in London."

"You do?"

He threw her a lopsided smile which riled Pete up the wrong way. "I was whisked away to England by a witch."

"So are we going then?" Pete interrupted, staring daggers at the demon.

"Yep. Claire, I'm sorry, but you'll need to wake Jasmine up. It's best if she's conscious to teleport."

Claire nodded, then went back to the log she'd been sitting on.

Pete followed her, leaving Pueblo and Jerrod looking at the map on the phone. "I don't know if I like this," he said to her quietly.

"It's flying – of course you won't like it. We have no choice. Jasmine ... Jasmine, honey." She stroked their daughter's cheek.

"We're trusting a demon?"

"He did just save our lives."

"I don't like him."

She threw him a knowing look.

He frowned.

A smile grew across her face, and she pulled an arm out

from under Jasmine and snaked it around his neck, pulling him down until his lips met hers.

It was a splash of beautiful water to all the raging destruction of fire. It was a moment of rest amid the ongoing turmoil. He sighed into her kiss, wishing it would never end.

When he pulled back, her smile was a full-on grin. "I know you don't like him," she whispered, her eyes twinkling as she read his jealousy correctly.

"Can't hide anything from you, can I?"

"Nope. And I'm your open book, too. Because I'm yours."

"Mummy?" Jasmine stirred, blinking her way out of sleep.

They both turned to her, and Pete knelt down, ignoring the tightening of his chest at being so near to her, knowing what she was capable of. Love and fear warred in his heart. Could Claire see *that* about him? How scared he was of their own child? He hoped not. It was a travesty, and it made him feel disgusted with himself.

"Jasmine, sweetie, we're going to teleport. I need you to wake up."

She rubbed her eyes. She was still clutching the single bit of material left of Marlo, but she didn't seem to notice – nor did she let it go.

"Elky's gone. He can't ever hurt you again, I promise. But we need to leave now, and Jerrod's here to help us do that. He has a friend with him who'll help us, too."

She yawned. "Okay, Mummy," she said sleepily.

Claire lifted her back into her arms as she stood.

Pete noticed Jasmine's eyes – normal again apart from their odd colouring – take in her surroundings even as they remained glazed with sleep. Her gaze fell on the crater she'd created. Did she remember?

She said nothing.

Claire carried her as they walked back to Jerrod and

Pueblo. "We're ready."

Jerrod smiled widely at Jasmine. "Hey, kid. Ready for a wild ride?"

She smiled a little, but nestled her head into Claire's shoulder.

"Yeah, I feel the same way," agreed Jerrod.

Pueblo laughed.

Claire turned to him, and looked at him almost shyly. Yeah, it got Pete's goat. He knew he was being unreasonable, but the wolf in him wouldn't leave it alone. No female of his should be looking at a cat like that. He held back the growl that threatened.

"I wanted to ask you about the creature that swooped in and took Elky," she said.

"Aah." The demon looked at the sky.

"Was that ... what I think it was?"

"Dragon," whispered Jasmine.

They both stilled, then Claire stroked her back. "Honey ... do you remember?"

Jasmine said nothing else.

They gathered themselves in a circle, following Pueblo's instructions for the teleporting version of 'lift off'. It involved holding the demon's fucking hand.

Pete was *not* okay with any of this, but he did as instructed; didn't let out the very unmanly scream he wanted to when he felt the sudden change in his body, as if air was getting *inside* it and pulling his molecules apart. *Jesus.*

Just before they 'took off' he looked at Claire and then at Jasmine. He didn't miss it – the look on Jasmine's face; desolate; newly guarded; armoured – and he had no clue whether he wanted to comfort her or run from her when he followed her gaze and saw what she was staring at, just before their bodies were whipped away into the air: Diego's burnt remains.

Chapter Nineteen

Her new clothes were a little bit too small. They belonged to a girl called Layla who was only three years old. Layla's mummy – she had long red hair and lots of freckles – had pulled out Layla's biggest clothes and said she could borrow them until Mummy and Daddy had bought new ones that fit her.

Jasmine liked Layla, except Layla was a bit annoying sometimes because she was young. She talked a *lot*. But she was happy and smiley all the time, a lot like her mummy. Layla's daddy smiled a lot, too, but he was huge. Bigger than huge. He was like a giant with a million muscles – even bigger than her own daddy.

But Layla had more than one dad, which Jasmine thought was a little lucky. Back at school, there had been a girl in her class who had had two mummies. One of the other kids had teased her about it, but Jasmine had thought it was a good thing. Why wouldn't it be good to have lots of parents?

Everyone who lived here was a wolf like Daddy.

They had arrived here just a few hours ago. It had been morning, even though it was nearly night when they had left America. Jerrod, and Jerrod's slightly scary-looking friend with the weird necklace, had said goodbye to them outside on the road. They hadn't wanted to come in. She knew she might never see them again – she was getting used to having to leave people behind.

Layla's mummy had answered the door and had looked very shocked to see them at first, but she had soon started smiling and laughing and hugging both Mum and Dad. Jasmine had gotten a hug, too.

Layla's giant daddy had also hugged everyone. Her other tall daddy with almost white hair had shaken everyone's hand, and her third daddy hadn't said too much. He'd looked a little sad, but also happy to see them. He was very quiet.

Layla's mummy – she was called Lydia – had shown her mum where everything was, and her mum had given her a bath and changed her clothes while Daddy had had a meeting with all Layla's daddies. Mum had said Daddy was trying to see if they could stay and live here.

'Here' seemed okay from what she could see. Right now, in the October afternoon sun, she stood at the end of the driveway to the big house. Daddy had said it was safe to play here, even though it was so big. He had told her to stick with Layla and her brothers – they knew their way around. There was lots of grass all around her and *lots* of trees – some really big woods – it was a little bit like Aiden's home but humongous.

"Jasmee?" For some reason, Layla couldn't say her name right, even though it really wasn't that hard. "Would you like to come and play with my brothers and with Richard?"

Layla had lots of brothers. They looked quite different to her. They all had really blond hair and pale blue eyes like her tall dad; Layla's hair was almost black, although her eyes were a beautiful purplish-blue like her mother's, and very big in her round face. She looked at her now with those eyes, very hopeful she'd say yes. Layla *really* wanted to be friends with her.

Jasmine blinked and looked around her. Her heart hurt a bit. She felt cold. Too cold. She didn't want to be around lots of children and lots of noise. "Where are you going to play?"

Layla pointed into the woods. "Through there. There's a field in the middle of the trees. Richard's meeting us there. After playing, we'll come back for tea."

She didn't know who Richard was. She pressed her hand against the pocket of her trousers and felt the bulge there. It made her heart hurt more. The cold she felt threatened to turn to ice. She couldn't make everything that had happened disappear. Playing wouldn't help – not anymore. "I need to do something first, but I can meet you there."

Layla looked unsure for a moment. She frowned, deeply, but then she looked up and nodded. "Okay."

"Okay, see you soon." Jasmine turned and walked away, heading for the woods, but away from where Layla had pointed. Looking back once, she saw Layla standing there, uncertain, shuffling her feet, but then there was a huge whoop behind her and two of her brothers came flying out of the house, sprinting for the woods and what Jasmine assumed was the field in its middle.

Layla squealed her delight and sprinted after them, shouting her annoyance at them being bigger and faster.

Jasmine walked a little quicker, then finally slipped through the trees and kept going until the quiet that surrounded her, relieved her. She looked around for a suitable place to do what she wanted to do.

A soft patch of earth under some pine trees caught her attention. It didn't look like it would be difficult to dig.

She placed herself in front of it, and then knelt down and began to move the earth with her hands. She had been right – the dirt was loose, and before long, she'd dug herself a little hole just big enough for what she wanted.

She blinked away her threatening tears as she reached into her pocket and pulled out what was left of Marlo. She had to stop crying – no more crying allowed. Monsters didn't cry.

She hugged the piece of fabric to her. "Goodbye, Marlo," she whispered. And then she placed it in the hole and shifted the dirt back until it was all covered up.

Mum and Dad thought she couldn't remember, but she remembered. Most of it, anyway. All the bad bits.

Really, really bad.

She pressed her hand on the mound. "I'm sorry I burnt you up."

She couldn't be friends with Layla … not after…

No – she couldn't be friends with anyone. She hurt people.

You kill people.

She felt the shadow, rather than saw it.

Turning sharply towards it, she stood up, trying to ascertain exactly what she'd felt. You couldn't *feel* shadows, could you?

Scanning the woods around her, she tried to find the feeling again.

And there it was.

She wasn't scared; she was curious. She took a step forward, following 'the feeling'. It was like when you thought someone was standing behind you, and when you turned around, they were.

She found a path through the trees. When she looked along it, she saw that beyond the woods was a hill – a large hill – and it was quite far away, but that's where the feeling was coming from: the shadow feeling. It brought a cool darkness that was comforting rather than scary, and soothing rather than lonely; that in some ways felt more of a friend than Layla's bubbly cheeriness. It was … in pain. It *was* pain, and it stirred her own pain in its familiarity. Whatever was causing the shadow, it would understand her.

And Jasmine couldn't hurt what was already hurting.

She was gone before she knew it, only this time, there was a sense that she *made* the flying happen; she *controlled* where she wanted to go. She'd never done that before, but when the world had finally stopped whizzing past her and she had regained her balance, she looked up to find she was on that hill.

And the 'shadow' was closer than ever. *Not a shadow.* Now she was near it, she could sense a presence; a person perhaps. But its pain permeated everything, including her own hurt in her heart.

She walked, following nothing but the feeling, knowing it would lead her to something she needed to find. She made no noise with her steps, her feet small enough to find her footing among the stones and fallen foliage, and she was light enough not to snap twigs if she stepped on them.

She knew she was getting close. Nevertheless, she almost missed her. It was the afternoon sun gleaming off her reddish-blonde hair that alerted Jasmine to the woman. She had her back to her, and was looking out over the hill through the trees towards the big house and the woods she'd just teleported from. Two big, full bags lay by her feet.

A woman – not a shadow – but there was something shadow-like about her. Her hair shone almost unnaturally, its waves falling down her back, so shiny it reminded her of water. *She has hair like the ocean.*

And something else. Some kind of darkness clung to her. *Just like it clings to me.*

The woman suddenly turned, and visibly jumped with a gasp when she saw Jasmine right in front of her. She froze.

So did Jasmine.

Their eyes locked.

Hers, in the sunlight, were the colour of a brand-new penny. "Hey," she said, still not moving a muscle; still staring. Then, finally, she looked around, searching for ... her parents? "Do you ... live here?" Her eyes landed back on her.

Jasmine shook her head. Only ... that wasn't true, was it. She *did* live here now. She nodded instead. "I moved in today." She looked down at the bags by the woman's feet. "Are you moving in, too?"

The woman looked surprised for a minute, then seemed to make up her mind about something. She knelt down so she was the same height as her, like all grown-ups did. "No. I'm just leaving actually. And if you don't mind, I don't want any-one to know I was here."

"Why not?"

She stalled. Either she didn't know the answer, or she was trying to make one up.

It didn't matter. Jasmine knew the answer. She'd known it when she'd first sensed her presence. "Is it because you're a monster, too?"

The woman looked shocked, but that's how everyone looked when they realised you knew their secret. "What do you mean?"

Jasmine looked down. Diego's face flashed through her mind and worse ... the state she'd left him in.

She didn't want to talk about it, but also ... she did. The pain was too big. But she could feel this woman's pain was big, too, so... "I have a monster in me. It's my fault we came here."

The woman's eyes filled with sadness at her words. And understanding. "Who's 'we'?"

"Mummy, Daddy, and me. They're talking to the wolves that live here. They told me to play with the others while they talked."

"But you found your way here, instead?"

She nodded. "I'm scared to play. The monster inside me killed a boy, and I'm not supposed to tell anyone."

The woman sat down on the grass, looking straight at her. "We're even then. I know something about you I'm not supposed to, and you know I was here even though you're not supposed to."

Jasmine shrugged. "I guess."

"I'm going to tell you one more secret, though. If you want me to, that is. But you can't tell anyone – ever."

A part of her died at the thought of yet another secret to keep. But at least this time, she'd been given a choice – she could just say she didn't want to know. Except she *did* want to know about this woman with hair like the ocean who understood her pain. "I won't tell, I promise."

The woman let out a sad smile. "You were right: I have a monster in me, too. It's also killed people – the bad feeling from that never really goes away, but … that's not my secret. This is." She reached into the pocket of her jacket and brought out a small, velvet box. She opened it, and Jasmine took in a sharp breath at the most beautiful ring inside it. The setting sun that peeked through the trees caught the diamond.

"Wow."

"Yeah. This was given to me by a very special man who loved me *in spite* of the monster in me. He didn't care, you see. The monster couldn't make me ugly to him; he just saw all the good stuff inside me, and the way he loved me was like … *real* love, you know? Like people *should* be loved. He loved me so much, he asked me to marry him."

Like Daddy and Mummy. Jasmine smiled.

"Well, I *can't* marry him, but that's not the point. The point is that no matter how big, bad, and scary that monster in you gets, someone out there will still love you. I'm going to give you this ring because I want you to remember that."

She gasped, her eyes widening. "You're going to give me the ring?"

The woman took it out of the box and held it for her to take. "Yes. But you have to keep it a secret, and you have to *promise* that every time you look at it, you'll remember the story, and that there are people in the world who will love you no matter how big that monster gets. Do you promise?"

She thought of how Mummy loved Daddy in spite of his scars; maybe … they could love her too, even if she killed all those people.

She took the ring, scared she might ruin it by touching it. "I promise."

"Good."

"But I have nothing to give you in return." Guilt panged her chest. This woman could be a friend, but would she want to be her friend if she couldn't give her anything in return? "Mummy says when someone gives you a gift, you should give them something back if you can."

"There's no need to give me anything." Then, she paused, thoughtfully. "But there *is* something you can do for me."

"There is?" Jasmine felt hopeful. She wanted to do it.

"It's just a little thing, but … since you're going to be living here… There's an old wolf who also lives here called Richard."

Oh, yes! That was the name Layla had mentioned.

The woman suddenly looked sad. She turned her head away, blinking. "Look out for him, please? As best you can? But don't *tell* him you're looking out for him, because he always likes to think he can look after himself, even when he can't."

Jasmine smiled, and nodded enthusiastically. "I'll look after him, I promise." And she meant it.

"Thank you." The woman stood.

"You're going now?"

"I have to."

She felt a twinge of sadness about that. She was the first real friend she'd made here. "What's your name?"

"It's Je—er ... Laura. My name's Laura. What's yours?"

"Jasmine."

"That's a pretty name – one of my favourite flowers."

Jasmine beamed with pride, and maybe it was contagious, because the woman gave her a huge smile back. She was really, *really* beautiful when she smiled.

"Will you be okay finding your way back to the house?" she asked.

"Yes."

"It's a long way – are you sure you can walk it?"

She was still smiling, clutching the ring to her. It was the best gift. It was a piece of true love. "I didn't walk."

"Oh." Laura looked a little confused, but didn't ask her what she meant, thankfully. "As long as you're careful along the steep bits, okay?"

Jasmine nodded, fervently. "Bye-bye, Laura."

Laura placed her rucksack on her back and grabbed her other big bag. "'Bye, Jasmine." She headed towards a small path through the trees that Jasmine assumed would lead out to where she needed to go. She should go, too. She felt panic at the thought of Mum and Dad thinking she might be lost again.

No sooner had she thought that, than the air changed and began to move around her; past her; wind tousling her hair in a delightful way until it all stopped. She was starting to become used to it – teleporting. It was starting to feel familiar.

She opened her eyes and found herself back on the driveway to the house, exactly where she'd last spoken to Layla.

She still held the ring. It was the most precious thing she'd ever been given. She kissed it, then put it in her pocket where Marlo had been. She'd keep it safe, and she would keep it a secret, and she *would* keep her promise: when she was feeling sad, she'd remember that some people loved you no matter what. True love existed.

With a smile, she turned and suddenly stopped, unsure, when she saw a man sitting on the front step of the house watching her. It was one of Layla's dads – the quiet one. Her heart leapt. Had he seen the ring? She didn't think so – she'd had her back to him. But he might have seen her teleport.

Jasmine took a deep breath, smiled at him, and waved.

He looked surprised for a minute, then smiled back. It was a kind smile, and she had the feeling that maybe rather than staring at her, he'd been deep in thought. She could see the green of his eyes from here – a very warm green – the same green the colour her left eye now was. Maybe living here would be okay after all.

Feeling better than she had in a while, she turned and ran into the woods where Layla said she'd be with her brothers and with Richard. She could hear their laughter from here. She had a mission: look after Richard. She was going to do that.

The could feel the ring in her pocket as she ran, and it warmed her up, chasing away the cold she'd felt when she'd first arrived.

Amid secrets and monsters and fire and death; amid every uncertainty; love existed. Love was real. It was the *one* certainty. Mum and Dad were proof of it; the ring in her pocket was proof of it.

"...no matter how big, bad, and scary that monster in you gets, someone out there will still love you."

Where monsters lurked, love also waited.

Bigger than any monster could be.

Epilogue

She was beautiful. He'd thought so from the first moment he'd laid eyes on her, and nothing ever shone a light on it so brightly as a life and death situation.

Pueblo made his way to Amy, sleeping so far under the duvet only the tips of her blonde hair peeked out the top. He was planning on waking her gently, but she beat him to it the moment he sat on the edge of their bed, depressing the mattress.

She leapt up, mostly asleep, yet still managing to pounce – all right, *half* pounce – on the intruder in the bedroom. He was damned lucky no chant left her lips.

"Hey, babe ... Amy. It's me. It's me."

The sleep fell from her eyes in an instant. "Pueblo." She threw her arms around him in relief, though a tinge of anger coloured her words. He hid a smile at her innate sense of indignation over his actions. "Where the *hell* have you been?"

"You weren't here for me to tell you."

"Yeah, 'cause I was taking our son to school."

"There was no time to leave a note. Jerrod called – he needed me."

"In Nevada?"

"Yes – near there. I had to go. The woman and her

daughter I told you about – the ones who turned up at the Birthlands..."

"What about them?"

"They needed help. And if I ever see another shaman again it'll be too soon."

"*You're* a shaman."

"I'm a reluctant shaman. Listen, the girl – the daughter – she's special, Amy. She's something else."

"When did you get back? Brennan's been asking and I haven't been able to tell him a thing."

"I'm sorry. I got back late this afternoon, but I needed to check in on something before I came home. Amy ... I think it's begun."

Her blue eyes widened as she sat up straighter in the bed. "What do you mean?"

"I'm talking about Brennan. I'm talking about what we always knew we'd have to face one day."

"No. Pueblo, nothing's changed." She lowered her voice, no doubt because Brennan was sleeping in the next room. "He's shown no signs of anything yet – no shapeshifting, no magic – nothing at all."

"Amy, listen to me ... do you remember nine years ago, Elena mentioned a man called Ri Tian?"

She blinked, then nodded. "Wasn't he the one who made the necklace Mary wore?"

"Yes. He passed away early this morning. It's what I was checking on. I needed some answers."

"So, he passed away. What does that have to do with Brennan?"

"Aside from the fact that he wears Mary's necklace?"

"Don't use that tone with me."

He sighed. He was fucking tired. "I'm sorry. I didn't mean it that way. Amy ... I saw it. I saw the dragon."

That shut her up. She pulled herself to her knees and took his face in her hands. "Say that again."

"I saw the dragon." The same dragon none of them had seen since the day Brennan was born.

Amy's eyes filled with tears.

"I swear it's somehow tied to the girl. It appeared *for* her. And her eyes ... they were two different colours."

Amy gasped. "Like the dragon's eyes."

"Exactly."

"But ... what does that mean?"

"I have no idea."

Something fell in Brennan's room, causing a muffled clatter.

They stared at each other. Amy was the first out of bed, running for the bedroom across the hall from theirs. "Brennan?" she called out, though she refrained from shouting.

They both listened at the door, but couldn't make out any further noise.

Amy placed her hand on the door handle, and turned it slowly ... quietly.

As gently as she could, she pushed the door forward.

Pueblo tried to steady his nerves. They'd been shot to bits from the moment he'd found himself standing on hot rocks, summoned by a woman wearing wolf's blood.

As the door swung its full arc, he heard Amy suck in a breath.

His heart fell to his feet.

Brennan stood by the window, a silhouette in the dark with his back to them. But he turned when he heard them at the door. "Mum, Dad ... I had a dream that was just ... it was out of this world. I dreamt I was flying. I was a dragon – I was *actually* a dragon."

They said nothing. Well, Amy squeaked – that was the

nearest to words they managed. Because the room was not as dark as it should be at two o'clock in the morning – Brennan's eyes were alight with flames. In his right hand, he balanced a small ball of fire. His son was grinning from ear to ear. "Dad, look." He held up the fire. "Look what I can do. Just like you! It just happened. I didn't even have to try."

He was shifting fire.

They'd been waiting for this moment – waiting to see how it would manifest – and had it not been for the fact he'd just seen a five-year-old girl kill four people with the exact same ability; had it not been for the fact he'd seen the dragon they feared they'd never see again ... *because* of that girl ... he'd be whooping for joy.

Instead, he swallowed hard, and forced a smile. "That's amazing, son. That's amazing."

Amy laced her fingers through his, but gripped his hand far too hard. He knew his words were replaying in her mind.

It's begun.

HAVE YOU READ…

After the Storm novelette series

After the Storm is a series of novelettes that take place at relevant points in the immediate months after *Eye of the Storm*. (You need to read *Eye of the Storm* first.) They concentrate on the healing our characters need to go through after everything that happened. They do not need to be read to understand the main story arc – they are additional reads for fans that also contain "Easter eggs" of what is to come.

The Witching Pen series
Plus the companion novel, Saving Eve.

Witches, angels, demons, Heaven and Hell all come together in a dizzying story of friendship, love and forgiveness. A titillating mix of paranormal romance and urban fantasy brings you a sensational series you won't forget.

Blood Surge
A Vampiric Urban Fantasy Novel

A beautiful library in a sleepy town in Hampshire is the perfect place for Sophia to escape a fraught childhood and forgotten past until an old lover borrows a book, a woman dies, a ridiculously gorgeous man keeps turning up around every corner, and a stately home party goes awry. It turns out Sophia's life (and past) isn't what she thought it was at all. *Passionate vampiric urban fantasy.*

Once Times Thrice

Practical Magic meets *Serendipity* in a beautiful, fun, and magical series about love, family, and second chances, set in Cornwall, England. Follow Merri, Jamie, Pippa, Jimmy and Candy as summer turns to autumn.

Contemporary romance with a touch of magic.

Broken Lights

One gunshot, one scramble for life, one unlikely couple, one very long night ... can one damaged woman and one ordinary man, find the extraordinary in the very last second they're given?

Broken Lights is a standalone short novel of what's really worth fighting for, when one second is all you have left.

To keep up with all new releases, works in progress, and general writing updates, please visit Dianna's website (diannahardy.com), or join Dianna on Facebook (facebook.com/authordiannahardy).

Acknowledgements / Author's Note

Thank you to Amanda Pederick, my editor, for listening to my grammar rants and 'getting' my style. You are fab.

Thank you to my *Aftershock* beta readers – Maureen Hoar, Pam Appleton, Elizabeth Morgan, and Sami Rae Pfleider – for your invaluable and timely feedback. It was hugely appreciated.

Thank you to Gareth for your assistance with a medical query which saved me a re-write at the last minute.

Thanks to my ARC readers for your continued love of my books and leaving those hugely important reviews so others know about my stories.

Thank you to Alastair for your constant and undying support of both my books and me; for understanding how important writing is to me; for seeing all the dark and still loving me.

And massive thanks to my readers for being so patient and for your endless enthusiasm for my characters. I strive to write and publish two books a year. I don't like to turn out more than that because I feel the quality of my product will suffer if I do, and in this very fast-turning industry, I'm incredibly grateful you're still here, enjoying my stories with the same level of passion I have when I write them. Each book means the world to me in some way or another, so it brings me much joy to know there are readers who get a lot out of them. Thank you!

Yours,
Dianna Hardy
October, 2018

Also by Dianna Hardy

Blood Shadow
Blood Never Lies, #1

Five years after her life changed forever, Jennifer Warren has put her past firmly behind her – at least, she's tried. A few sweaty nightmares here and there are a small price to pay for the freedom she won. No longer a werewolf, but human, she works as an office manager for a health and beauty spa in York, and keeps herself to herself. It's barely enough to pay the bills, but it's quiet and safe, and the clique of the staff means she's left well enough alone – no one asks her questions; no one wants to get to know her better.

David, her tender, kind boyfriend of two years is all she needs ... and she doesn't really need him, which suits her just fine. Never mind the occasional guilt that she doesn't really love him; he'd never hurt her in a million years – that's worth its weight in gold.

But Jennifer's just received another note – one of those that her mysterious, anonymous 'friend' likes to leave her every now and then; warnings of things to come, people not to trust... Her elusive friend has saved her more than once the past five years.

Only this note has left her breathless; her chest tight. A Super-moon is coming – the first in thirty years – and with it, a total lunar eclipse.

Jennifer's disowned her past, but it hasn't disowned her. As the earth shadows the full moon, her own shadows threaten to turn on her.

Can you ever escape what you truly are?

Blood never lies.

~*~

For a full list of Dianna's books, including the Eye of the Storm series and The Witching Pen series, please go to:
www.diannahardy.com/books.html

About The Author

Dianna Hardy is an international bestselling author of (cross-genre) fantasy fiction, most notable for her dark (often explicit) paranormal fantasy and the raw, intense *Eye of the Storm* series. But her heart-warming *Once Times Thrice* series proves she thrives in the light as much as the dark. Whatever your poison, what she loves most is to bring you stories that are action-packed, fast-paced and not short of heat, with the focus on character development, relationship dynamics, and the plot. She writes full-length novels and short fiction.

In December 2012, *Releasing The Wolf* hit the Kindle Paranormal Fantasy charts in both the US and the UK, where it stayed for three months, enjoying a highest ranking of #20. Both books in the *Eye Of The Storm* series have enjoyed success in the top 100 of Fantasy charts on Kindle US, Kindle UK, and iTunes (Australia, top 40). *The Witching Pen* series, *'Til Death Do Us Part* and *A Silver Kiss*, have also hit the top 100 of iBooks (Apple Books) charts in Fantasy, Romance, and Horror in ten different countries worldwide.

Although quite active online, Dianna prefers the quiet company of nature and animals to the hustle and bustle of people. She loves anything paranormal (she doesn't really consider it "para"), organic food, walking barefoot, the smell of the woods after rain, and summer days.

However, she is also sustained by coffee, chocolate and the occasional vodka.

Having graduated from Richmond Drama School (London) in '98, she spent the next few years in a multitude of jobs (both acting and non-acting), studying anything that fascinated her, searching her soul, and finally found her passion where it had always been: at the end of a pen.

She currently lives on the south coast in England with her partner and their daughter, where she writes full time.

Official site:
www.diannahardy.com

Facebook:
www.facebook.com/authordiannahardy

X:
www.x.com/thewitchingpen

www.ingramcontent.com/pod-product-compliance
Lightning Source LLC
Chambersburg PA
CBHW022154170626
46807CB00005B/2206